C.

LEADVILLE LADY

LEADVILLE LADY

LESLEE BREENE

FIVE STAR

An imprint of Thomson Gale, a part of The Thomson Corporation

THOMSON

GALE

Detroit • New York • San Francisco • New Haven, Conn. • Waterville, Maine • London

LIBRARY OF CONGRESS CATALOGING-IN-PUBLICATION DATA

Breene, Leslee.
  Leadville lady / Leslee Breene. — 1st ed.
    p. cm.
  ISBN 1-59414-546-6 (hardcover : alk. paper) 1. Silver mines and mining—
Fiction. 2. Colorado—Fiction. I. Title.
PS3602.R443L43 2006
813'.6—dc22
                                    2006019025

U.S. Hardcover:
ISBN 13: 978-1-59414-546-9
ISBN 10: 1-59414-546-6

First Edition. First Printing: October 2006.

Published in 2006 in conjunction with Tekno Books.

Printed in the United States of America on permanent paper
10 9 8 7 6 5 4 3 2 1

For my mother, with love.
Nancy Jane Cole Carlson.

ACKNOWLEDGEMENTS

There are always sources aside from the author's muse that contribute to the process of completing a final manuscript. My heartfelt thanks to the following.

Leadville: Colorado's Magic City, by the late, longtime resident Edward Blair, was a priceless material source from start to finish of *Leadville Lady.* While writing *Leadville Lady,* I took the delightful liberty of inserting actual historical personages such as Lt. Governor Horace Tabor and his then mistress, Baby Doe, into the storyline. The madam, Sallie Purple, is mentioned as well as a popular restaurant, Tontine's. My intent was to create as true-to-life 1880 Leadville as possible.

For her editorial expertise, I am grateful to Alice Duncan.

Special thanks go to Kay Bergstrom, aka Cassie Miles, and my critique group for giving me thoughtful advice. To Janie VanDerSchouw, aka Jane A. Westwood, and George VanDerSchouw, aka Jackie Vann, who generously shared their knowledge of Leadville history.

CHAPTER ONE

Leadville, Colorado, 1880

Marshal Cody Cassidy ducked into the shadowed alley behind O'Connor's harness shop. He was out of breath after dashing the two blocks from Drago's gambling hall where he'd gotten the tip of the break-in tonight. He wiped the sweat from his forehead.

In the twilight, he saw Peg O'Connor's back door standing ajar. Fierce barking punctured the summer night.

Sure enough, someone was in there now.

He whipped the Colt from his holster. His boots kicked up dirt as he bolted across the alley.

The smell of musty leather filled Cody's nostrils as he slipped inside—just in time to hear the sound of breaking glass. His pulse quickening, he moved along the dark hallway toward the front room.

Gotta save Peg before they get to him.

Through the shattered window, a man peered inside the shop. At a wolfhound's persistent barking, he backed away.

"Hold it right there!" Cody hollered to the vandal's retreating back.

Then a blunt object, like the toe of a boot, struck his wrist. Pain seared up his arm. Seeming to leap from his hand, his gun misfired, sending a bullet through the side wall. He lunged for the blurred shape of another man careening toward him. The gleam of a knife blade slashed the air. Cody felt a sharp sting and grabbed his shoulder.

In the shadows, he could only guess the assailant's description. About six feet tall, lean, and fast. And already disappearing down the alley.

"Damn devil!"

The wolfhound trotted to the back door then turned to face Cody, its eyes glowing amber. A growl rumbled from low in its throat.

"That you, Marshal?" Peg O'Connor clambered downstairs from his second floor living quarters carrying a kerosene lamp. A shock of red hair fell over his wide-set eyes; his rumpled nightshirt hung askew. The lamp shed a wavering light over Cody and the beast.

"Yeah, it's me. Better call off your hound."

"Come here, Digger, me boy," the Irishman called. The wolfhound retreated to Peg's side but continued to regard Cody with wary eyes. "Did the yella dog get away?"

"Afraid so. You all right, Peg?"

"Aye, I'm still alive." He hobbled over broken glass to the front window favoring his wooden peg. "They would o' killed me in me bed if ol' Digger hadn't taken to barkin', and you showed up."

"Hope my deputy got the one that busted your window."

Peg let out a disgusted snort. "These lot jumpers keep attackin' us, tryin' to take away our businesses—even burnin' down our shops to get us out. You've got to stop 'em, Marshal!"

"Lot jumpers or claim jumpers, they're filthy parasites," Cody ground out. "I'll round up every spare officer on the force."

Peg's ruddy face split into a malicious grin. "Aye, and maybe we'll call out the vigilantes."

Cody recalled last year's vengeance, the rush to hang men. "No. Better wait on doing that, Peg."

When Cody reached his office, big Jim Hacker, his first

deputy, was just marching a shackled prisoner inside. "I chased this coyote from O'Connor's as far as those bawdy houses up on State Street."

"Good job, Jim. My luck wasn't so great. The one inside got away." He held the door open for Jim with his boot. "You can lock him up. We'll hold him till the judge gets back next Monday." He pressed his hand to his throbbing shoulder. "The devil nicked me. Would you get something to clean up this shoulder?"

Jim nodded and shoved his disheveled prisoner into the back cell room.

Cody scuffed across the rough-hewn floor to his desk in the corner and dropped his long frame into the chair. Damn, he was tired. He'd been on duty for the past ten hours. But he had to come up with a plan to ambush these marauding lot jumpers. Their after-dark attacks had grown more daring in recent weeks, and nearly fatal this time.

Jim Hacker swung through the door from the back room with a bottle of carbolic acid and a towel. Cody shrugged off his shirt. He winced when Hacker dabbed at his cut shoulder. "Ain't deep," Jim said. "You'll live." He pointed a beefy finger toward the desktop. "Think ya better read that telegram, Marshal. It come today for Ned, but since he's gone—"

"Ned's gone? Gone where?"

Hacker grinned knowingly above his thick, dark beard. "Gone to get hitched."

Cody massaged his forehead. "Shoot, thought that wasn't until the end of the week."

Ned Saunders, his new deputy, had no sooner taken the job three months ago than fallen in love with a young woman working in her uncle's hardware store. Cody exhaled an exasperated breath. "Seems like everybody's running off to get hitched." His younger brother had eloped with a saloon gal only last week.

He leaned forward, holding the telegram near the desk lamp, and stared at it. "This is all I need."

Hacker scowled. "Bad news?"

"Bad enough. Ned's cousin is arriving tomorrow. A woman from Ohio. Guess it's a woman. Not many men go by the name Sky." Cody tipped back his Stetson. "Ned must have forgotten when she was coming. How long will he be gone?"

"Not sure." Hacker swiped a hank of black hair from his brow. "Think he said they'd visit Cindy's folks in Laramie."

Cody bristled. "Great. With all the lot jumping and claim jumping going on around here, and I'm shorthanded, all I need is some stiff-necked eastern gal coming to town." He stood and paced over to the dust-streaked window and gazed out at the traffic on Front Street. "The telegram said she'll arrive early tomorrow morning from Denver." He envisioned this proper young miss getting off the train in Leadville, her curious eyes gazing up and down the platform, looking for her cousin.

"Ya want me to meet her, boss?"

Cody observed his hulking deputy, a man who at first glance looked like he'd just lumbered down from a mountain cave. With his chest-length beard and uncut hair, Hacker resembled the back end of a bear. Cody's take-charge instinct prevailed. "No, thanks, Jim. You'd probably scare her half to death. I'd better take care of the lady myself."

Sky Saunders stepped off the train onto the platform of the new Leadville station. A midday breeze cooled her perspiring brow beneath her Sunday straw brim. She turned, amidst the throng of fellow travelers, and stared out over the valley to the breathtaking, snow-dusted sapphire mountain range rising above her. Leadville. The last stop on her journey to meet her cousin and start a new life.

Come west, Sky, and join the silver rush! Ned had urged in his letters. She gulped in a deep breath of the sweet mountain air and felt a rush of expectancy. Well, she was here now and she would be a part of it. She'd left her past and all her sad, bitter memories behind.

"Be careful, Sky. Ned's words may sound promising, but he always was impulsive—just like you." Granny Saunders's voice pricked her conscience as she worked her way down the crowded platform toward the baggage car. "You could be jumping into another kettle of fish!"

Sky shook her head indignantly. *But you know I had to leave Placerton, Gran. Had to get away from the town gossips—after Thomas allowed me to file for divorce.*

Her soon-to-be former husband, vice president of the town bank, had taught her accounting skills when she showed an eagerness to learn. He'd permitted her to take a job at the bank as bookkeeper.

She laughed to herself now. As pinchpenny as Thomas was, she knew her job had been a way to pay for her keep.

Rubbing her elbow, still tender from the "accident" a month ago, she realized fate had forced her to look ahead to her loveless, bleak future. Now a quiver of excitement rushed through her. On her person were several documents—proof of Thomas's crimes that had prompted an early settlement and ensured his finalizing the divorce.

At last, she was nearly free.

Ahead dusty male travelers crowded around the pile of unloaded baggage. She found a place at the end of the line.

After she claimed her two trunks and a baggage handler told her she could pick them up at the front of the station, she walked into the small train depot. Once inside, her empty stomach did a nervous flip-flop. Was she really here, gambling her future in this strange, faraway place?

In her haste to escape Thomas, and to start a new life, she'd accepted Ned's offer to help her find employment in this bustling mining town. She'd even sent most of the settlement money ahead so he could locate a room for her and set up a small bank account.

His last letter had revealed the most exciting news about the mine, and cinched her decision to make this journey.

Pausing by an alcove, she scanned the faces of passing travelers, looking for her cousin. Above the jostling crowd, a white western hat caught her eye. She blinked. What she saw sauntering toward her, not fifteen feet away, had to be an illusion.

Beneath the hat, deep-set eyes stared from a sun-bronzed face directly at her. A full, tawny mustache draped above a clean-shaven, strong jaw. A gun swayed in a low-slung holster. Denim jeans molded to long, muscular legs. *A cowboy.*

Why was he coming straight toward her? A tremor of anxiety slid down her spine.

The man came to a halt not three feet away—and he was no illusion. His prairie green shirt stretched smoothly across his upper chest and broad shoulders.

To her dismay, her heart did a triple spin and wedged into her windpipe.

His voice, low timbred, spoke her name. "Miss Saunders?"

She straightened and looked up into sparkling hazel eyes. Blood roared in her ears. "That's my name." Her voice sounded oddly foreign. "And who are you, sir?"

The tall cowboy touched the brim of his dusty hat and made a stilted bow. His hint of a smile was distracting. "I'm Marshal Cassidy. Your cousin Ned is one of my deputies."

Her gaze dropped from the earnest hazel eyes to the silver star on his vest. Lettering on the star read: *Marshal, Leadville, Colorado.*

Sky's limbs turned the consistency of crabapple jelly. "Dear Lord. Where is Ned? Has something happened to him?"

"Ned's fine," the marshal's voice reassured. "He's on his honeymoon. Your telegram just missed him by a day."

"Honeymoon?" The inference of intimacy from this disturbingly powerful and handsome man sent heat rushing up her neck to her face. She tried to make sense of the unexpected development. "He did mention a girl he'd met, but I had no idea. Then, I am arriving earlier than he expected."

Several bearded, boisterous men muscled past them and the marshal steered her out of their path. They observed her curiously, one scanning her traveling dress from bodice to hem. She sent them a reproachful look, feeling like a goose just before it's served for dinner.

"Miss Saunders, I know you've traveled a long way. I can help with your arrangements. First, let's get out of here. Where's your luggage?"

"It's outside. The baggage handler loaded it on a wagon."

He shook his head. "Never leave your belongings alone here. Things can disappear quicker than gold dust."

Sliding his large, tanned hand under her elbow, he guided her toward the open front door. If she wasn't agitated enough, his touch made her skin tingle.

Suddenly they were outside on the wide dirt street with masses of people, mostly rough-looking miners, carrying furniture, bedding, all manner of tools, and open wagons trundling noisily past. Dust hung on the warm air.

Sky searched the bustling scene and spied her trunks atop a loaded baggage cart. "There they are." A bewhiskered handler eyed her quizzically when she hurried up to him. "Can you find me an available rig?"

"Just a minute, miss. I've got a wagon here." The marshal's decisive voice came from behind her.

Sky opened her mouth to object. She wanted to hire her own vehicle. She must remain independent and not place herself in a compromising situation. But he was already loading her trunks onto his wagon.

"Really, you don't need to do this." Her voice faded into the din of ongoing traffic. "I can pay for a rig."

He gave her a swift boost aboard the vehicle. She hit the wagon seat with a hard thud, her lace petticoats flouncing up around her knees.

"Please, Marshal Cassidy," she said, modestly arranging her skirt as he climbed aboard and sat down next to her. "I would like to find a boarding house."

"You'd be better off staying at our place with my dad and me, until Ned gets back."

His strong thigh brushed uncomfortably close to hers and she focused her eyes ahead, frustrated at how to proceed with her request. "Thank you, Marshal, but I think I should find a room at a boarding house."

She didn't want to stay with his family. That would certainly make her obligated to him. The thirty dollars tucked away in her purse wasn't much, but it should pay for a decent room until Ned returned and she could straighten out her finances.

The marshal's brows converged. "You can't stay in one of these bawdy houses. They're not fit for a lady." Without waiting for a response, he snapped the reins smartly over the horses' rumps and urged them out onto the crowded road.

"Very well then." Her short reply was lost amidst the clatter of steel-rimmed wagon wheels. She could only clasp one hand on her hat and the other firmly on the splintered edge of the wagon seat.

The driver of a six-mule team wagon kept them from entering the tangled thoroughfare. His whip cracked the air, sounding like a barrage of pistol shots going off next to her ear. She cringed, her shoulders jumping up like a scared cat's.

"Sorry, miss. But this is Leadville. Hundreds of get-rich-quick miners come through here every day." His gaze, as well as his words, was blunt. "You'll be glad not to be visiting for long."

"Well," she huffed, indignant at his assumption and his tone. "I'll have you know I may be staying for some time." She raised her voice for emphasis. "I've recently invested in a silver mine!"

Cody arched his eyebrows in surprise. "What mine is that?"

"It's the Lucky Lady. Ned knows all the details. He wrote me that he's invested my money very wisely in a promising claim."

An alarm went off in Cody's head and his jaw tensed. He knew her affairs weren't any of his business, but he couldn't help his curiosity. It came with his job. "Did Ned tell you the name of your mining partner?"

She straightened on the seat as if her spine were reinforced with a steel rod and answered him coolly. "I'm sure he did, but it doesn't come to mind at the moment."

All right, he thought matter-of-factly, don't tell me. It's your money you're throwing to the wolves. He shrugged. "Guess it's none of my business."

Her chin lifted a notch. "Thank you for your concern, Marshal."

Cody slanted a glance at the young woman seated next to him, her eyes as blue as the Leadville sky and focused dead ahead. No doubt she was a lady, outfitted in that trim-fitting dress the color of a robin's egg, her dark auburn hair tucked up beneath her flower-covered hat and twisted into a neat braid at her creamy nape. She couldn't be compared to the women who followed the hard-edged men into this booming mountain town. Not by a long shot.

The minute he'd seen her waiting inside the station, so prim and out of place, he'd known she didn't belong here. What had Ned Saunders gotten her into? If she were smart, she'd turn tail and run.

This young woman had about as much business "investing in

a silver mine" as he would racing in the Kentucky Derby.

He was willing to bet it wouldn't be long before she'd be on a train to Denver and back to where she came from.

CHAPTER TWO

Rocking down the heavily traveled road, grasping the edge of the hard seat, Sky fell into a tense silence. Just where was her new mining interest located? Ned hadn't revealed it, only that the mine was situated in the mountains outside of Leadville. Well, from her view, there were mountains as far as the eye could see. As to her mining partner, a Mr. Gunther was the miner Ned had glorified as "sitting on a king's fortune. But keep this under your hat," he'd warned.

"How was your train ride from Denver, Miss Saunders?" the marshal asked, interrupting her thoughts.

Her uplifted gaze met his, a kaleidoscope of golden-greens, and a strange palpitation started beneath her corseted bodice. Shaking off the unwanted reaction, she replied, "Not as bumpy as this road. But longer than I would have liked."

He flicked the reins, urging the horses around a lumbering team of oxen. "Don't think you would have appreciated the old stage route. It took over twelve hours."

Was he being insolent? She observed him cautiously.

From somewhere deep in his throat, he chuckled. "And most folks complained when they had to jump down and push the stage out of the mud."

"Push the stagecoach?" Sky balked at the miserable image. "Even the women?"

"Yes, ma'am."

She could swear he smiled at her response as he looked in

the other direction. Had he told her the truth or was he just pulling her leg?

She sat up straighter on the hard seat, realizing she'd have to curb the good manners Granny taught her, to reply when someone made a comment. She did not want to appear a naive fool.

On the outskirts of town, the marshal guided the team off the road. "Here's our place."

A rustic two-story log house, built much like its neighbors, only larger, stood back from a wide-open front yard. Flat-roofed sheds flanked a fenced corral and a small barn. The few straggly trees and barren dirt grounds sent an unwanted wave of nostalgia washing over her. In her mind, she remembered Placerton, with its neat maple-lined avenues and verdant, groomed lawns.

A keen smell of barnyard permeated the air. "Do you raise horses?" Sky asked expectantly as the marshal assisted her down.

He gave a short laugh. "Horses are too good a name for most of our plugs. My dad's in the wagon-building business. We trade and sell a few nags and mules on the side."

"Oh?" Sky felt a twinge of disappointment. This place was not at all like Placerton.

"I'll have your trunks brought to your room, but first I'll show you inside," he offered briskly.

He led her up the rough-planked porch steps and into the log house. She blinked, her eyes adjusting to the interior, as she walked across a crimson and black Indian carpet bordering a large room with a stone fireplace and man-sized leather furniture.

"You'll be staying in my brother Will's room. Actually, it's not his room anymore." His voice was tinged with sarcasm. "He moved out sooner than anyone expected."

Sky followed behind him, her gaze settling briefly on Marshal

Cassidy's striding hips, his snug-fitting denim trousers. He was an impressively built man. The sound of his boot heels clicked across the hardwood floor.

"When did you say Ned will be returning from his honeymoon?" she asked as they entered a bedroom at the rear of the house.

"In about a week. He'd better get back here soon. I need his help."

"And so do I." She'd entrusted most of her early divorce settlement with Ned and she did not plan to be a silent partner.

The marshal blew out a long breath. "I know this isn't what you expected, Miss Saunders. My kid brother ran off with a saloon gal last week, which didn't sit too well with my dad and me. We sure weren't expecting it."

She looked up at him in astonishment; his tall frame filled the doorway. "I should say not."

An awkward silence fell between them. On the bureau, sunlight glimmering on a silver-framed photograph caught her attention. She went over and touched the frame. "Such a beautiful woman. Is she . . . ?"

"She was my mother." Cody stared at the photograph and the unreadable eyes of the woman he hadn't seen in twenty years. "She left us when I was very young." Not wanting to reveal his vulnerability to such an old wound, he shrugged. "That's life, I guess."

His eyes met hers, and he saw that she studied him with a curious intensity mingled with what he thought was compassion. An uncomfortable tightness gathered in his throat. For some strange reason, he felt an impulse to throw her off guard.

As he turned to leave, Cody sent her a devilish grin. "I hope your reason for coming all this way is gonna be worth it, Miss Saunders."

Heat inflamed Sky's cheeks, flooding downward inside her

bodice. My, he was outspoken. "Thank you, Marshal Cassidy. I trust that it will." She closed the heavy door, embarrassed at her flustered reaction and amazed at what she and the marshal had in common.

With arms held stiffly at her sides, Sky paced the length of the room. Back and forth, back and forth. Her current situation couldn't be more perplexing.

What do I do now, Gran? Now that I'm suddenly beholden to a total stranger—and Ned won't return for at least a week!

Beloved Gran, who'd taken Sky in after her parents drowned in a raging flood, raised her to the age of thirteen, before Gran's heart failed and Sky had been sent to live with her aunt and uncle, and five spiteful cousins. Ned being the exception. He'd become as close to her as a brother.

In the surrounding silence, no answer came. Granny Saunders must have been "plumb out of advice." Only the forlorn braying of some wretched mule in the outer yard reached Sky's ears.

Folding her arms across her waist, she stared out the dusty window to the looming mountain range. In Placerton, she'd determined that she would move away and start over. A place where no one knew her, where she could create a new identity.

She removed her hat and set it on the bureau, recalling the marshal's earlier curt remark: "You'll be glad not to be staying long." Should she take him seriously?

Should she stay and take her chances in this wild, unsettled town, or demand that Ned return her investment and tear out of here on the next train bound for Denver?

The thing that impressed Sky about Frank Cassidy, aside from his impressive height and gravelly voice, was his straightforward handshake. When he walked into the large living room with his son Cody that evening, she turned from the stone fireplace and the senior Cassidy took her hand warmly in his.

"Welcome to our home, Miss Saunders," he said, his gray eyes etched at the corners with nature's lines. "Hope your stay is comfortable, though I hear you found an unwelcome surprise when you arrived."

Sky lifted her chin. "Thank you, Mr. Cassidy. Sometimes life is full of unwelcome surprises."

Next to his father, standing a few inches taller, the marshal smiled at her from behind lively hazel eyes. "At least Miss Saunders didn't have to push the stagecoach uphill to get here." His voice held mischief. And, again, she didn't know whether to believe him.

"Now don't agitate our guest any further, Cody." Frank Cassidy obviously smothered a chuckle under his breath.

"Mr. Cassidy, sir." A jolly-looking, red-faced woman appeared at the threshold to the hallway, wiping her hands on her neat white apron. "*Ja*, the venison is ready. Ready as he ever vill be." She grinned, showing a gap between her front teeth.

"Fine, Gerta. We're looking forward to it."

The marshal came up beside Sky and lightly touched her elbow. "Miss Saunders, let's sit down and enjoy some of the best cooking this side of the Mississippi." His smile was warm, and she was startled at how her body responded so favorably to his touch.

After a fine meal, Gerta served them a pungent coffee.

Adding a generous amount of milk to her cup, Sky addressed Frank Cassidy. "You were interested in my life in Ohio; now please tell me about Leadville." She had mentioned living with her aunt and uncle, and given credit to Gran, but had left out Thomas all together. "What is it like to live here?"

Father and son looked at each other and lifted their brows.

"It's a miracle city," Mr. Cassidy enthused.

"It's a raving boomtown," the marshal added.

Sky cocked her head. "What does that mean, 'a miracle city'?"

The senior Cassidy set his coffee cup down on the table. "Well, we've got a steady stream of men making a lot of money up on Fryer Hill. Lots of mining and lots of rich silver discoveries."

"Some lose their last dime, too," the marshal said. "There are no guarantees."

His father shook his head. "But look at the Robert E. Lee. In less than two months, that mine produced a quarter of a million silver dollars!"

"My, that is a lot of money," Sky agreed.

"Our own former mayor, Horace Tabor, sold the Little Pittsburg to his partners last year for one million!" Frank Cassidy continued. "Now, he's the state's lieutenant governor and ready to make even more on his Matchless mine."

He leaned toward her. "If I was ten years younger, Miss Saunders, I'd be up there breaking my back in the mines myself. This land you're on right now is the richest soil in the damn country! If you'll excuse my cussing, miss."

Sky sat back in her chair, the thought of immediate wealth sending an exhilarating thrill up her spine. "I had no idea, Mr. Cassidy."

"You've got stars in your eyes, Miss Saunders," the marshal observed. "Just like all the hopeful tinhorns who come up here."

"And what is a 'tinhorn'?"

He shrugged. "Oh, just a gambler who thinks he has abilities, able to beat the odds."

An uncomfortable surge of heat flushed up her neck above her lace collar. She didn't care for his hasty comparison. "It sounds like many who come here are more than tinhorns."

Mr. Cassidy pushed his chair away from the table. "Guess I'll excuse myself and go have a smoke." He got up. "You're welcome to stay as long as you like, Miss Saunders."

"Thank you."

"I've got a feeling Miss Saunders will be leaving shortly, Dad. She's probably going to miss the comforts and safety of home."

The senior Cassidy gave a quick wave and ambled to the front door.

Fuming inside, Sky rose from her chair. She didn't take to his presumption of the time she would be leaving. "It's late, Marshal. I should get some rest after my long journey."

He shot to his feet, towering above her. "Yes, ma'am." He walked with her to the hallway that led to her back bedroom.

Sky paused at the threshold and forced a pleasant demeanor. "I found our dinner conversation fascinating. It made me recall some wise words from my grandmother."

"It did?"

"Yes. She always told me that women were as capable as men."

His brows arched upward. "If they could swing a pickaxe like a man, they sure would be."

"My granny could have. Goodnight, Marshal."

Sky entered her room, her thoughts swirling with snatches of Frank Cassidy's words. *A miracle city—the mine sold for a million dollars—the richest soil in the country.*

She would count the days until Ned returned, but meanwhile she'd search for her new mining partner, Mr. Gunther. The marshal's prediction of her early departure was wrong.

She didn't plan on leaving Leadville any time soon.

CHAPTER THREE

Just after dawn, Cody descended the stairs from his second-floor bedroom. He heard female voices below: Gerta's and Miss Saunders's.

As he reached the last stair, Gerta scurried out of the pine-paneled dining room and back into the kitchen to fix his breakfast.

Miss Saunders stood, gazing out the front room window, but turned to face him as he entered. A fine-figured woman she was. Narrow waist, slightly flaring hips. Her sensibly fashioned dress, a shade of deep green, complemented her creamy skin and vibrant blue eyes. Eyes that lifted to meet his from beneath a sweep of feathery dark lashes.

Instantly, he was wide awake. "Good morning, Miss Saunders."

Her features brightened. "Yes it is, Marshal. I've been enjoying this captivating view of the mountains."

Well, she was in a fine mood. He stepped closer. Did he smell the scent of lilacs? "No mountain views where you're from?"

"Oh, no," she said. "Just tree-lined streets." A blush the shade of wild roses tinted her cheeks. "You know, I would really like to see more of the city now that I'm here."

"There's not much to see." Attempting to hide his reluctance, he shifted his gaze to the mountain range. Why couldn't she put this raucous, untamed place behind her and return back east where life was more civilized? He didn't have time to take her on a buggy ride.

"Goodness. After your father's wonderful description of Leadville last night, it sounds terribly exciting!"

He smothered the urge to smile. Frank Cassidy had glossed over the tough life here, the raw day-to-day existence. Everyone struck it rich, according to him. Cody knew better. But, not wanting to insult his father or appear inhospitable, he acquiesced. "If that's what you'd like, Miss Saunders, I certainly will oblige."

Gerta's voice, accompanied by the aroma of frying bacon, announced from the kitchen. "Your coffee is ready, Marshal. Yust the way you like it. Hot und black."

Cody's mouth watered. "Thanks, Gerta." Before moving toward the kitchen, he addressed his houseguest. "I have to make a stop at the jail and question a prisoner. After that," he said with a wry grin, "I'll swing back and show you what a god-forsaken mining town looks like."

Sky straightened on the wagon seat, her eyes surveying the town and panoramic mountain range ahead. The team rumbled down a wide dirt road, bordered on either side by one- and two-story frame business establishments. Everything around her was alive and in motion: the mule teams pulling loaded wagons, the men driving them, the men on foot. "So this is Leadville."

"Yes, ma'am." The marshal glanced her way, his powerful shoulder moving against hers as he guided the team through congested thoroughfare. "We're on Harrison Avenue, the main street in town."

She nodded, absorbing his aroma of pine soap mingled with road dust. Although surrounded by strange men, in all manner of attire, this man's physically commanding presence provided a sense of security. Well, after all, she thought, he was the marshal.

Along the street, signs advertised lamp goods, crockery and

glassware, ales and liquors, books and stationery, drugs and clothing. A few restaurants blended into the mix. They passed a meat market where twenty plucked chickens and half a dozen small pigs dangled across the open double doorway.

"Up here's the finest theater between St. Louis and San Francisco." The marshal angled his head to the left as they approached a tall red brick building on the next block. "Tabor's Opera House."

Holding onto the brim of her straw hat against a sudden gust, Sky craned her neck. "It does look grand."

"Our former mayor had a fancy opening here a few years ago." The marshal's mustache lifted at the corners. "But he didn't count on that vigilante hanging right across the street."

"A vigilante hanging?" Sky croaked.

"Some poor devils got their necks stretched while the society folks paraded by in their swell clothes, gawking and making the biggest commotion."

Sky gasped. "Did you catch the vigilantes?"

He shook his head. "I wasn't the marshal then. Just heard about it."

"Oh." She hunkered down, adjusting her skirts around her. "Are there many hangings here, Marshal?"

He nodded. "Lots of 'em, Miss Saunders."

Her recollection of Ned's correspondence came to mind. He'd described Leadville as "a booming mining town filled with ladies and gentlemen from the East, who come out here for the adventure of experiencing a new frontier."

He'd obviously exaggerated about the eastern gentlefolk and failed to mention the hangings.

The part about the "new frontier" was true enough, however. All around her men were arriving to make their fortunes. Couldn't women too? She'd just forget about the hangings. No town was perfect. Her new mining partner, Mr. Gunther, must be working in their mine right now.

"Marshal Cassidy," she suggested suddenly, "please take me up to the mines."

His expression tensed. "You aren't serious?"

"Well, of course I'm serious."

"I can't do that, ma'am."

"Why ever not? There must be hundreds of them."

He guided the horses over to the boardwalk at the end of the street. Swiveling, he met her gaze with indignant hazel eyes. "Because, Miss Saunders, a mine is no place for a woman . . . that is, a lady."

Sky sent him a chiding glance. "Well, I am a lady. But that has nothing to do with viewing the mines." Her spine stiffened. "If I were a man, Marshal Cassidy, would you deny me the opportunity of seeing Leadville's most obvious source of commerce?"

His eyes widened beneath the brim of his western hat, his features reddened. "You could fall in a mineshaft—or break a limb."

"Very well, Marshal." She deliberately leaned in toward him, gazing upward through the veil of her long dark lashes. "But I would think that after my long, arduous journey to get here, you wouldn't refuse my one request."

Her words stroked Cody like a velvet whip. "Well, I . . ."

She was a stubborn woman who needed a comeuppance or a kiss. And he knew if he tried either one, he'd surely get his jaw slapped. It wasn't decent how close she sat to him, her enticing lips tilted upward, only inches from his.

"Thank you, Marshal." She smiled, obviously pleased. "I won't be the least concerned about the dangers of the mines when you'll be there to protect me."

He winced at her ignorance and bit back the urge to tell her what he thought of willful eastern women. She'd be as awkward traipsing around a mine yard as a sheep in quicksand.

Frustrated, he cracked the reins over the horses' rumps. "All right, Miss Saunders. I'll take you on a short tour. But don't make me have to remind you, this was your idea."

As they rode out of town, he couldn't help notice the satisfied look on her face. Her city-fashioned hat dipped over her forehead, she gazed out at the distant sloping foothills like a princess going to inspect her properties. Just wait until she got a whiff of that slag up her snoot. The harsh reality of the mines would send her on her way back home in no time.

After a while, Sky glanced over at the marshal to determine his mood. He'd been awfully quiet since they'd left the outskirts of town. She hoped he wouldn't hold her spontaneous curiosity against her; it was simply in her nature to ask questions and explore possibilities. She wanted to find out all she could about these silver-rich mines and maybe find Mr. Gunther in the process. The marshal's tanned face remained stoic.

For the sake of conversation, she asked, "Who's watching your prisoner, Marshal, while you're away?"

"My deputy."

"Oh." The constant motion of the wagon caused his hip and thigh to graze hers, which sent discomforting tingles down her leg. She scooted a few inches away. "What was the prisoner's crime?"

"He broke a shop owner's window the other night. We think he's a member of a gang of lot jumpers. So far, he's been tight-lipped."

"What are lot jumpers?"

"Thugs who attack a business owner, usually after dark. They chase him off his property; then they claim land rights."

"Does that go on often?"

"Too often." His voice hardened. "Leadville is full of bunco artists, thieves—better known as footpads—as well as claim jumpers."

Her brows drew together. She wished he hadn't revealed quite so much of the town's dirty laundry so soon, especially since she was considering taking up residence here. "You don't have an easy job then, do you, Marshal?"

He cast her a sardonic look. "Some say it's an impossible job. The last marshal got backshot."

A chill scampered down her spine. She glanced nervously through the surrounding sparse trees. "I hope they pay you well."

His responding laugh held sarcasm. "If you can call a hundred and twenty-five dollars a month well paid."

"With the risks you must take, Marshal, it sounds like you should ask for a raise."

He urged the team around a fallen log jutting into the middle of the road. "You might have a point there, Miss Saunders."

The washboard road climbed higher, the air thickening with a strange odor. "Are we nearing the mines? I smell something foreign."

"This is Carbonate Hill. You're smelling the slag . . . what's left of the ore after the silver's mined out of it."

She looked out over sooty-looking piles of debris. Several men working on the hillside stared back at her curiously.

"Where's the biggest mine in this area?"

He shrugged. "North of here, on Fryer's Hill, there's the richest."

The word "richest" piqued her interest. "Please, show me."

Cody saw a spark light up her sky-blue eyes. She was a determined woman. "Guess we might as well take the full nickel tour, now that we're up here," he said, wondering at how easily she maneuvered him, and why he let her. And why she'd even want to be up here.

They approached a hillside the color of charcoal, dotted with at least a dozen outbuildings, stacks of logs, and mounds of metal slag. Tall smokestacks jutted from some of the buildings, belching gray smoke clouds into the air.

He drew the horses to a halt. "Here it is—one of the richest square miles on earth. Originally, a prospector sold the claim to old man Fryer for a six weeks' grubstake."

Fascinated, Sky took it all in. Although tempted to mention her grubstaking Mr. Gunther, she recalled Ned's warning to be discrete and decided she'd better not. "Does the owner live up here?"

"Nope. After Fryer made his fortune, he sold out and moved to Denver. But he used to live up here in a squatty little cabin with a dirt floor. Cooked his meals in a rough stone fireplace."

"Kind of an old hermit."

"Yeah, they say he was bull-headed, but friendly to some down on their luck. Fryer didn't pay attention to the experts who said he'd never make it. He sensed there was silver here and he proved it."

Sky breathed in the strange ore smell. The smell of success. The aroma of independence. She could identify with old man Fryer. With only the sweat on his brow, raw determination, and some luck, he'd attained his goal. Now he was a rich man. No one could look down on him again.

She tried to imagine what it would be like mining silver out of these mountains. "Can we go into the mine?"

The marshal reared back on the seat. "There is no sane reason why a woman would want to go down a filthy mineshaft, Miss Saunders."

She knew she was testing his patience. Glancing over at him imploringly, she revised her request. "Well, could we just drive up and *look* into the entrance?"

"What for?" Exasperation reflected in his eyes.

"I want to see where the silver comes out."

Cody threw up his hands. "The silver doesn't come out; it's mined out."

Why in the hell had he ever let her talk him into this fool's chase? And why would a proper eastern lady be so curious about a damned black hole?

Her smile was radiant. He'd swear it was warm enough to melt the biggest chunk of ice in his father's icehouse. "Could we just drive near the entrance?"

With strained control, he held back his rising temper. "You try a man's tolerance, miss." Slapping the reins over the startled horses, he drove them uphill, past an armed guard, and into an outer yard. "This is as far as I go."

"Would you assist me down, please, Marshal?"

"Why?" he snorted.

"I'd like to see where the miners work."

Cody slowly rubbed his jaw, his teeth clenched. "Only for a minute."

Reluctantly, he jumped down and went around to the other side of the wagon. He grasped her around her midsection and set her on the ground, surprised at how his large hands nearly spanned her small waist. Her chin tilted upward, just reaching his shoulder. She was a tall woman, with a high, well-formed bosom, and warm beneath the fabric of her traveling dress. He cleared his throat, not expecting the resulting attraction her nearness provoked.

"Thank you, Marshal. I won't be a minute."

He watched her turn, lifting her forest-green skirt, and sashay away into the yard. She hadn't taken more than four or five prissy steps, when her ankle twisted awkwardly beneath her and she pitched forward into a pile of smelter slag.

Cody stood transfixed, pressing his mouth shut to avoid laughing out loud, half expecting his houseguest to let out an unladylike scream. Surprised when she didn't, he watched for a second or two while she struggled to right herself, her dress bunched up above her shapely stockinged calves, her lily-white gloved hands flailing in the black slag. Darned if it didn't serve her right.

As she pushed herself into a seated position, her straw hat cocked askew and now a shade of charcoal gray, he rushed to her. "Miss Saunders, are you all right?"

She blew out a long, defiant breath. "Aside from my pride, and my ankle, I'm just fine, Marshal." She glared up at him, her face smudged with smelter dust. "If you'll help me up, I can make it back to the wagon."

He grabbed her arm and lifted her to her wobbly feet. "Well, now, I hate to say it, but I tried to warn you."

She coughed, and he saw the flush of color on her cheeks. He guided his hand under her elbow, hoping she wasn't going to bawl. He couldn't stand it when women bawled.

Pulling her arm away, she forged ahead, limping over the rocky ground. But in only a few paces, she weaved sideways, and he caught her around the waist. "It's my ankle." She winced in obvious pain. "I'm afraid I've twisted it." Her voice sounded less stubborn, more vulnerable.

"You shouldn't put any more weight on it, miss. We'd better head back and get you off of that foot." Before she could object, Cody swept her up in his arms. She felt light as a prairie dove. Beneath his nose, the aroma of lilac water blended with smelter dust.

Sky reeled with embarrassment and discomfort. The marshal's arms around her, holding her body so close to his warm, hard chest, made her lightheaded. "I'm, I'm sure I'll be fine once I can soak my ankle in some Epsom salts." Her face felt gritty, her nose and throat clogged with dust. She knew she looked a wreck.

He set her on the wagon seat and hopped up beside her, extremely agile for a man his height. She was about as agile as a newborn calf. She'd made a fool of herself. "I shouldn't have gotten off the wagon and tried to walk on such uneven ground," she confessed.

The marshal gave a slight smile, his mustache lifting. "Well, at least you didn't fall down a mineshaft, Miss Saunders. That would have given us a whole lot more explaining to do."

When they neared the bottom of the hill, another team approached, traveling at a hurried pace.

"Aren't they going too fast?" Sky asked.

"Looks that way."

Their lead horse whinnied and both horses sidestepped nervously off the narrow, rutted road, causing the wagon to tilt at an angle. She slid to the edge of the seat. To the right, a deep ditch yawned up at her. The marshal caught her by the arm, but not in time to prevent her from throwing weight onto her twisted ankle.

She gasped as pain streaked from her injury up her calf.

"Watch where you're going, man," the marshal barked to the oncoming driver.

The other driver swerved and slowed. "Sorry, Marshal. We're checking on a report of a deserted claim," he replied from between protruding lips, his voice like grating sandpaper. The man's companion sat next to him mute as stone.

Sky didn't care for the looks of the driver. Beneath his shabby bowler, wisps of greasy black hair sprouted from the sides of his head. His wide-set, bulging eyes roamed from her face downward over her bodice. Green eyes the shade of dark cesspools. Despite the heated flush of her cheeks, evoked by his intimate gaze, a tremor of apprehension chilled her.

The marshal squinted impatiently at the interloper. "Then go about your business. But slow down."

The bulging eyes flickered. "Will do, Marshal."

Edging his team alongside them, the driver tipped his grimy hat, his murky gaze swiveling to the road ahead. His companion smirked, exposing a missing front tooth.

"Jackasses," the marshal muttered under his breath and urged the team onward.

She stared after the departing men, grateful she'd been sitting next to a powerfully built officer of the law. "Who was that?"

"Think his name is Wickham. He's just a flunky who works in the city clerk's office."

She shuddered. "I wouldn't want to meet up with him on a dark street."

"Then you don't mind that I didn't introduce you?"

"Not in the least."

She reached down beneath her petticoats and rubbed her throbbing ankle. All she wanted was to get back to a comfortable chair and a bucket of warm Epsom salts. Then, she could think of ways to seek out Mr. Gunther in this booming mining town. In spite of Leadville's seamier side, the seduction of finding adventure and wealth here boldly sparked her senses.

Why couldn't she make her fortune here like others had? Her hush-money from Thomas was tied up in her investment in the mine, so she'd have to find work. She was well equipped to find a bookkeeping position to support herself. Certainly she could manage.

Yes, striking it rich might not be such an impossible dream. Becoming an independently wealthy woman would suit her just fine. No man could ever mistreat her again.

Glancing over at Marshal Cassidy's strong profile, Sky decided he would be a most beneficial ally, once she informed him of her intentions.

CHAPTER FOUR

"There ve go." On the enclosed back porch, Gerta helped Sky into her wrapper and assisted her from the side of the metal tub to the wicker chair. The small woman's pudgy arm steadied her as she settled herself into the welcome cushions.

"Thank you so much, Gerta." Sky managed a smile in spite of the continued throbbing from her twisted ankle. "That bath and the salts were relaxing."

"You're velcome, miss." The Cassidys' cook straightened. "Dat vas quite a fall ya took traipsin' around the mine yard." She shook her head, giving Sky a look that said, *Why in the world would you do such a thing?*

Sky nodded. "Yes, it was. I guess I should have considered the old saying, 'Curiosity killed the cat.'"

Gerta grinned, revealing the gap between her front teeth. "Ya. I tink so. The marshal shouldn't a let ya do it."

Boot heels clicked across the kitchen floor and the marshal himself stuck his blond head around the doorframe. "Hello, ladies. Is something burning in the oven?"

Gerta's eyes rolled upward and her plump hands flew out beside her like airborne birds. "Oh, m' Got. My pies!"

Marshal Cassidy sent Sky one of his unexpected winks as the harried housekeeper raced back into the kitchen. "And how is your ankle, Miss Saunders?"

Sky felt a twinge of embarrassment about being caught in only her underwear and robe. "It's a little better," she said, drawing her light cotton wrapper together over her breasts. "Aren't you home a bit early, Marshal?"

"No, ma'am. Deputy Hacker has things under control, along with several of the police officers helping him out." He angled his rugged features toward the kitchen. "By the smell of things, supper isn't too far away."

"Oh, of course." Sky glanced beyond him to the hallway, wondering how she was going to make it to her room and get dressed.

The marshal's gaze settled on her ankle. "Looks like you've got some swelling there. You should have it propped up."

"Well, Gerta was going to . . ."

He held up a finger. "Just hold it a minute. I'll be right back." Before she could respond, his broad-shouldered frame disappeared from the doorway. In a short time, he returned, carrying a roll of gauze and a green bottle in one hand, and a footstool in the other.

"Got just what you need." He squatted in front of her, lifted her leg onto the worn footstool, and set the gauze and bottle next to it.

"Really, Marshal, I don't think . . ."

He opened the bottle and reached for her foot.

She tensed, pulling it inside her wrapper. "What is that horrible-smelling potion?"

He grinned. "It's liniment. Great stuff." Paying no attention to her anxiety, he took hold of her foot, eased it toward him and began slowly rubbing the pungent liquid into her swollen ankle.

She tried to object, but his large, sun-browned hands seemed so capable and the bath had left her lethargic after the long ride in that bouncing wagon. She sighed, despite herself, his warm stroking fingers making her forget the pain. "Yes, it is nice." The palms of his hands caressed her ankle and then worked upward to her calf. She shouldn't let him touch her leg—her limb. But, it felt so relaxing.

"That's good," Cody drawled. He saw her eyelids flutter and her pretty head nod back against the chair. She was enjoying his touch. Hell, he was enjoying it himself. Her calf fit nicely in the palm of his hand. "This should help take away the pain."

The marshal's hands and words soothed her. Sky closed her eyes. She'd never much liked Thomas touching her; she'd merely accepted his early attempts at affection as her wifely duty.

She was aware of the gauze being wrapped around her ankle. Suddenly, behind her closed lids, she saw Thomas's long, pale fingers like sharp blades slapping her. Little slaps at first. Then stronger—stinging—on her shoulders, her back, her buttocks. Her eyes flew open and she jerked her foot away from him. "What did you say?" she snapped.

The marshal sat back on his haunches, a look of surprise on his face. "I said I use it on my horse all the time."

"Your horse?" She held her ankle protectively close to her beneath her wrapper. "Really, Marshal. I should be getting dressed for dinner."

As if taken aback by her abruptness, he rose to his feet. "Yes, ma'am. I'll help you."

She allowed Cody to help her from the chair, but when he offered to carry her, she declined, insisting that she could walk by taking his arm. Every step was painful, but she didn't want to become dependent on his help.

"I'll be looking for employment as soon as my ankle heals," she remarked as they approached her room.

"That'll be fine. There's no hurry." He assisted her across a braided rag rug and settled her into an armchair.

"I'm a very competent bookkeeper."

She leaned over to adjust the gauze bandage and Cody caught a glimpse of the swell of her lovely ivory breasts above her shift.

"Yes, ma'am," he murmured, his heart rate quickening at the seductive sight.

"Here ve go." Gerta popped up behind him holding a bulky towel. "Here's some ice to keep da svelling down. But she needs to be in bed vit her foot up."

"If that's where she needs to be . . ." Without waiting for permission, he slipped his arms around Sky and carried her across the rug to the quilt-covered bed. She let out a cry of protest.

The housekeeper rushed to his side. "Vait, vait! Let me roll down da covers."

Cody noticed Sky's cheeks blush the color of prairie roses while he held her closely to him and Gerta bustled about readying the bed. Darned if the gal didn't feel just right in his arms.

"I'm not a mustard plaster, Mr. Cassidy!" she vented in a burst of objection and tried to pry her upper body away from his chest.

"All right." He chuckled. "I'm putting you down." He plopped her unceremoniously against the pillows at the headboard.

"Thank you." His houseguest dismissed him with a quick look from beneath long, curving eyelashes.

"Shoo now, Marshal." Gerta started to push him good-naturedly toward the door. Her head came to just above his elbow. "Ve'll be fine. I'll bring Miss Saunders's supper to her in da bed."

Cody shook his head in mock resignation and ducked out the door. He'd never seen so much fuss over a twisted ankle. The gal hadn't even appreciated his best remedy. And she'd pulled away from him like she'd been snake bit when he'd been so gentle with her. What was it about his touch? The few times he'd visited Sallie Purple's pleasure house, other women never reacted that way. They always wanted more.

Frustrated, Cody barged out the front door, his stomach growling as loud as a starving grizzly's.

After Gerta left the room, Sky lay back against the feather pillows, trying to get comfortable. The ice-filled towel draped over her throbbing ankle like a dead weight. Not that she wasn't grateful. Everyone was trying to make her comfortable.

Except she felt just the opposite. Her mind buzzed with confusion. The places on her ankle and calf still tingled where the marshal had massaged them. How could she have such a reaction to his touch? She thought a man's hands would never feel soothing on her body. She'd never wanted a man to touch her again after Thomas. But the marshal's fingers, strong and firm, and seemingly caring, were so different from Thomas's long pale fingers and clammy touch.

The men were as unalike as night and day. She recalled Thomas when she'd first met him. Older widower, impeccably dressed, bookish, and bespectacled. He'd always been careful not to show affection in public. Spoke to her in low but assured tones. Fatherly. A mentor, she'd thought. A rescuer, she'd thought, from her aunt's constant demands.

How wrong she'd been. When she married Thomas she'd only traded one set of demands for another.

She closed her eyes and willed her ankle to heal quickly so that she could concentrate on job prospects. She must leave this house where a man's touch could make her sigh, and his mere presence could deliver a warm flush.

Cody finished his breakfast and headed toward the front room. He had to get over to the jail. It irked him that his prisoner would only be fined for Peg O'Connor's broken window. The thug had been lounging in a cell, eating three square meals a day at the citizens' expense, and neither he nor Jim had been able to pry anything out of him. These lot jumpers were a sly, secretive bunch—about as likeable as a gang of marauding coyotes.

Worse yet, the vandal would likely skip town before Peg saw any compensation.

As Cody reached the front door, he heard Miss Saunders's voice greeting Gerta in the kitchen. Funny, he seemed to just miss her at breakfast the last three mornings. At dinner, she was polite but subdued. He guessed she was anxious about her cousin's return.

Yes, he thought, as he made his way down the front porch steps and sauntered over to his waiting buckskin, everyone would be relieved when the deputy groom got back to town.

Maybe, after their reunion, Ned could convince Miss Saunders that she didn't belong here.

Before dinner that evening, Cody entered the front room and saw his houseguest sitting on the chamois leather sofa, chatting amiably with his father. Light from the elk antler chandelier gilded her auburn hair, done up in a flurry of curls on top of her head.

A half hour before, Cody had jumped into the back porch tub for a quick bath to wash off the day's sweat, and even lathered up his hair with some fine smelling soap Gerta had left on a towel draped over the wooden stool. Refreshed and invigorated, he looked forward to a companionable evening of conversation. He had to admit Miss Saunders's presence this week had added luster to a rough-around-the-edges, male-dominated house.

"Sit down, son." Frank Cassidy gestured to the wine bottle and glasses on a tray in front of him. Wine the Cassidys brought out on special occasions. "Miss Saunders has good news."

Cody quirked a brow and reached for the wine bottle.

"What's your good news?" He seated himself on the sofa next to her.

Her deep blue eyes sparkled. "I've just been offered a new position."

"Oh? Where?" Cody held the wine bottle suspended over a glass on the side table.

"My ankle is so much better," she continued as if she hadn't heard his question. "I'll be moving out tomorrow."

"Tomorrow?" He attempted an encouraging expression, but his face felt stiff.

Her gaze danced from him over to his father, her features glowing. "I knew you'd both be pleased."

"Sure, we're pleased." He poured himself a glass of wine. "Just wonder how you found a position so fast."

She smiled, a satisfied twinkle in her eye. "Gerta passed along a tip from her brother-in-law."

Cody took a swallow of the tart red wine. Miss Saunders was enjoying her little secret, keeping him in the dark. "Well, now, you're leaving tomorrow." He sent her a challenging glance. "I'll be glad to move you to your new place first thing in the morning."

Her pretty face puckered, as though she was weighing his offer. Then she gave a slight shrug. "That would be very helpful, Marshal."

Pensive, Sky sat on the rocking wagon seat, mentally kicking herself for getting stuck in this precarious position. She never should have agreed to let the marshal deliver her to her new place of employment. She should have found someone else to bring her. What if she didn't like the place or her new employer? How embarrassing to find that out with the marshal watching!

Granny Saunders was "tsking" to herself right now. Sky was stuck in another pickle that Gran couldn't get her out of.

Now the marshal caught her eye from beneath his slanted hat brim. His smooth-shaven jaw and clean aroma, akin to a pine breeze, engaged her senses. Why did his presence distract her so? "You said this place is down Harrison Avenue?"

Sky studied the scrap of paper Gerta had given her with roughly drawn directions. "It's up here at Chestnut Street. You turn west."

They reached the end of the block and Cody guided the horses around the corner. "Now will you tell me the name of the place?" he asked, growing more impatient. He assumed, being she was a bookkeeper, she'd work at a bank, but they'd driven right by the First National Bank and she'd said nothing. Why was she being so darn secretive?

One thing he did know. Women were unpredictable. The bitter memory of his mother's sudden departure flashed in the back of his mind. He'd learned a hard lesson about women at the tender age of ten when his mother ran off with that no-good miner. His dad had never really recovered from her departure. Never remarrying, he'd lost himself in his wagon-building business and left most of the raising of his younger son to Cody.

"It . . . it's called Burtram's Gaming House." Sky's voice wavered. "I think I see it, up here to the right." Her gaze settled on a boldly lettered sign across a two-story clapboard building in the middle of the block. Even at midmorning, entertainers mingled with passing pedestrians. A raggedly dressed magician juggled cards in front of the tall, narrow windows in the front. Sky gritted her teeth, waiting for the reaction she knew was coming.

The marshal's large frame jerked as if he'd been kicked by a mule. His sudden reaction caused one of the horses to brush against a passing pedestrian, who waved his fist angrily. "What?" he blustered. "You can't work here!" He snapped the reins across the animals' rumps.

"Stop, Marshal," Sky demanded, grasping his muscular arm. "This is the correct address." She shivered, dreading the imminent confrontation with a man she respected.

Swerving the team over next to the boardwalk, he brought them to a halt. "You can't be serious, Miss Saunders." His tanned features flushed red with anger. "This is a gambling hall!"

"I realize that, Marshal." She straightened her spine. "And the offered pay is very generous, as well as the inclusion of board and room." That was the information Gerta had passed along.

"Board and room!" The words shot from his mouth like a barrage of canon balls. "You can't be serious!"

"I couldn't be more serious," she fired back. Her voice held firm, but her knees shook beneath her dress. "Now, please assist me from this wagon or I'll be forced to jump out of it."

A responding growl rumbled in the marshal's throat, then escaped in a muttered curse. He sat immovable as a giant tombstone and scowled ahead.

How could she defy such a man? He'd taken her in when she had no place to go and treated her as a privileged houseguest. Quavering inside, Sky still held her determined expression. The pitiful funds left over from her settlement money, now invested in some unknown mine, wouldn't last more than a week. She needed this job, and she needed it immediately.

"Well, I see we've come to an impasse." Sky exhaled a fretful breath and glanced over to the magician a few yards away. The stocky man was pulling cards out of his slouchy hat and making exaggerated expressions of joy, as if he'd just won a lucky hand. She leaned toward him. "Sir! Could you help me, please?"

The man grinned widely at her, displaying a set of incomplete teeth, and hurried over to the wagon. The marshal, seemingly unaware of her request amidst the street noises, continued to stare ahead grumpily. She offered her outstretched hand to the man and, with a flourish, he assisted her to the boardwalk. Thanking him, she snatched her valise from the rear of the wagon.

"Hey! Where are you going?" the marshal demanded as she started to turn away.

"I'm going inside to apply for a position."

He leaped from the wagon seat and stood towering above her, his eyes shooting hazel sparks from beneath his hat brim. "Miss Saunders—you can't work here. It's just not the right place for a lady." His large hand clamped down over hers on the valise handle. "Let's get back on the wagon and we'll talk."

The warmth from his flesh sent heat tendrils scurrying up her arm. "I have no intention of climbing back on that wagon, Marshal." Setting her chin defiantly, she tugged her valise toward her. But the marshal had a mighty grip.

"Well, good morning, folks." A gravelly voice greeted them in the midst of their tug-of-war. "Could I be of some assistance?"

Sky tore her exasperated gaze from the marshal and darted a glance at the big-boned, dark-haired man approaching them. "I do hope so. Are you Mr. Burtram?"

The man's thin lips lifted in a semblance of a smile. "Yes, ma'am."

"I'm Sky Saunders and I'm here to apply for the bookkeeping position, if it's still open."

"No, she isn't." His hand still over hers, the marshal nudged her back toward the waiting team.

"Please, Marshal. This does not concern you." She yanked the valise forcefully out of his grasp.

The proprietor's watery gray eyes switched from the marshal back to Sky. "Job's open if you got the right credentials, miss." He wheeled and headed toward the open door of the gambling hall. "C'mon inside."

She looked up at the marshal imploringly. "I need this job. At least wait while I talk to Mr. Burtram."

"All right. You've got five minutes before I unload your luggage on the sidewalk."

The hairs rose on the back of her neck. How dare he treat her so high-handedly? With a quick nod, she turned and hurried to the door of the gambling hall.

A young Mexican boy hovered in the doorway as she approached. Thin and disheveled, he watched her with only a hint of curiosity, his mouth expressionless. When she smiled, he averted his wide brown eyes and darted away into the shadows.

Aside from the cigarette and cigar smoke, alcohol fumes, and stale body odor, the noise most affected her senses. Men wearing slouch hats and dust-covered clothes sat at scattered tables about the hall and gathered in clusters at the long bar. A boisterous air permeated the place, a place inhabited strictly by men. It seemed half of them stared at her standing inside the doorway, alone and feeling queasy at her stomach.

What if the marshal was right? This was certainly not a likely place for her to work. She closed her eyes for a moment, wavering on which direction to go: forward or backward, out the door to the lawman waiting for her.

"Miss Saunders?" The proprietor came to her side. She noticed he at least wore a clean shirt and had combed his thinning dark hair. "Would you come back to my office, please?"

She allowed a moment to compose herself. She could listen to what he had to offer. Gerta had assured her the pay here would be better than at a bank or store. "Show me the way, Mr. Burtram," she managed. He led her through the noisy patrons and she wondered if anyone here might know the whereabouts of Ned's miner, Dan Gunther.

As Burtram started along the hallway past the kitchen, Sky glanced over her shoulder to the front entrance and saw it filled with the broad-shouldered physique of Marshal Cassidy. She felt a jolt of anxiety. He cared enough to be concerned for her, but she had to seek her own way.

The pay Burtram offered was better than she'd expected. "Thirty dollars a week," he mumbled from around the short stogie stuck in his mouth. At the bank at home, she'd made twenty for a five-day week; this would be six.

She smiled affably. "And you're including room and board."

Burtram's puffy eyelids lifted above his slightly bloodshot eyes. He appeared to be a man who needed a good night's sleep. "Room plus two meals a day. Kitchen's closed on Sunday." He cleared his throat, his voice still sounding like footsteps on gravel. "Cook ain't bad. He makes a tolerable bear stew."

"Oh." Sky attempted an enthusiastic tone. Realizing the five minutes were drawing short, she pressed him. "Could I see the room now, please?"

They climbed to the second floor. He showed her a small room above the office. Her eyes took in a made-up cot in the corner, a chair, an upended box serving as a side table, and an oil lamp perched on it. "Ain't no curtains on the window . . . but we can put some paper up there for ya."

She swallowed. Not exactly home. But then home was a place she'd left in the past. "This will be fine. I'm very good with a needle and thread." Wanting to appear professional, she stuck out her hand. "I'll take the job, Mr. Burtram. Of course, I'll want a lock put on the door. When do I start?"

Still chewing on the stogie, he nodded. "Call me Jack. You can move right in and start today, miss." He shook her hand, adding, "I'll put the lock on m'self. No one will bother you, and that's a promise."

Sky rushed to the front door. She knew she'd tested the marshal's patience, but surely he'd understand her need for the interview. Her optimism fell as she stepped outside into the bright morning light and saw her two trunks stacked on the edge of the plank walk. The marshal was long gone.

CHAPTER FIVE

Sky climbed the stairs behind two of Burtram's hired men who carried her trunks. They left them in a corner and shuffled out the door, leaving her standing alone in the center of the small room. For a moment, she couldn't believe she'd actually done this daring thing. Moved away from the shelter of the marshal's comfortable home and into this . . . this place.

She swallowed hard.

At least it was her room, her space. The day long ago when, at thirteen, she was placed in her aunt and uncle's house surfaced in her mind. She'd had to share a cramped bedroom with her two snickering female cousins. Even now, Sky felt the scalding embarrassment as the two older girls cast critical stares at her, the orphaned cousin, exchanging whispers about her unruly hair and homespun dress. She squeezed her eyes shut, closing out the humiliating memory.

Determinedly she removed her straw hat and stepped across the rough plank floor to the upended crate box. Blowing the dust off the crate, she moved the lamp aside and plopped her hat next to it. She sat down on the cot and was surprised that it felt fairly sturdy beneath her. Then she wondered: how clean were the sheets and had someone slept on them before? Did the blanket have lice?

Shuddering at the thought, she made a mental note to find out where she'd do her wash and ask Mr. Burtram to put in a few pegs to hang her dresses on the far wall.

It irked her that the marshal had left in such a huff. He was too arrogant for his own good. But what if he was right? She had no business working here. Could she trust the proprietor to treat her well? Gerta wouldn't have given her his name if he wasn't respectable, but then Gerta was passing along a tip from her brother-in-law and had probably never set foot in Burtram's Gambling Hall before.

A lively din floated up from the street and Sky couldn't resist opening the dust-streaked window wider and leaning out over the sill. Thriving humanity moved below her. Miners, mules, and mayhem. All kinds of businessmen. A tinkling of piano keys wafted from a saloon up the block. Fortunes were to be made here.

Her miner was out there somewhere. A shiver ran down her spine.

She breathed in Leadville's promise on the morning breeze and girded herself. *Well, I'm here. I've thrust myself right into it like a tadpole jumping into the middle of a frog pond.*

Her cousin and his new bride came to mind. Off on their carefree honeymoon. She sighed anxiously. *Ned, come back soon.*

"Oh, these books!" Sky let out an exasperated groan and swiped a lock of hair out of her eyes. Two days on the job, and she was having no luck balancing last month's receipts. Whoever had done the bookkeeping for Burtram must have been asleep at the switch. It would take weeks to set things straight. She scoffed to herself, thinking she should have asked for twice the salary her employer had offered.

Through the half-open door to the office, she heard a familiar timbred voice coming from somewhere up front in the hall. Her ears pricked up. *Good Lord. It's the marshal.* Well, if it was the marshal, she didn't care to see him. Her pride was still bruised at the way he'd up and left her and her trunks in the dust.

She stretched, then pushed her chair away from the overflowing desk. What she needed was a cup of Cookie's strong coffee before once again tackling the unbalanced books.

After smoothing her hair back behind her ears and pinching her cheeks, Sky moved to the door. She told herself she wouldn't look out toward the noisy hall, just slip over to the kitchen.

But just as she stepped across the threshold, the voice reached her ears again, and, despite her vow, she looked down the hall. It was him, all right, talking amiably to Jack Burtram, his stance relaxed as he leaned his tall frame against the polished wood bar. He had no business being here or looking so self-assured in a light blue denim shirt, his white western hat slanted just so over his forehead.

Her first thought was to escape. She couldn't trust herself to be polite to him.

Sky turned to make her way to the kitchen, but not soon enough. His greeting lassoed her and his easy grin caught her eye as she glanced over her shoulder. "Good morning, Marshal," she returned, trying to tamp down the sudden fluttering in her breast.

He sauntered over toward her, touching the brim of his hat. "Guess I owe you an apology, Miss Saunders, for leaving so fast the other day." His gaze briefly skimmed the floorboards, then settled back on her face. "It wasn't the gentlemanly thing to do."

Not quite ready to accept his apology, she lifted her chin a notch. "You did leave in a hurry."

"Sorry, ma'am. I want you to know, I . . . I'll be at your service whenever you might need assistance."

Blast, if his hazel eyes didn't sparkle, even in the low light of the long hall. "Thank you. I'll remember that."

"As a matter of fact . . ." He shifted his weight onto one hip and lowered his voice. "I understand Bill Crocker is looking for a clerk up at his general store right now."

The hackles rose on the back of her neck. How dare he try to interfere with her decision? "Really, Marshal. As you can see, I am already employed by Mr. Burtram."

A tic appeared in the marshal's clean-shaven jaw. "I understand that, ma'am, I just thought you might like something more . . . ah . . ."

"More what?" Despite herself, a cool anger hung on her words. "More respectable? I don't care what people think of the work I do, as long as it's honest work."

He raised a hand in placation. "Oh, I didn't . . ."

She cleaved him with a look of disdain. "Yes, you did. I came from a small eastern town, Marshal, where small-minded gossips could make life miserable for those who didn't comply with their ideas of respectability. Here, I can see things are different."

"Don't take me wrong, ma'am. I know you're a lady." His expression was contrite. "That's why I . . ."

Behind the marshal, Sky saw Burtram approaching. "Don't bother concerning yourself, Marshal. I have to get back to work now." As she turned away, she heard the marshal's retreating boot steps and his warning.

"Burtram, I don't want to hear about any of these sidewinders giving Miss Saunders any trouble. If I do, you'll have me to answer to."

Sky whirled around to see the marshal's broad-shouldered frame push through the swinging doors. He was a powerful man, used to giving orders and being obeyed. She would not let him manipulate her; yet, the intensity of his concern sent an undeniable rush of satisfaction racing through her.

Cody dived through the swinging doors and charged up the crowded boardwalk. He was hot under the collar and it looked like there was nothing he could do about it. This was the second time in the last two days she'd caused his temperature to soar. First, she wouldn't listen to his advice, and now she was stuck in a thankless job in a second-class gambling hall. How could Gerta, his own housekeeper, have suggested she apply for work there? A gambling hall! He couldn't imagine her practically *living* in that place, let alone working there. A beautiful, refined young woman like Miss Saunders.

The mere thought of it had the same effect as taunting a bull in a holding pen.

Well, wasn't it just like a woman? He recalled the nights when his mother had visited gambling halls in another mining town and ended up running off with that no-good miner. There was nothing his father could do or say to stop her. Wincing at the memory, he shoved it to the back of his mind.

Even the prospect of a decent position in the general store hadn't appealed to the independent Miss Saunders. He gave a cynical snort, the image of her determined, steel-blue gaze and upswept auburn hair still fresh in his thoughts.

Cody strode the uneven boardwalk along Harrison Avenue, heading toward his office on Front Street. He reminded himself that he had no business interfering in her business. Yet, because she was a naive, tender greenhorn, vulnerable to any hoodwinker that came her way, he felt compelled to keep an eye out for her.

He cursed under his breath. His dang deputy had better get back to town quick and talk some sense into her stubborn little head. She had to get out of that gambling den before it turned into a hornet's nest.

During the following days, Sky spent any free time exploring the neighborhood, and soon learned the cost of living in Leadville was high. Boarding houses charged from eight to fifteen dollars a week. Hotel fares averaged four dollars a day for a single bed. To think she could be spending at least half her weekly salary on room and board made her feel lucky after all. Being able to pocket nearly her entire earnings would enable her to put away a considerable nest egg.

Cotton pillows sold for a dollar apiece. A pair of blankets ran two and a half dollars. She would definitely invest in a new pillow and blankets as soon as she received her first week's pay. Material for window curtains was a necessity. She'd hung up a towel temporarily so no roving eyes could see her undressing. In a fabric shop up the street, she spied a bolt of blue floral gingham that would do nicely.

Now if she could just get used to the ceaseless clamor of humanity bursting from the gambling hall day and night. During the day, balancing the books completely absorbed her. The nights were the worst. Stomping, bellowing, cursing, and breaking bottles assaulted her senses, invading her room. Cigar smoke seeped through the cracks in the floorboards. She'd tried stuffing her ears with wads of cotton to no avail.

Sleeping in late was the result of restless tossing on her narrow cot half the night. Shameful for someone who'd always prided herself on waking at sunrise. Now she crawled out of her cot at nine o'clock and wouldn't appear downstairs until nearly ten, grumpy and ready for a cup of Cookie's strong coffee.

The last few days, she'd seen the marshal riding past out front on his spirited buckskin. Straight as an arrow in the saddle, his hat at a jaunty angle over his brow. He never looked in the direction of the gambling hall but kept his eyes focused ahead. She avoided glancing out the window but still found herself watching for him. Anticipating that little tingle that would start deep inside. Yet, she told herself she didn't care if he rode by or not. She was merely glad he was doing his job, keeping the streets safe for the citizens of Leadville.

She hoped to see Ned ride up any day now. How long could

he stretch out that infernal honeymoon? It'd been well over a week.

Late the next morning, Sky hunched over the books, intent on balancing the previous night's receipts. Suddenly, from behind, a pair of warm hands slid over her shoulders.

"Hey, Bluebird," a familiar male voice teased. "When did you fly in?"

She bolted upright just as the tanned hands spun her around in her chair. "Ned! You're back!" Sky leaped from the swivel chair into her cousin's welcoming arms.

"Hi, kid." Ned gave her a rough hug and then held her at arms' length. "Sure sorry you missed our wedding, but I've got someone here I want you to meet." With a grin as wide as the Rockies, he pulled a shy girl from the doorway. "This is Cindy, my new wife."

Cindy offered a friendly smile. A pale blond braid draped over one side of her simple lavender muslin frock.

"Well, now." Sky smiled back, grateful to see her cousin at last returned and looking happy and healthy. "Hello, Cindy. If I had known you two were thinking of tying the knot, I'd have gotten here sooner."

Ned threw his hands in the air. "Guess it just happened kind of fast."

"I guess. You missed my telegram telling when I would arrive. The marshal met me at the station and very kindly offered his home."

Ned raised his sandy-colored brows. "He told me. Think he would've liked it a whole lot better if you'd stayed there."

"It wasn't his decision to make, Ned. This position came up and I needed the money." She made a fist and cuffed him in the shoulder. "Someone spent my money to grubstake a miner."

Ned nodded enthusiastically. "I sure did, Sky. It's a durned good mine ol' Dan's workin' on. He's already mined out a little profit."

"That's good. When do I get to meet 'ol' Dan'?"

Ned's eyes lit up beneath his shock of brown hair. "The marshal's gonna keep me pretty busy chasin' down these lot jumpers, but I'll introduce you, soon as I can."

Sky gave him a skeptical look. "It had better be real soon."

As fate would have it, she didn't have long to wait. Saturday night, after a late supper in the kitchen, she climbed the back stairs to her room. The idea of a brisk walk to unkink her leg muscles had entered her mind, but she dared not venture out on the street after dark. Even a man wouldn't feel safe walking alone without carrying a ready pistol on his person.

Once inside her room, she bolted the door and lit the kerosene oil lamp. Then, boot steps clicked on the stairs and someone pounded heavily on her door. Her heartbeat rising in her throat, she picked up the lattice-back chair and held it in front of her like a shield. "Who is it?"

"Sky?"

With relief, she recognized Ned's eager voice. "I'm coming, Ned." Dropping the chair, she rushed to the door and unlocked it.

Ned barged past her. "What on earth?" Her nose smelled alcohol before her gaze settled on his boyish, excited features.

"He's here, Bluebird. C'mon downstairs."

She blinked. "Who's here?"

"*Dan.* Dan Gunther."

"Oh!" Realization hit her. Hurriedly, she glanced in the small rectangular mirror on the wall near the door. She reanchored the tortoiseshell comb beneath her topknot and dashed out into the hall behind Ned.

"He says he's anxious to meet you." Ned grinned, his whiskey breath invading her nostrils.

She locked the door and dropped the key in her skirt pocket. "Say, cousin, does Cindy know you're out on the town tonight?"

Ned looked sheepish. "Well, not exactly. She's at her uncle's for dinner, and he's so long-winded, I had to get out of there. Told her I wanted to see a guy about some property."

"Ned! Don't start off your marriage telling little white lies. Cindy will smell that whiskey a block away." He might be two years older than her, but she could still give him a piece of her mind.

"Geez, Sky." Ned frowned. "I know, you're right. I just happened to run into ol' Dan." He tapped her playfully on the cheek. "Thought you wanted to meet him."

An exasperated sigh escaped her lips. "I do."

"Well, c'mon—he's waiting for us."

Downstairs, the nightly hullabaloo had begun. Faro dealers with greased-back hair worked crowded gaming tables; men rolled chuck-a-luck dice from tinhorns. Dust-laden poker players bent over their cards like coyotes at feeding time.

Sky wrinkled her nose at the pervasive odor of stale sweat and hard alcohol. Didn't these men have a bar of soap and a clean change of clothes?

In one corner, a makeshift band ground out a raucous tune above the surrounding din. Shaded eyes gawked at her from beneath slouched brims. She was glad to be escorted through the boisterous male throng by a marshal's deputy.

Halfway to the front of the hall, Ned shouted in her ear, "There's Dan, coming in the front doors."

Following behind Ned across the sawdust floor, Sky peered through the smoky crowd. In the thick haze, she made out the stocky frame of a man pushing through the swinging doors. A gambler's boot sticking out from beneath a table almost tripped her. When she looked back up, the slightly stooped man was moving their way.

Her eyes focused in the dim light from the overhead chandeliers. Her mouth dropped open. Could this be the prosperous miner Ned had bragged about? Had grubstaked with her settlement money?

The man wore a beat up slouch hat crammed down over gray bushy sideburns and full beard. Red woolen underwear protruded at his collar from a frayed flannel shirt hanging half out of baggy canvas trousers. He was caked with grime from head to toe.

"Hey, Dan!" Ned waved amiably.

The old miner stopped in his tracks and let out an ear-splitting whistle over the din of the hall. Heads swiveled, eyes stared.

The old coot approached them. "Well, howdy-do?" His snappy dark eyes took Sky in full measure. Breaking into a grin that showed several empty gaps, he chuckled heartily. "They don't call me 'whistlin' Dan Gunther fer nothin' "!

CHAPTER SIX

Sky cringed, still in disbelief that this gray-whiskered, squint-eyed mountain man could be her miner. Never had she seen such an aberration.

"Well, I've told ya my name, miss. What's yers?" Whistlin' Dan moved closer, the pungent smell of whiskey and male sweat surrounding him.

"This is my cousin from Ohio who helped grubstake you," Ned said with enthusiasm, temporarily rescuing her. "Miss Sky Saunders."

She forced a smile, glad that Ned had used her maiden name. "Hello, Mr. Gunther. I understand that you—" She saw him extend a grimy paw toward her and blanched. How could she politely get out of shaking it?

Oblivious to her reluctance, the shaggy codger grasped her hand and a dynamic energy bolted from his hard callused palm to hers. She nearly jumped out of her skin. "Sure nice to meet ya, ma'am." His dark gaze crackled in the dim light.

"And you," she replied, slightly breathless. "Ned tells me you've staked a claim on a promising silver mine."

Dan Gunther cocked one bushy brow and leaned closer. "That's right. She's up on Stray Horse Gulch. The Ol' Lady Luck, I call her."

"Oh. Yes." Sky withdrew a step, his whiskey breath nearly overwhelming her.

Dan's gaze swiveled around the long hall. "Let's find us a

cozy corner where we can talk." One of his gnarled paws clamped onto her arm, and she found herself being led through the smoky throng.

"Get us another bottle of Wild Turkey, Ned," the miner hollered over his shoulder, then charged ahead. Ned waved and disappeared into the haze.

Painfully aware that she was one of the few women on the premises, Sky followed along grudgingly. This was not her idea of a civilized meeting place. She brushed against hard foreign bodies, avoiding leering stares and foul language.

Dan Gunther had no qualms about clearing a path. He roughly elbowed anyone who stood in his way.

"Watch who yer pushin'!" a man wearing soiled overalls growled.

"Yeah. Somebody's gonna knock the rest of your teeth loose," another warned from the side of a chuck-a-luck table. Raucous laughter burst from that clustered group.

Sky was relieved to spy a free table and a few chairs over by the far wall. But just as they approached, two grizzled men hunkered down into the chairs, placing their drinks on the table.

"Hey, you coyotes," Dan bellowed. "That table's taken."

An uncomfortable twinge started at the base of her stomach. Where was Ned?

One of the men, burly and black bearded, rose from his chair. "This is our table, weasel face. We're gonna play us some poker."

"Nope." The craggy miner shook his head. "This is our table. You boys come up jest as we was gonna get it."

Sky nervously tugged at Dan's sleeve, but he ignored her.

The black-bearded tough stole a glance at his big-nosed friend. "Boys?" Cords on his massive neck twitched. Then he and his partner roared with coarse laughter. "Maybe we look like boys to a stale old fart like you."

"Watch yer tongue in front of the lady." Dan shoved Black

Beard and, despite his bulk, the man staggered backward a few feet.

"Hey! You old—" Black Beard lunged forward swinging his doubled fist. Dan dodged, the fist glancing off his shoulder. The momentum of the blow sent him reeling back against Sky.

With a surprised shriek, she lost her balance and toppled backward onto the lap of a faro player. Chuckling at her dismay, he tipped his bowler hat. His honey-eyed gaze sent her scrambling to her feet just as Dan Gunther flew past her and landed in a heap on the sawdust floor.

"Dan! Are you all right?"

Her question was lost in the surrounding hoots and cheers. "Get him, Gunther!" a raspy voice urged.

Startled, she saw Dan lift a chair and crash it over Black Beard's contorted face. Blood spurting from a cut over his eye, the man snarled and slammed into Dan like a battering buffalo.

Then all hell broke loose around her. Voices shouted obscenities. Fists flailed in the air. A bottle whizzed by her nose and struck a poker player on the side of the head. His body slumped, his face dropping forward into his cards.

Her heart pounding like a locomotive, Sky swung around, looking frantically toward the bar. Where was Ned?

Someone shoved her sideways and she fell into a chair, knocking it over and her with it. As she fell, she struck the back of her head against the edge of a faro table. Sharp pain ratcheted around inside her skull.

Suddenly a pair of large, strong hands reached for her. Stars shimmering in front of her eyes, Sky tried to focus on the familiar features of the man kneeling down at her side. "Marshal?" He helped her to stand on wobbly legs.

Hazel eyes stared into hers. "Hold on. I'm getting you out of here."

The room and its tumbling chaos rocked around her. "I'm
. . . fine . . ."

The next thing Sky knew, she was being hoisted over his
muscular shoulder and carried toward the swinging doors. Gazing down at the undulating crowd, she felt a wave of nausea
surge through her. She thought she was going to be sick.

Out on the boardwalk, the marshal set her down unceremoniously. "I'm not a sack of flour," she said, her head hurting and
her stomach queasy.

"I saw you fall in there." His voice was brusque. "Did you hit
your head?"

She winced, remembering. "Yes, I hit it against a table."

He slipped his fingers up beneath her hair and examined the
back of her skull. She let out a yelp when he found the injured
spot. "You've got a little goose egg. You'll live."

She frowned irritably, fingering the bump herself. He didn't
have to be so indifferent. "It feels like a big goose egg. And, my
stomach . . . I feel sick."

He pushed his hat back off his forehead. "I told you, this is
no place for a . . ."

Two entangled men barreled out the doors, grunting and
cursing. They rolled past Sky and the marshal, still slugging it
out. "Like hogs in a barnyard," the marshal muttered.

Ned followed, dragging Dan Gunther. He held the miner
under his armpits, keeping him barely on his feet. Ned looked
at Sky with concern. "Are you all right? I tried to get back to
you, but the crowd was too thick."

Marshal Cassidy put a protective hand on her shoulder. "She
bumped her head, but she'll be okay. It's a good thing one of
the gamblers tipped me off. I brought several police officers to
settle things down."

"Where's the Wild Turkey?" Dan Gunther mumbled through
cracked and bloodied lips.

Ned grinned over at him. "Think you've had enough of that stuff tonight, partner. I'm taking you home with me to sleep it off in the barn." Holding Dan's slouch hat in his free hand, Ned waved to Sky and the marshal. "I'll put him on his mule. He's not gonna feel so good in the morning."

Sky nodded, still feeling lightheaded herself. "I've got to get back . . ."

The marshal stood before her, tall and commanding. "I can't let you go back in there yet. Not till it settles down."

"Well, I can't stand out here all night."

His mustache quirked up at the corners. "You need some fresh air, Miss Saunders."

She started to object, but a glance inside the front window at flying hats and bottles made her stop. And his hand on her arm was insistent. He turned her toward his buckskin waiting at the hitching post. With one swift motion, he scooped her up into the saddle and swung up behind her. The sudden feel of his strong chest brushing her back, the piney smell of him, made her senses reel. "Where are we going, Marshal?" she asked, with a slight quaver in her voice.

"We're going to take an evening tour of Leadville. Someplace where you've never been, Miss Saunders." His lips close to her ear sent gooseflesh skipping down her bare neck.

He flicked the reins and they started up Chestnut Street, into the hubbub of Leadville's nightlife, past hotels and noisy dance halls. Chandeliers glittered from inside clouded windows; tinny notes from a piano drifted out onto the night air. In front of one saloon, a man and woman dressed in garish costumes sang a bawdy song, and as they finished, the man smacked the woman boldly on her switching derriere. Instead of reacting with disdain, the woman tossed back her crimson locks and bellowed gleefully. Her randy partner chased her inside.

Sky's face flooded with hot embarrassment and she looked

away. So this was what the city was like after dark. A mixture of contempt and magnetism overtook her. She felt like someone peeping through a forbidden keyhole.

"Not exactly like home," the marshal noted with a trace of humor.

He expected her to be shocked, and he was enjoying it. She sat up straighter and focused ahead, choosing not to answer him. Where was he taking her? She was dying to ask, but held her tongue, knowing the town marshal wouldn't dare put her life in peril.

They came to the edge of town and he turned the horse up another road inhabited with one-story cabins and tall, scattered trees. The giant moon above washed everything in a silvery light. The sky was so clear, she thought she could count the flickering stars. Sounds of crickets echoing, the steady clop of the horse's hooves, and the creak of the marshal's boots in the stirrups filled her ears.

The sense of being the only two-footed creatures of sky and land pervaded her senses. Although eerie, it also mesmerized her. Sky breathed in the waxy smell of saddle leather and pine-scented air.

Time lost meaning and the anxiety she'd lived with in her new unpredictable environment faded. The marshal's closeness provided a cloak of temporary shelter.

At last, he drew his horse up beneath a few clustered trees. An owl hooted from overhead and the sound of rushing wate' arose from somewhere nearby. "Where are we?"

"A place called California Gulch." He dismounted, the reached up for her. "C'mon down and I'll show you."

She hesitated. Riding into a starlit night was fine when it v two people on a horse. A man and a woman alone on ' ground, in the dark, could be another matter. Still, he was marshal—she had to trust him.

His strong arms came around her waist as he lifted her from the saddle. His hands seemed so sure and steady. "There's enough light tonight to see the water." He guided her ahead to an elevated ridge.

She saw the reflection of the moon hovering over a creek below. "This is a lovely place." Sky inhaled a deep, sweet breath. "Out here, you feel free from everything."

"Yeah, I know," he said quietly. "I thought it'd do you good to get away. Put some space between you and that place."

She sighed, glancing up at him, and saw his gaze had settled on her. Somehow she wanted to make him understand at least a part of her goals. He had given her his hospitality when no one else would have. "I know you don't approve of the gambling hall, but the pay there will be better than I could make in a store or at the bank. With my board and room included, I'll make enough to set aside most of my earnings."

Sky stopped short of repeating her plan to grubstake a miner. She knew the marshal wouldn't approve of a lady doing that. Actually, she didn't know if she wanted to support a man like Dan Gunther, if he was inclined to squander his money on alcoholic spirits. "That way," she continued, "I'll be able to support myself, with no one else's help."

In the moonlight, she saw his dubious expression. "You sure are an independent woman, Miss Saunders. I can't help but wonder what made you so determined."

She stared at the glimmering silver water in the gulch and felt a shiver slide down her spine. A creek could be so calm. Then so deadly. "I guess life just forced me to be," she said, not really answering his question.

He cocked his head as if she'd piqued his interest. "Whatever it was didn't seem to hold you back."

She became introspective, sensing this man could relate to

the tragedy of her early years, and decided to reveal a hidden memory.

"My parents had gone to town to get supplies and were returning along our county road when they were caught in a sudden spring storm. A very violent storm. By the time they got to the creek near our farm, the bridge had washed out. I was a toddler then. Granny Saunders was taking care of me at my parents' cottage. She became frantic with worry, but couldn't go for help because of the storm."

Sky brushed away a tear spilling over her cheek. "Afterward, people guessed my folks tried to cross the creek at a low point, but the horse got caught in the fast current. They found the poor animal and the wagon not too far downstream. They didn't find my parents' bodies for almost a month because of the heavy mudslides."

Even now, a lump formed in her throat as she recalled Gran's revelation to her when she was old enough to understand. She felt the marshal's hand, warm and comforting, come to rest on her lower back. "Although I don't remember my mother and father, Gran told me many stories about them so I felt I had known them. And, fortunately, I had their photographs."

She paused. The marshal stood quietly beside her on the ridge of the gulch like a tall pillar. It was almost as if he understood her loss without having to say so.

"My grandmother was like a mother to me for thirteen years, until she died and I went to live with my aunt and uncle. That's where I came to know Ned. But Gran and I were so close. We cooked together, sewed quilts, read books—and laughed about life. No one could tell Bible stories better than Gran. And, she taught me to stand on my own." Her voice trailed off, giving way to the rising tide of emotion from carefully laid to rest memories.

He was so silent, it was almost as if he was no longer there.

But then he said in a low voice, "My mother left us when my brother Will and I were very young. I took on the responsibility of steering him in the right direction when Dad went off mining, and then started the wagon business."

"I remember her portrait on your brother's bureau. I'm sorry."

Sky sensed an empathy pass between them. Each of them had suffered a great loss as children. She half turned, her eyes misty. "Taking care of your brother was admirable of you."

"Too bad he didn't listen to some of my advice."

The marshal moved closer, lifting her chin with his fingertips. He lowered his lips slowly until they lingered above hers. His action was a surprise, yet she could sense what he was going to do and was powerless to stop him. She tensed from head to toe.

"You are beautiful in the moonlight, Miss Saunders." His kiss was like a whisper, his mustache soft on her mouth. Tentative. Then he withdrew for a moment, yet only a breath away.

She stood transfixed like a cornered rabbit, not knowing whether to stay or run. He answered her confusion; one hand moved up her back, the other went to her shoulder, guiding her closer. Her body betraying her fears, she melted into the long muscular length of him.

Sounds of the rushing water below magnified in her ears while her body quivered in response to his enveloping arms. But her mind fought a terrible tug-of-war. Much worse than when she let him massage her twisted ankle and didn't want him to.

His lips found hers once more, now hot, seeking. Seeking something she could not give. Her heartbeat raced to a gallop inside her breast. *Wait. This can't happen.* Even if she'd wanted to, she wasn't free to share her physical favors with any man.

Not when she was still legally a married woman. Nor could she trust any man. Not even the marshal. He might set a trap for her, and then when he'd caught her, treat her with the same indignities and offenses that Thomas had.

"Please, Marshal." Flushed with a strange heat his kiss had ignited, Sky disentangled herself, pulling away on a ragged breath. "I don't need sympathy . . . or anything else from you. Take me back to town." She pivoted and headed back toward his horse.

Looking after her retreating figure, Cody felt her words sting like a slap across his face. What had he done wrong? Told her she looked beautiful in the moonlight? Kissed her? He knew she'd felt some of the same reactions to the kiss he did. The jolt of heat shooting through him—like lightning. Even if she'd first been stiff as a stick, she'd felt it too. The way her body leaned into him on the second kiss, her lips softening beneath his.

His head spun. He just couldn't figure her.

Why, he'd even known an immediate kinship to her when she'd related the loss of her parents.

Cody followed her back across the ridge to his horse, waiting in the dappled shadows of the trees. He assisted her up into the saddle without speaking, not trusting himself to respond to her rejection. Dammit, she was a stubborn, unpredictable woman!

He loosened the reins from a low hanging branch where he'd tethered them and swung up behind her. Digging his heels into the buckskin's sides, he turned the horse back to the road, urging him into a trot. Miss Saunders gripped the saddle horn and jounced along, he knew uncomfortably, her hair flying free down her back.

Stray tendrils brushed backward, caressing his cheek, smelling faintly of lavender. He jerked his head to the side, cursing the pleasant reaction her silken hair aroused in him. Why had he brought her out here? An eastern woman with rigid principles. He should have known better.

Cody's jaw clenched in resolution. He was Leadville's marshal, and that was where his responsibilities were—to his job. Not chasing after contrary, independent women. Errant footpads, claim jumpers, and thugs ran loose every night in this bawdy town. He'd better set his priorities and his mind straight, and get back to the job he was hired to do.

They rode back without speaking, accompanied only by the bright moonlight over their shoulders, the horse's steady hoof beats on the hard dusty road, and the echoing call of crickets on the night breeze.

CHAPTER SEVEN

On the ride back to town, Sky wondered whether she should have let the marshal kiss her. All the while she wondered, his strong, muscular arms encompassed her, his hard-muscled thighs moved rhythmically alongside hers as they straddled the buckskin. How could she possibly weigh her lack of willpower when their bodies still touched, his chest brushing against her back? The warm musky smell of him drove her to distraction.

It would have been far more preferable to take this impromptu ride in a buggy. At least then she could have kept her distance. Wishing she'd never come along with the marshal, she held onto the saddle horn, her senses shamefully aware, her nerve endings tingling every place their bodies grazed.

He'd said nothing since they left the gulch. She knew he was angry, probably would have liked to leave her behind and let her walk back. Rejecting his affections as she had. But she'd had no other choice. Keeping her self-respect was mandatory.

Yet questions slowly formed inside her: Why did she feel drawn to this man? Why didn't she fear his touch as she had Thomas's?

Upon returning to Leadville, the lights and noise from the gambling establishments blared as boisterously as when they'd left, with no sign of abatement. Miners and gaudy women still crowded Chestnut Street.

Despite her staunch resolve to stay cool and self-possessed in the saddle, she'd found the steady rhythm of the horse's hooves on the long ride had lulled her into unwittingly leaning back against the marshal's broad chest. Sky sat upright, her muscles complaining from her bottom down to the insides of her legs from the constant rub of saddle leather. The thin layers of her petticoats had provided little protection.

They pulled up in front of Burtram's Gambling Hall and Sky waited as the marshal slid to the boardwalk. As he assisted her to her feet, the space between them vibrated with tension.

She lifted her gaze to his. "Thank you for the ride . . . and for rescuing me." Her stubborn forthrightness had faded since withdrawing from him at the moonlit gulch.

Something unreadable flickered across his shadowed features. "It's late. You'd better get inside." He briefly touched the brim of his hat before moving back to his horse. Once he'd lifted his tall frame into the saddle, Marshal Cassidy urged the buckskin up the congested street, leaving her shivering on the boardwalk in the chill night air.

When Sky climbed out of the cot the next morning, her head ached as well as numerous muscles throughout her body. *Well,* she thought, stretching like a cat, *that's what I get for riding horseback all over creation in the dark of night.*

As she went about her morning ritual, washing up and brushing her hair before the makeshift bureau of stacked wood crates, flashes of her moonlight rendezvous with the marshal haunted her. The intense empathy reflected in his features. Empathy changing to desire. She could still feel his firm hand on the small of her back, the fullness of his mustache brushing against her upper lip, and the softness of his lips on hers. His body heat.

A sudden tingle shimmered outward over her limbs. *You are shameless,* she chided herself while peering into the rectangle of mirror on the wall. Exactly the admonishment Granny Saunders would have chosen.

A respectable young woman didn't allow such worldly images, even if she was almost divorced. Sky blushed, realizing she'd never before known these hidden reactions to a man. Thomas was the only caller her aunt and uncle had permitted to come courting.

Well, she'd better abandon all stimulating thoughts of Marshal Cassidy if she wished to keep her self-respect.

She wound her waist-length hair back into a coil at her nape and fixed it with pearl-tipped hairpins. Her stomach grumbled.

A good breakfast was her first priority, then paying Ned a call. She needed to discuss and decide whether further grubstaking Dan Gunther was truly a good idea.

Downstairs, the kitchen was empty. It was Cookie's day off. But she heard a shuffling sound as she passed and stopped to look back into the room. Who would be there on a Sunday morning when Mr. Burtram was gone and the hall was closed? Her nose detected the smell of cooking grease and day-old coffee.

In a far corner, a small figure moved. "Hello," she called.

A young Mexican boy stepped into the light shining from the window over the work counter. He resembled a miniature scarecrow, wearing tattered clothes that hung loosely on his thin frame. He held his hands behind him, a sheepish expression passing over his dusky-skinned, drawn face, and swallowed something he'd been chewing. "Morning, *señorita.*"

"Good morning." She recognized him as the cleanup boy who mopped floors and helped Cookie with errands. "What's your name?"

"Antonio." His hesitant voice betrayed his deeds, his dark-eyed gaze darted into the hallway behind her as if looking for an escape.

"I'm Miss Saunders. I do the bookkeeping for Mr. Burtram."

At the mention of their employer, young Antonio's mouth twitched and he quickly scampered past her to make his getaway, his back pockets bulging. *"Adiós."*

"Adiós," she replied, the unfamiliar language pleasant on her tongue. As the boy disappeared out the back door, Sky smiled, amused to see the tin breadbox left open on the counter. But then she wondered why he'd taken stale biscuits when he could have eaten at his own home. He must live nearby.

Her stomach reminded her of its empty state. Forgetting about Antonio, she hurried toward the front door and the closest restaurant.

At the intersection of Harrison and Chestnut, Sky approached a uniformed officer, asking him where she might obtain a horse and driver to take her to Ned's place on Chicken Hill.

While she talked with the officer, a rig pulled up alongside them. Assuming the driver was parking the rig, she focused her attention on the officer. After a moment, the man leaned toward them.

"I can take the lady to Ned Saunders's place," his raspy voice interjected. "Know just where it is."

She turned and was surprised to see the bug-eyed, greasy-haired man she and the marshal encountered on Fryer Hill the day he'd taken her up to look at the mines. She didn't remember his name, nor did he identify himself, only tipped his grimy hat.

Her stomach clenched uncomfortably. She hadn't liked the character's looks then, and she didn't like them now. It was fortunate that the officer caught her wary expression and waved away the driver with a curt, "Mind your business, Frog. The lady don't want your company." The driver scowled and pulled in ahead next to the boardwalk.

When a man and his wife came by on a buckboard, traveling eastward out of town, the officer flagged them over. Sky welcomed the couple's invitation to join them.

Boris Wickham's gaze riveted on the young woman as she gathered up her skirts and hopped into the back of the couple's wagon, her deep auburn hair coiled neatly beneath her bonnet. Fuming inside at her high-toned airs and the way she and the officer so easily snubbed him, he twisted his lips into a grimace. "Frog," the nickname some townsfolk called him, especially rankled. Someone should teach them some manners.

She was an eastern woman, no doubt. He remembered her immediately from the day he'd seen her with Marshal Cassidy up on Fryer Hill. The two of them riding so cozy together. He smirked to himself.

That day, he'd been inspecting the mines for improper claim recordings as he often did as a sideline to his job in the county clerk's office. Not that he got paid extra for it. Not that he got paid a living wage. Nothing close to what the marshal made.

The law had cheated Wickham out of his claim on Fryer Hill, two years back. He'd filed the claim incorrectly, they said.

Since then, he worked a night job. It had paid well, so far. Lot jumping and claim jumping could be very profitable. With the assistance of his secret committee, and during the cover of darkness, he had succeeded in amassing several choice properties in town. By being discreet in who he hired, Wickham had kept his identity a secret. He sat up straighter on the wagon seat. He'd even avoided being caught by Leadville's incensed, self-proclaimed vigilantes last year.

Just thinking about his luck made his heart race. No one wanted to fall into the hands of the vengeful vigilantes. They'd stretch your neck faster than a badger could snare a rabbit.

At least the marshal had curbed vigilante activities. Yet it was only a matter of time until Cassidy sniffed him out. The man was a human coyote, new on the job, and pressured to stop the crime wave everyone complained about. One of those straight lawmen—the kind he couldn't stomach.

Wickham pulled a half-smoked cigar butt out of his coat pocket. Well, he wouldn't let the marshal get in the way of his livelihood. The way times were now, a man had to take advantage of every opportunity coming his way.

He lit the cigar and puffed thoughtfully. Too bad he couldn't have given the marshal's new lady a ride. She might have tipped him off as to how much the marshal knew about his committee.

Slapping the reins across his horse's scrawny rump, he merged into the ongoing traffic up Harrison Avenue. He'd keep his eyes wide open and his ears alert. No tinhorn marshal was going to stop Boris Wickham.

Beneath the warmth of a lazy July sun, Sky rode out of town with a miner and his wife, headed toward Chicken Hill. Bouncing around in the back of the couple's wagon wasn't her most favorable means of transportation, but their company was far preferable to the first offer she'd received. She shivered in the heat, recalling the first driver's wide-set bulging eyes and protruding lips, and considered herself lucky. "Frog," the officer had almost snarled at him. The name was fitting.

Gazing ahead, she recognized, according to Ned's directions, his log cabin and small barn. When the miner pulled his team to a stop at a fork in the road, she hopped to the ground and thanked the couple for coming to her aid. Tilting her Sunday straw brim forward over her brow, she moved up the dusty road, her mind turning over questions she wanted to ask her cousin about that old coot, Dan Gunther.

"Sky! What a great surprise!" Ned called from behind a rail fence he was repairing.

Waving hello, Sky hurried the last several yards to greet him. "I'm glad I caught you at home, Ned," she called, slightly out of breath. "We need to discuss the character of your miner friend."

He grinned and set his hammer down next to a jar of nails. "You mean ol' Dan? Why, that man's got character to spare."

"Don't make fun of me." She retrieved a handkerchief from her skirt pocket and wiped her perspiring forehead. "If he's got money to throw away on spirits the way he did last night, I don't think he needs my support."

Ned's expression became more serious. "That only happens once in awhile, Sky. A man works as hard as he does, has to let off some steam now and again."

She huffed at his logic. "You men! I should know you'll always stick together."

A melodic whistle suddenly rose on the summer breeze. Sky lifted her hand to shield her eyes as she looked in the direction of the sound. From the small barn to the side of Ned's cabin emerged the stocky, bowl-legged frame of Dan Gunther leading a scrawny gray mule. The familiar notes of "She'll Be Comin' 'Round the Mountain" surrounded both man and beast.

She smothered a smile. Well, he didn't look any the worse for wear, if that was possible.

"Good mornin' to you, Miss Saunders," the disheveled miner crooned as he approached. Sweeping off his crumpled, dusty hat, he held it to the front of his flannel shirt and bowed from the waist. "A fine mornin' and a fine-lookin' woman all make for good luck." He cocked his head and squinted amiably at her, deep laugh lines fanning out from the sides of his bloodshot eyes. "Or, so I've been told."

"Thank you, Mr. Gunther." Noticing his tobacco-stained teeth and the bulge inside his lower lip, she said, "I hope you aren't feeling too much under the weather today." She knew he couldn't mistake her meaning.

From the corner of her eye, she saw Ned meander back along

the fence. He didn't want to be caught in the middle of any altercation.

Dan half-turned and spat a stream of tobacco juice into the knee-high weeds. He swiped his faded shirtsleeve across his mouth. "Well, ya know, miss, I should of held my liquor better than I did last night." A mischievous twinkle glinted in his dark eyes. "I sure hope you'll accept my apology."

Sky cleared her throat and steadied her gaze. "Mr. Gunther, I will gladly accept your apology for one indiscretion. However, I will need some assurance on your part that you intend to stay sober while working your mine . . . if I agree to grubstake you further."

Dan Gunther stroked his bushy graying beard, his tongue making a strange clicking sound. Behind him, his mule twitched its funny lop ears as if also considering her ultimatum.

"You sound like a downright sensible woman, Miss Saunders. And, ol' Dan can't help respectin' that." He reached into his baggy pants pocket and fished out a small leather pouch. Loosening its drawstrings, he stuck weatherworn, stubby fingers inside the pouch and fished out several shiny objects. Extending his hairy bear paw of a hand, he opened his callused palm, revealing glittering silver ingots of varied sizes.

Sky gasped in surprise. To look directly at the silvery chunks in the stark sunlight hurt her eyes. What must they be worth?

"The ol' Lady Luck is showin' real promise. This is just the beginnin' of a big strike, miss." His face lit up with excitement as he slipped the nuggets back into the pouch.

She let out a long breath, wanting to believe him. "Well, I will reconsider my offer of support—after I confer with Ned, of course."

Dan gave an agreeable nod of his bushy head. "I'd be obliged." He mounted his lop-eared mule. "Me and Miss Fanny gotta be headin' back to the hills."

Sky couldn't hold back a little chuckle. "Miss Fanny?"

"You betcha!" Dan scratched the mule behind one of its ears, causing the animal to break into what Sky could only describe as a buck-toothed grin. "She's my girl. Sorta unpredictable, but ain't she a beaut?" He urged the mule toward Sky. "Get a look at them long eyelashes. Not meanin' to offend, miss, but she's got more of a fetchin' eye than any woman I ever knew."

Observing the mule's charcoal-fringed brown eyes, she had to admit the old miner was right. "Miss Fanny is the most attractive mule I've ever seen." She didn't add that judging mules was not her strong suit.

The disheveled miner let out a long whistle and waved at Ned, still working along the fence. "Good day to ya," he called to Sky, raising a stubby finger to his hat as he suddenly wheeled his mule and headed off across the field toward the road.

"Mr. Gunther, we really should discuss your mine . . ." she called to his disappearing back.

"Damnation!" she muttered and kicked at a dry mule chip. There were so many questions she wanted to ask about his mine, and he was leaving already. She stared after the old coot and his loping mule, now a cloud of dust in the distance.

When he'd be back in town was anybody's guess.

CHAPTER EIGHT

Sky loosened the pins from her hair and let it fall freely around her shoulders. She'd just climbed the stairs to her room after a long day balancing the week's books. Jack Burtram was a taskmaster when it came to making the figures balance to the last penny, and her eyes burned from staring at rows of numbers.

From the street, voices raised on the thin night air. Why did they have to congregate in the alleyway right beneath her window? Irritated, she moved across the room and pulled apart the gingham curtains in order to close the half-open window.

Her ears caught the shout below. "Marshal Cassidy's been shot!"

Her back stiffened. *The marshal?*

"How bad?"

"Don't know. Just heard about it." The first man's voice sounded out of breath as if he'd been running.

Sky shoved the window up and stuck her head outside. "Where is the marshal now?" she hollered to the gathered group.

Several bearded faces angled upward. Someone whistled. The first man stepped forward. "They're takin' him to his office, ma'am."

"Thank you," she called and pulled herself back into the room, her heartbeat fluttering against her ribs.

The marshal's been shot!

The alarming statement echoed through her brain. Jamming

two combs into her hair, she snatched a light wool shawl from the wall peg and lunged out the door.

Her feet fairly flew down the bare wood stairs to the back hall. The marshal! How badly was he hurt? Who shot him and why? Without questioning her own immediate concern or what motivated it, Sky raced up Chestnut Street to the corner of Harrison Avenue.

Bad news spread fast. Along the street, people spoke in grave voices. Hangings and shootings were common in Leadville, but the marshal was its highest law enforcer, and this was of concern to all citizens.

As she hurried up the avenue, she heard one old miner boast to another, "He's the best marshal we've had yet."

A tight knot of onlookers had clustered in front of the marshal's office on Front Street by the time Sky got there. A redheaded man with a peg leg was gesturing to the man next to him, and she moved up to them.

"Aye, 'tis not lookin' good. They ambushed 'em up on Fryer Hill, the bloody cowardly dogs. Tryin' to jump a claim, they was."

"Has anyone called a doctor?" Sky blurted, unable to stand back with the others.

The red-haired Irishman turned to her with a dubious expression. "Aye. Big Jim. Even though he was grazed in the shoulder 'imself, he went chasin' for Doc Potter."

"Potter's probably in his cups again," the other man scoffed.

Apprehension coursed through her. "Then who's tending the marshal?"

The Irishman raised his bushy brows. "His other deputy Ned loaded 'im up on a buckboard and took 'im out to the Cassidy place."

"Ned Saunders is my cousin and he doesn't know a thing about gunshot wounds." She flung back a lock of her tumbling hair and called to the bystanders. "Who can take me out to the marshal's place?"

It didn't occur to Sky that she'd had little experience herself with such wounds. The only puncture wound she'd tended was when her uncle accidentally drove a nail into his foot while working in his toolshed. But she did know some home remedies—and she had to do something.

"I've got me rig just up the street, miss. If ye don't mind an old peg-legged man drivin' ye."

Sky grabbed the Irishman by his shirtsleeve. "That doesn't bother me a whit, sir. Just get me out there."

Ned looked surprised when Sky burst through the Cassidys' front door. She strode toward him. "Where is he?"

"We've sent for Doc Potter and he should be on his way any minute."

"Hah," she bristled. "From what I've heard, ol' Doc could be drunk as a skunk tonight. Where is the marshal?"

"He's in the back room, but you can't—"

Sky slipped past him and through the hallway into the rear bedroom. Expecting to see the senior Cassidy here, she was taken aback to find the marshal alone, lying on top of the bed covers. He did not resemble the virile man she knew. First she saw his face, ashen, drained of the robust, natural glow of health, then his broad chest, rising and falling in an effort to breathe. Then she saw the blood. It covered his pants from his upper left thigh to his knee. The makeshift bandage Ned had applied was soaked through.

The marshal groaned, gritting his teeth in obvious pain, then drifted into an unconscious doze.

Dear God, he was in bad shape. She turned as Ned entered the room. "Have they got some carbolic acid and some clean rags?"

"Carbolic acid?" Ned looked like she'd asked for a magic potion.

"Please run out to the sideboard in the dining room and get some whiskey, the strongest alcohol they've got. Hunt for some clean rags in the kitchen."

Ned started backing toward the door. "Okay . . ."

"Go. Now!" she demanded. "If we don't hurry, he's going to bleed to death!"

Swiftly Sky removed Ned's tourniquet. She snatched off her shawl, twisted it, and tied it as tightly as she could around the marshal's upper thigh. Drawing a clean handkerchief from her skirt pocket, she wiped the sweat from his forehead. "You're going to be all right, Cody," she whispered, realizing this was the first time she'd called him by his given name. "The doctor is on his way."

Then she prayed that it was true

Several minutes later, Ned rushed into the room, his face flushed. He held a bottle of whiskey in one hand and a fistful of rags in the other. "This is the strongest whiskey I could find, almost eighty proof."

Sky bit down hard on her lower lip. "Good." They both stared at the prone figure on the bed. "We've got to remove his trousers," she said with more confidence than she felt. The thought of seeing the marshal in his under drawers gave her pause, but the urgency of the moment chased away any false sense of modesty.

"Yep, we do." Ned set the whiskey and rags on the bureau next to the marshal's gun holster he'd removed earlier. He untied the now crimson shawl and unbuttoned the marshal's pants, stiff with drying blood. Sky knew Ned, at medium height and of wiry build, would have difficulty lifting and sliding the jeans off Cody Cassidy's more than six-foot frame.

Her heart thrumming in a quickened rhythm, she went over

to the bed to help Ned remove Cody's heavy boots.

"Hello!" a male voice called from the front room. "Marshal back there?"

"Come on back, Doc," Ned answered.

Sky looked up to see a stocky, heavily mustached man carrying a black satchel cross the threshold. She shuddered a sigh of temporary relief.

Ned straightened. "Sure glad you made it, Doc. We've got our hands full." He gestured toward Sky. "My cousin, Sky Saunders. Doc Potter."

With a brisk nod, Potter immediately gave his attention to the marshal's wound. "Looks like he's worse off than Deputy Hacker." He pulled a stethoscope out of his satchel.

Sky watched anxiously. "How does he sound?"

"He's got a stronger beat than I'd expect from the looks of it. We'd better get them pants off." He glanced over at her. "Did you say you was family, ma'am?" Doc Potter asked, a faint aroma of spirits on his breath.

Sky tore her gaze from the marshal's unconscious form. . . . "Ah . . . no, I—" The doctor angled his head toward the door. "Think you'd be more comfortable stepping outside now. I'll have to clean the marshal's wound."

Irritation pricked her. "Well, I am here to help."

But the doctor's back was already to her as he cut away the pant legs. Then the two men slid the upper portion of the marshal's pants and his drawers down over his hips. "Hold on, boss," Ned said quietly.

Between Ned and Doc Potter, she caught a glimpse of a well-formed right buttock, and her insides quivered. Without another word, she left the room as Doc pulled a bottle of some kind of antiseptic from his black satchel. He'll need hot water, she thought, and hurried to the kitchen.

As she lit the stove, she wondered if she should have stayed at the gambling hall and let the deputies and the doctor take care of Marshal Cassidy. The doctor appeared sober enough to take care of him now. Gerta would come in the morning; she'd be an excellent nurse for his needs.

Finally, the bedroom door opened and the men emerged, somber but wearing more relaxed expressions. Sky knitted her fingers together, palms damp with sweat. "How is he?"

Doc Potter set his satchel on the edge of a hall table. "The marshal's lucky to be alive. He lost plenty of blood from the gunshot and more when I cleaned out the wound. But the bullet didn't hit a bone; it went right through the other side."

Her stomach did an anxious somersault.

"What are his chances, Doc?" Ned asked.

The doctor stroked his drooping mustaches. "Don't know right now. He's a powerful man, in excellent physical condition. I'd say if he makes it through tomorrow, he's got a fighting chance."

"I'll watch him through the night," Sky confirmed. She owed it to him. He'd given her a helping hand when she first arrived here. Now, he needed one. "Tell me what I should do."

"Well, you better keep his knee bent so the air can get to both the top and backside of his leg. I cleaned him up pretty good, but if the bleedin' starts again, you'll need to apply the alum I'll give you. Keep the wound swabbed out with this." He handed her a dark brown bottle.

She took the bottle. "I'll do my best."

Doc Potter hadn't finished. "Watch for any putrefaction and if you see any, run for my place like your heels are on fire." He snapped his satchel shut with stiff, large-knuckled hands and added further instructions. "Keep his fever down best you can. He'll have a lot of pain when he comes to. We'll deal with that when we come to it. Try to get him to eat somethin'." His bright jet eyes studied her. "This ain't a job for the fainthearted,

85

ma'am. Think you can handle it?"

"Everything but setting my heels on fire," she replied dryly, her fast-tripping heart belying her calm exterior.

The corners of Doc Potter's mustaches turned up. "I'll drop by later to see how you and the marshal are doin'."

"Thanks for your help, Doc."

When Ned entered the kitchen a short time later, she was searching the pantry shelves for herbs to make poultices. "Where is Mr. Cassidy?" she asked. "He should be told about his son."

"Jim Hacker said he went down to Denver on business and won't be back until the end of the week. I'll get over to the telegraph office tomorrow and send him a wire."

"Good." She removed a jar from the top shelf and examined the label. "Ergot," she murmured, trying to remember if her aunt had used it to pack wounds.

"Do you want me to stay or will you be all right for a while on your own?"

She glanced over at Ned and saw dark purple shadows beneath his eyes. He'd been through a long, tough day. "I'll be fine. Gerta will be here early in the morning."

Ned's features relaxed. "Okay. Glad the marshal is in good hands. Cindy will be worried and waiting up for me."

After Ned left, she went back to the marshal's sickbed, found a folded quilt on top of a cedar chest and, wrapping it around her, settled into a corner rocker. If he needed her, she'd be close by.

Before dawn, she awoke, her eyes gritty, her mouth dry. The light from the kerosene lamp on the bed table flickered, sending long ominous shadows across the far wall. She hesitated, absorbing the reality of the moment, her gaze traveling over the marshal's muscular frame lying the full length of the narrow bed. Beneath the sheet, two firm pillows bolstered his left leg, keeping the knee bent.

It amazed her that a thug's bullet could leave the marshal in this prone, helpless position. A man with such physical strength and vitality. He would need a lot of grit to pull himself through.

She got up from the rocker and went to his bedside. His breathing came softly and shallowly. The low light glinted over his tawny hair, called attention to dark gold beard stubble across his jaw. A sheen of sweat glazed his exposed chest and arms. She reached out tentatively to touch him and found his flesh radiated an unhealthy inner heat.

Quickly, she fetched a bowl of vinegar water from the kitchen and sponged his face, neck, and torso down to his waist where the sheet stopped, then left the cool compresses on his forehead hoping to bring down his fever.

Now she had to check his wound. At the thought, her palms broke out in a cold sweat. She knew he lay naked beneath the sheet.

Holding her breath, she lifted a corner of the sheet. Arrows of flame pierced every inch of her at the sight of his exposed masculinity. He was magnificent. Dear Lord. A year of nursing her uncle had never prepared her for this! She swallowed hard.

Ignoring her shaky hands, she folded the muslin fabric diagonally back across Cody's stomach, his genitals, and right leg. After snipping the gauze bindings, she gently peeled away the bandage, applying more of the vinegar water to loosen the cotton that stuck to his wound. The bullet had hit him high on the inner thigh; and now as the bandage fell free, she saw blood oozing once again from the wound.

At first glance she knew she must work quickly or he would bleed to death.

Rushing to the kitchen, she lit the stove and spooned alum into a frying pan, shaking it over the hot range until it smoked and darkened. A rooster crowed in the side yard.

Where are you, Gerta? Come soon, she prayed. *I need you!*

She sprinkled the burnt alum onto a fresh piece of gauze and hurried to the bedroom with the poultice. But as she went to apply it, she gaped in horror. Bright new blood welled in the bullet hole, then streamed downward into the valley of his groin, where thick tawny hair caught and held it.

Temporarily paralyzed, she hovered, watching for a long moment, then recoiled in a jerk. "Get hold of yourself, girl." Gran's voice came to her. "You've got to stop that bleeding!"

Once again, she bathed the wound, staunched the flow, and prayed. Perspiration dampened her face and trickled down her sides as she repeated the process, fighting against time.

Vaguely she was aware of the front door closing and footsteps tapping down the hall. "Who's dere? Marshal, is dat you?"

Sky's head snapped up. "Gerta—in here," she called. "Come quickly. The marshal's been shot!"

The Scandinavian cook appeared in the doorway. Her blue eyes widened with disbelief as they took in the chaotic scene: the marshal's half-naked body on the bed, Sky in her blood-smeared apron, the disarray of gauze bandages, vinegar cruet, and medicine bottles on the night stand.

"Oh, my Got!" She rushed to Marshal Cassidy's bedside. "Vat happened?"

Sky explained the ambush on Fryer Hill the night before, while she finished staunching the wound and applied the alum poultice.

Gerta listened in obvious shock, then wrinkled her nose. "Vat is dat stink?"

"It's burnt alum."

The cook poked the air with a pudgy finger. "You should try dried ergot. It's goot for vounds like dis." She turned and scuttled back down the hall.

In the kitchen, Sky watched as Gerta made a poultice of the dried ergot from the jar she'd found earlier in the pantry. The purplish powder derived from rye was far more agreeable to the nose than the stench of the alum.

Together they packed the marshal's wound with the ergot poultice. "Dis vill bring out da poisons." Gerta patted the bandages gently and looked into the marshal's sallow face. "Such a goot man."

"He's been unconscious since last night. Do you think he'll wake up soon?"

"It's hard to know." Gerta shook her head. "But ven he does, he'll sure need somethin' for his strength."

Sky swabbed his still-feverish forehead with an alcohol-moistened cloth. "What can we feed him?"

A light shone in Gerta's delphinium-blue eyes. "Elk brot!"

"Elk brot?"

"Come." With a swivel of her wide hips, Gerta waddled out the door.

A head taller than the bustling housekeeper, Sky followed closely behind, through the back-porch door and out to the icehouse.

Emerging moments later, Gerta held up a chunk of meat. "We yust butchered an elk," she announced, heading back to the kitchen.

After energetically beating the steak with a mallet, she put it into heated salt water to steep. "Elk brot, ya?"

The aroma of the simmering meat made Sky's mouth water. She hadn't eaten anything since dinner the night before. But she smiled at Gerta, standing at attention over the stove, her plump cheeks flushed. "Yes, a strong broth." Gerta's matronly presence buoyed her sagging spirits.

She and Gerta shared a hurried cup of chamomile tea and buttered scones before going back to check on the marshal.

"He's still got a fever," Sky said worriedly as she touched his wide brow. She doused another cloth with alcohol and blotted the perspiration from his face. Gerta watched with puckered features and just shook her head.

From out front, a horse whinnied. *Maybe it's Doc Potter,* Sky thought. *He'll know what to do.* But when someone pounded on the front door, calling in a loud voice for Gerta, her hopes fell.

At the sound of her name, Gerta dashed out of the room.

"Papa's been hurt bad in da mine! You got to come, Mama."

Gerta's painful cry punctured the air.

Sky froze in place, disbelieving the frantic voice. She dropped the wet cloth and rushed down the hall to the front door. A gangly youth stood inside the doorframe, holding Gerta by her rounded shoulders. "Don't cry, Mama. Yust come."

"What's happened?"

The youth's anxious gaze swept from his mother to Sky. "My pa's mine caved in. He's got some broken ribs and they tink his leg is broke."

"Ohhh . . ." Gerta wailed into her handkerchief.

"Come *now,* Mama!"

Gerta blew her nose loudly and looked with despair at Sky. "I'm sorry. I have to go."

Sky stared at the two of them. The young messenger of doom and her strongest hope of saving the marshal's life. She said with attempted conviction, "Of course you must."

From the doorway, she watched Gerta's son assist her into a decrepit rig. "Yust give him da brot and keep his fever down," Gerta called to her. The young man hopped onto the driver's side and slapped the mottled gray horse into a trot.

Don't go, Gerta. I don't know if I can do this by myself. I don't know if I can do this.

CHAPTER NINE

Bracing her shoulders and taking a deep breath, Sky confirmed her resolve. Like it or not, she was in charge now. Without Gerta, it was up to her to give Cody a chance to survive. Back in the kitchen, she poured the steaming elk broth into a large soup bowl and set it on a tray. The broth's enticing aroma made her mouth water. Adding a napkin and spoon, she quickly carried the tray to the back bedroom and set it on a small table next to the bed.

In the morning light, Cody's color was pale against the pillow, his features contorted. If she could just get some nourishment down him . . . he'd lost so much blood.

She strained to lift his head, then propped the pillows behind him. He groaned and suddenly tossed beneath her. As she straightened, his muscular left arm swung outward. His large-knuckled fist smacked her alongside her eye and cheekbone. With a stunned gasp, she was propelled sideways against the soup tray. A geyser of hot broth erupted everywhere, some splashing onto her hand. The bowl flew across the braided rug, crashing to the hardwood floor; the spoon and tray clattered nearby.

A sob catching at the back of her throat, Sky grabbed up her apron and wiped at her burned hand. Unwittingly, her mind flooded with painful memories of the times Thomas had hit her in their bedroom. "By accident," he'd sometimes said afterward. She could still see his ruddy, smug face when he was slapping her, leaving scattered bruises on her body where no one could see them but her.

"I hate you!" she hollered to the corners of the room. Then her eyes focused on the prone, unconscious man lying on the bed and she covered her face, realizing her mind had just played a cruel trick on her.

Taking quick gulps of air, she knelt and picked up the spoon and broken pieces of crockery, and set them back on the tray. She sopped up some of the spilled broth with the napkin, her left eye stinging from Cody's involuntary blow. Before leaving the bedroom, she paused at the door and stared a moment at him. There was no comparing the two men, her former husband and the marshal. They were as different as night and day.

"I'm sorry. I know you didn't mean it," she murmured, knowing he couldn't hear her.

Her eye and cheek throbbed, but she ignored them and busied herself in the kitchen, reheating the elk broth on the stove and preparing a new tray. She worried that if she couldn't get something down Cody, he wouldn't have the strength to fight back. He hadn't eaten in over two days.

She tried again to feed him, pushing his chin down and coaxing the spoon through his slightly parted teeth. But the broth only spilled from the side of his mouth and dribbled onto the pillow lip, staining it a meek brown. Another attempt and the broth trickled down his neck and into the hair brushing his shoulder. He made a gagging sound. "Damn! Drink it!" she cried.

But it was no use. He'd choke if she continued the forced feeding.

Swinging away from him, she stared at the rough-hewn wall, tears of exasperation welling in her eyes. She had to do something! What would work?

She tore back to the kitchen, searched cupboards and drawers. Finally she found a small gravy baster. Yes! That might work. She could drip the broth down his throat like a mother bird feeds her young.

She poured another bowl of broth. Standing over Cody, she drizzled a few drops into his mouth as she held his jaw open. Then she massaged his throat. Perspiration dampening the bodice of her dress, she kept up the procedure several times until admitting it was going to take longer than she'd thought. Growing impatient, she left the baster on the tray and paced the floor, her pulse beating against her temples.

In the front parlor, the grandfather clock gonged twelve times. Noon. The day was half gone. Her stomach made a complaining growl but she ignored it. Cody needed nourishment far more than she.

Determined, she returned to the bed, pried his mouth open again. Sucking up the broth into the baster, she squeezed the liquid into his mouth. Gently, she massaged his throat. "Drink this, Cody. Please!"

After a few more attempts of holding his chin back and dripping the broth, he made an involuntary swallow. The broth seemed to be absorbed. She blotted the perspiration from her forehead onto her sleeve. It was a tedious procedure, but at least it was something. She managed to get him to swallow a few more times.

She took the tray back to the kitchen and returned to check on him before she fixed herself something to eat. When she entered the bedroom, she found him thrashing from side to side. Then, before she could stop him, he'd rolled over onto his left leg. His injured leg! Panicking, Sky pushed him slowly onto his back, then fell across him, panting with the effort. He was a tall, muscular man, and unconscious, he was nearly impossible to move.

Catching her breath, she lifted herself up from the bed and

peeled the rumpled sheet from his lower body to check his wound. Her heart pounded against her ribs at what she saw. He was bleeding again—profusely!

Dear God! She touched her throbbing temples. *Gran. Gerta.* Either would be a better nurse than her. Certainly stronger.

The battle was far from over. There was no one near who could help. With renewed effort, she began to fight once more: burning the alum, cleansing his wound, staunching the blood, applying the ergot poultice. While she labored, she prayed the blood flow would stop.

As the afternoon wore on, Cody seemed to fight his own uphill battle toward consciousness. His eyelids flickered; his hand moved sporadically across his torso. Each time he moved a limb, she poured her strength on him, willing him, then badgering him to lie still. The sweat from his fevered body mingled with hers: the palms of her hands against his broad, matted chest, her moist cheek once pressing against his.

Toward evening when he still hadn't gained consciousness, she stopped hoping he'd waken enough to drink the broth himself and repeated her feeding method of dipping and drizzling once more.

At least the bleeding had subsided.

Returning to the kitchen in a near trancelike state, Sky smelled the aroma of the elk broth still simmering on the stove. Suddenly ravenous, she lifted the lid from the crock. Inside, the slab of elk stewed in its own juice. She skewered it with a long-handled fork and plopped it on a plate. Hunger gnawing at her, she snatched the hot piece of meat up in her fingers and bit off a large chunk, chewing greedily, licking the juices that trickled between her fingers. Too tired to look for a clean napkin, she wiped her mouth with the back of her hand.

The elk satisfied her hunger but not her fatigue. If only she could get a few minutes' rest. Her eyelids felt heavy. She sat down at the kitchen table and wearily leaned forward onto her folded arms.

It seemed she'd barely closed her eyes when a male voice jarred her awake. "Miss Saunders?" Boot heels clicked across the front room floorboards.

Still groggy from sleep, she pushed her chair away from the table. "I'm in the kitchen."

Doc Potter stood in the doorway, his features flushed, his jet eyes staring at her intently. "I would have come by sooner, but there was a mine cave-in up on Stray Horse Gulch. How's the marshal?"

Sky got to her feet and brushed back a lock of stray hair. "I know about the cave-in. The housekeeper's husband was badly hurt. She had to leave this morning. The marshal's lost a lot of blood . . ."

The doctor's thick brows converged. "You've been here alone?" He came closer in the dimly lit room. "What happened to your eye?"

Touching her fingers to the tender eye, she felt the puffiness around the lid. "Oh, the patient objected to my cooking," she said, chagrined. "It's nothing."

He shook his head. "You'll need to put something on that." He started toward the hall. "First, I've got to check the marshal."

They moved through the shadowed house to the back bedroom where Cody lay, still on his back, but making low moaning sounds. Sky lit the bedside oil lamp and hovered behind Doc Potter as he examined Cody. Bending close, he pulled away the poultice. "Wound looks good . . . no bleeding."

She licked her lower lip anxiously.

"No fever and, as far as I can tell, no gangrene."

She exhaled a weary sigh. "Thank goodness. I guess the ergot poultices helped, and the elk broth."

"You fed him?"

"He was still unconscious, but I managed to get some broth down him with the gravy baster."

"Gravy baster?" The corners of his drooping black mustache lifted as he half turned to her. "You've done a first-rate job, Miss Saunders. I could sure use you as my assistant."

Cody would appreciate a woman doing that, she thought. *Nursing patients instead of working in a gambling hall.* She glanced around the disheveled room. "I never knew how hard it was to try to save a person's life."

The doctor's eyes shone with admiration. "You've got a lot of tenacity, Miss Saunders. The marshal will owe you a debt of gratitude. But he's not out of the woods yet."

Sky nodded, her shoulders sagging against the doorframe.

Before Doc Potter left, he handed her a bottle of laudanum. "He's gonna need some of this when he starts to waken. Dole it out best you can. It's hard to come by." His voice took on a confidential tone. "And I'd suggest you take a nip or two of whiskey before you turn in, miss. It'll sure help you sleep better."

In the flickering lamplight, Sky studied her patient's features: a wide forehead, long dusky eyelashes, a strong nose above a full mustache. An angular jaw dotted with two-day beard stubble. Absently, she thought how becoming the marshal's mustache was—how it added character to his face. Now it needed trimming.

"You need a shave, Cody. Tomorrow, after breakfast, I'll do that for you." She plumped the pillows beneath his head while addressing him as if he were awake. "And if you'd like me to trim your mustache, I'll do that too."

Somewhere behind his closed lids, he might hear her. Maybe her voice, her expectant tone might coax him from the snare
of his unconscious realm. The sooner he awoke, the sooner

she could get some food down him and rebuild his lost strength.

Thinking about shaving him caused an unexpected stirring in her. She hadn't shaved a man since her uncle was laid up one winter with a back injury. And the mere idea of having to shave Thomas's pale jowls gave her creepy gooseflesh.

To get her mind off Thomas, she went to the kitchen and heated some water. She filled a pan, set it on a tray with a clean cloth and a bar of soap, and carried everything to Cody's bedside. Careful that he lay still, she gently washed his face and neck.

When she glided the soapy cloth over his upper torso, crisp chest hair tickled her fingertips. An odd thrill skipping from her fingers up her arm made her step back. Why did this bathing seem like an act of intimacy? Worse yet, from a man she hardly knew? She rinsed out the cloth, quickly dried him with the towel, then drew the sheet up to his shoulders. Her body thrummed with a strange heat as she picked up the tray and carried it back to the kitchen.

Returning to the room, she pulled the small, armless rocking chair closer to the bed and sat down for a moment. If Cody needed her, she'd be close by.

In no time, her head lolled and she faded into a dream world where a strangely familiar man, with a tall easy stance, appeared in the doorway. He stood immodestly, bare-chested above close-fitting denim jeans. Smiling at her from behind a blond mustache, he moved closer. His broad shoulders hovered over her and she pressed her hands against his chest. His lips tempted hers but she avoided them, accusing him of being a thief. A laugh rumbled deep in his throat. He agreed that he was. And he wanted to steal something from her now.

An unwanted ache gathered low in her belly, but she pushed him away. *I hardly know you,* she argued.

You know me, he countered, his sensuous eyes staring into hers. He reached out to draw her to him.

"We've got 'em . . ." she heard Cody mumble. "Watch out, Jim!" His flailing limbs brought her shakily to her feet. Half asleep, she bracketed her arms across his chest, flattening his body.

"You've got to lie flat! Doc Potter says you must!" The vivid dream was strong in her mind as she felt his warm flesh beneath her own. She should not have allowed such a fantasy, yet how could she avoid touching him?

She stayed beside him, a vigilant guard through the night. Again and again, he tossed and she commanded, "Cody! Stay on your back . . . keep your knee up . . ." until she could fight him no longer.

In the wee hours of the night, she fumbled into the darkened kitchen, found more gauze, and tied his wrists to the headboard posts. Then, bone-weary, she sagged back onto the small, hard rocker. But some time later she arose insensibly, crawled over the end of the bed, and collapsed alongside his extended leg.

In the dream, Cody and his deputy Jim shambled up the scree slope to the rear of the mine yard. He knew the claim jumpers were hiding like yellow-bellied cowards, ignoring his call to show themselves. Two shots rang out. Like flaming arrows against the black of night. "Watch out, Jim!"

Light burned brightly beyond his eyelids. His eyes grated open. He saw a blur of shapes. Where was he? An acute pain pierced his left leg. He tried to move, find the source of the agony, but he couldn't. What the hell had happened to him?

His arms felt numb, rising above his head as if pinned by some unknown being. He writhed. A searing pain sliced through his thigh and he gave a guttural moan.

Then he saw the woman. At the end of the bed he was anchored to, she lifted in a foggy shroud. In the backlight, her spiked hair wafted about her head, her eyes purple-rimmed. What pit had he fallen into? What eerie witch had claimed him?

CHAPTER TEN

Cody fought to keep his eyes open and focused. But, as if lead-weighted, they dragged shut, leaving him wondering where he was and who had risen from the foot of the bed. He gritted his teeth against the scorching pain in his upper thigh, lifted sluggish lids again, then raised his aching head from the pillow.

A harpy cloaked in long flyaway hair gaped at him with wide eyes.

His last conscious thought was: *If she's a witch, she's a sadistic one . . . bound me up like a hog on a spit.*

Though he struggled, a black velvet curtain closed in around him. He took with him the image of the gaping witch, surrounded by an aura of light. Her distant voice nagged him, demanding feats of which he was incapable.

"Lie flat," she insisted. "Speak to me. Don't roll over . . ." Sometimes he dreamed her voice was honey-tinged, but then it rasped thorny-sharp again, until he finally escaped her altogether on a drifting gray cloud.

Sky despaired when Cody's head fell back against the pillow and he was lost once more into oblivion. "Cody, don't sleep now." She patted his stubbled cheeks. "Wake up! Wake up!" As still as a tree stump, he offered no response.

Groaning with disappointment and a feeling of failure, she swiped her tangled hair behind her ears. Her eyes felt grainy and her mouth tasted sour. Unable to tend to her personal needs for the last two days had left her irritable.

Cody's needs came first. After cleaning his wound, while shielding his private parts with the folded sheet, she applied a fresh ergot poultice and gauze bindings. Sometime soon, she would have to bathe his lower extremities. The thought of performing that task sent quivery tingles through her. She'd seen that part of him once, and still held a vivid picture of it in her mind. She contemplated untying his wrists from the headboard posts but decided against it; at least now he couldn't flip over onto his side.

In search of something clean to wear, she went upstairs to the second floor. The first room on her left was sparsely furnished and appeared to be Cody's. She went over to a pine bureau and gingerly opened the top drawer. Inside were several folded work shirts. She pulled a plaid one off the top, absently lifted it to her face, and sniffed. The clean smell of soap made her nose tingle and, for some reason, gave her a feeling of satisfaction.

In the kitchen, she made a pot of coffee and while the pot was perking, gave herself a sponge bath. Once over her head, the shirt almost dwarfed her, the sleeves hanging below her fingertips, the tail floating beneath her hips. She rolled up the sleeves and tucked the shirttail inside her skirt. The light cotton fabric along her arms and breasts felt smooth against her skin. Her face flushed with a sudden heat. Could the reason for her rising pulse be that she was wearing Cody's shirt? She whisked away the thought.

He was aware of the sounds first: birds chattering, a horse's whinny in the distance, perhaps a cup clinking against a saucer in another room. Then he smelled the aroma of fresh coffee and savored it for a moment before the dull, gnawing pain gripped him.

His eyelids flew open and he stared blankly across the room at a window curtain fluttering on a mountain breeze. He saw the rocker beside the bed. This wasn't his room. He blinked and took a deep breath, trying to get his bearings, trying to avoid the recurring pain. He was in his brother Will's room. But why? He turned his head on the pillow and saw that his arms were tied above his head with some kind of binding.

What the hell? He'd ended up in his own house, tethered to the damned bedposts! As if on cue, both hands started tingling and prickling at the same time. All the blood had drained out of them. He tried to flex his fingers. They felt like swollen sausages ready to explode from their skins.

Who had lashed him up like this? That gaping witch? Clumsily he tested the bindings to see if he could break them, but they were bound too tight.

Someone was moving around in the kitchen. Must be the housekeeper, he thought. Raising his head, he called, "Gerta!" his voice a raspy whisper. A knife-sharp pain ratcheted up his left leg at the sudden effort. He growled through dry lips.

Beneath the sheet, he was stark naked. His bent left leg throbbed when he tried to straighten it. What in blue thunder had happened to him?

"Cody, you're awake!" A cheery greeting and a plaid shirt. From the doorway, a young woman carried a tea tray. She placed it on the bedside table.

He tried to focus on her face. Wide-set, shadow-rimmed blue eyes, high cheekbones. A smile he remembered.

"Miss Saunders?" he managed, not believing she could have been the wild-looking witch in his dream.

"I've brought you some herb tea with honey and a warmed scone." She started to lift the teapot.

"To hell with the tea," he muttered, twisting his numb arms. He glared at her with all the strength he could muster and tried to sit up. "Untie my hands!"

She went big-eyed and leaped on him, her cool hands pressing him back against the mattress. "Please, Marshal," she pleaded. "Please don't. You're in no condition to move yet. If you promise to stay still, I'll remove the gauze bindings."

He watched her with dark suspicion, not about to promise anything, as she pulled a pair of scissors from the table drawer and snipped away above his head. She stepped back, holding the gauze strips, freeing him to move arms that seemed immobile. They dropped heavily to his sides.

"Oh dear, I am sorry. You're in a weakened condition from losing so much blood." She lifted one of his dead arms and began rubbing it, massaging the muscles. "It should be all right in a few minutes. Give the blood a chance to flow back."

Suddenly the blood pounded through his veins, racing to the nerve endings like a spring flood, shooting sparks of fire and ice to every surface. He let out a surprised gasp and arched his back. That triggered stabbing pain throughout the rest of his body. He uttered curses under his breath. If only he wasn't so goddamned weak!

She clasped his limp hand under her armpit while he lay there helplessly, listening to the sound of her beating the blood back into his arm, smacking it like she would a hunk of bread dough. *Geez!* Was she trying to torture him to death?

When she finished with that arm, she went around the bed and pounded away at his other one. Damned woman! If he had one ounce of strength left in him, he would tie her wrists to the bedposts. See if she liked being treated like a pathetic invalid. "What happened to me?" he demanded.

"You were shot—" Her voice wavered. "Up on Stray Horse Gulch. Something to do with claim jumpers."

"Shot?" He closed his eyes, the memory of pitch-dark night and gunfire flooding back to his brain. "Oh, God, yes." He tried to lift himself up on one elbow, but she immediately pressed him down. "What about Jim? Did he come out okay?"

She frowned thoughtfully. "I think so. Doc Potter came to look at you and said Jim was wounded, but not as badly as you."

"Oh. That's good." He concentrated on her face. One puffed eye, purple-rimmed, squinted at him. "Where did you get that?" He pointed shakily, wondering why he hadn't noticed it before.

Her hand flew upward to cover the injury. "Oh . . . you . . . hit me."

"I did that?" He was incredulous.

A rosy flush flooded her face. "You didn't mean to. You were tossing . . . and you were unconscious."

He exhaled an embarrassed sigh. "I can't believe I—Golly, I'm sorry, Miss Saunders."

She busied herself with the tea tray. "Don't worry about it. And why don't you just call me Sky? What you need now is a hot cup of tea before it gets cold." She whipped a cloth napkin off the tray and placed it on his upper chest. "I'll help you sit up a little."

"Okay . . . Sky." Slowly, he pushed himself forward so she could plump the pillows behind him. He felt as useless as a newborn calf. She brought a teacup and spoon on a saucer to the side of the bed. He smelled the aroma of cloves and honey, and his stomach rumbled. When she leaned toward him he noticed the plaid shirt she wore. It looked like one of his, as roomy as it was on her, hanging loosely over her shoulders and rolled up at the sleeves.

"Open wide," she said, coaxing his lips apart to slip the spoon inside. The steaming tea was soothing, and as she leaned forward, her high breasts pressed fully against her shirtfront. He could see the tempting crevice between them, above the third button on her shirt. Damned if he didn't feel a tightening in his groin, which caused a glaze of sweat to erupt over his entire body.

Sky was looking kind of blurry around the edges and his head wobbled back against the pillow. Again, a midnight velvet curtain started to close in around him. He struggled against it, clenching his fists alongside the mattress.

He was aware of her cool hand on his forehead, then a cloth smelling of alcohol wiping his face and neck. God, he hated this—having her nurse him like he was a frail old man. "I'm . . . I'm all right," he said, gritting his teeth against the new onslaught of agony.

Her soft features were masked with concern. "I know you're in pain, Cody. Doc Potter gave me something to take it away."

She drew a brown bottle from her deep skirt pocket and poured some of the contents into the spoon. She pressed it between his lips. Then another spoonful. It tasted slightly bitter, but he didn't care. If it would erase his misery, he'd drink the whole damned bottle!

A chain of giant purple peaks stretched above the valley, majestic beneath the midday sun. From the front room window, Sky gazed at them in awe and whispered a prayer of thanks. Cody was still alive! He'd wakened and spoken to her, and although he hadn't touched the tea, she'd make sure he drank some the next time he came around. Life was so precious. She'd lost too many people she loved: Her parents, whom she couldn't really remember, and Granny Saunders, whose death had affected her deeply. And last summer was devastating . . . when she'd lost the little one. A tremor ran through her and she hugged herself, chasing away the sad memory.

The nickering of a horse brought her attention to the side road where she saw an older man canter up to the house on a dappled gray. When he noticed her at the window, he waved, then dismounted and tied the horse to the rail in the front yard. She recognized the man's tan, craggy features and felt relief.

She smoothed back unruly wisps of hair from her face and greeted him at the door.

"I'm so glad to see you, Mr. Cassidy."

"I didn't get the wire till yesterday." Anxiety tinged his graveled voice. "I caught the first train out of Denver." He removed his hat and tossed it on a hall hat rack. "How's Cody?"

"Cody was shot in the upper leg and he's lost a lot of blood. He's better, but he doesn't realize how seriously he was wounded." She added, "He woke up this morning ornerier than a grizzly," then smothered a smile. "I had to tie his hands to the bedposts so he wouldn't flip onto his wounded leg."

Frank Cassidy's eyebrows raised inquiringly. "Is that how you caught that black eye, Miss Saunders?"

Sky blanched and touched her tender injury. She hadn't had time to look at it. How could she tell Cody's father that his son had backhanded her, even if it was an accident? "Oh, it's nothing." She pivoted and moved toward the hall. "Gerta's husband was injured in a mine accident and she had to go home to him, and I was rushing around in the kitchen . . ."

Before she could finish her explanation, Cody's hoarse bellow came from the rear bedroom. "Dad, come help me get out of this bed!"

Her heart pumping crazily, Sky hurried to the bedroom door, Frank Cassidy at her heels. To her dismay, her patient was sitting on the side of the bed. Both of his long bare legs dangled over the mattress edge, the sheet tangled around him and trailed to the floor. Blond mane askew, he stared at them from hollow, glazed eyes.

"Cody!" she admonished. "What are you doing?"

With quick strides, the senior Cassidy moved to his son and took hold of his broad shoulders.

"You'll start bleeding again," Sky warned.

Cody gave a weak scowl. "Glad you're here, Dad. She's been torturing me—even tied me to the bedpost."

"I'm sure Miss Saunders had your best interests at heart." His father gently inched Cody backward, lifting his legs up beneath the sheet.

Cody raised a large hand in protest. "I gotta get back to help Ned—stop those damned claim-jumpers!"

Frank Cassidy stood firmly beside the bed, a tall commanding presence. "I'm afraid you're not goin' anywhere, son, with that bullet hole in your leg."

Moving to the other side of the bed, Sky pushed Cody back into the pillows. "The laudanum must have curdled your brain. Now listen to your father and I'll go fix you some hot soup."

Cody muttered something and started to push himself up, but Frank Cassidy placed a steady hand on his chest. "There are two theories to winning an argument with a woman, son." He winked at Sky. "And neither one of 'em works."

Plinking piano keys from the front hall greeted Sky as she climbed the back stairs to her room. She'd entered through the back door to avoid having to elbow through the constant throng of milling miners eager to gamble away their most recent strike. After promising Mr. Cassidy that she'd return and continue nursing Cody during Gerta's absence, she'd come back here to get some clean clothes. Next, she must tiptoe around Jack Burtram to get his consent.

Her room was just as she'd left it, except for the dust. Her sensitive nose was offended by the filmy coating of Leadville grime that had blown in through the partially open window. She sneezed and blew her nose into a hanky and opened the window higher. What choice did she have? The room would soon be a furnace if she didn't allow a breeze to enter. After a sponge bath, she changed into a fresh white blouse and broadcloth skirt and went downstairs to the small office across from the kitchen.

Mr. Burtram sat at his chipped pine desk smoking the butt end of a stogie. His heavy-lidded eyes, revealing his chronic insomnia, lifted as she stepped over the threshold. "Miss Saunders," he boomed. "How is the marshal?"

The odor of the cigar made her queasy, but she managed a polite smile. "Marshal Cassidy has made much improvement. Fortunately, the bullet went right through his leg, but it's been a battle to keep him going." She paused, an emotional catch in her voice.

The furrows deepened in Burtram's forehead. "Hope you didn't get yourself too run down seeing to him. I don't like to fall behind on the books."

"No, sir." She seated herself at her desk and opened the weighty black ledger to the last page she'd finished, four days ago. It seemed like an eternity. "I'll work on them through tonight to catch up."

Someone came through the open office door and she glanced up to see young Antonio carrying a tray with a coffee pot, two mugs, and a plate of biscuits. Struggling with the effort, he set the cumbersome tray on a corner of her boss's desk. "Señor Burtram, Cookie made you some coffee." He cast a shy glance in her direction. "And also the *señorita.*"

Burtram grunted his acknowledgment and Antonio turned to leave. The boy's shabby shirt hung like a flour sack over his thin, hunched shoulders.

Sky felt a twinge of sympathy. "Thank you, Antonio," she called as he disappeared into the dim hallway. Then she poured the coffee into both mugs and burrowed into the work waiting on her desk.

Later that evening, Sky delivered the tray back to the kitchen and stopped a moment in the hall to massage a kink in her neck.

"Yep, they got their asses in an uproar over the marshal," a grating voice announced from the other side of the swinging doors.

The stark statement sent her reeling. She sneaked behind one of the doors and craned her neck to listen.

"You talkin' about that gang of devils up on Stray Horse Gulch?" another voice asked.

Sky peeked over the door, but could only see one of the men in profile. He was an old coot, wearing a bashed-in miner's hat and a yearlong beard.

"Yeah. One of 'em told me the marshal'd better not keep interferin' in their bizness, or the next time they'd send him straight to hell!" For emphasis, he shot an arc of brown spittle toward a spittoon near his muddied boots. "Maybe they won't wait till the next time."

Fear and anger knotted inside her. If only she were a man! She'd waste no time in tracking down these night crawlers and shoot them like the craven cowards they were! She inched away along the wall, fighting back the shiver of panic chasing through her. Cody was still flat on his back . . . and defenseless.

She had to get word to Ned that the marshal was in danger.

And she had to do it before it was too late.

CHAPTER ELEVEN

At first light, Sky bounced on the buckboard's spring seat next to Ned. After warning him last night about the threat she'd overheard at the gambling hall, he'd rounded up a spare uniformed officer and left Jim Hacker to cover the marshal's office. Hacker's arm was in a sling, but he was recovering quickly from his wound.

Then she'd received Burtram's grudging permission to take the monthly receipts with her so she could work on them. The large-boned Welshman had hollered after her, "But only until the first of the week! I'm not runnin' a charity hall here."

Now she glanced back nervously at the accompanying officer riding behind them and said to Ned, "I wish you could have lined up more than one man to guard the house."

"Benson isn't the best marksman, but he was the only man available." Ned rubbed the sleep from his eye with his free hand. "Hope Cody won't mind."

"Mind?" She swiveled on the seat and stared at him. "He needs protection from those claim jumpers."

"Yeah, I know, but Cody likes to do things his way."

"He can't be that proud," she scoffed. "Besides, he's in no condition—"

Ned shrugged. "He's a proud man, and he's never been laid up before."

Adjusting her shawl over her shoulders, she gazed ahead at the smoke rising from nearby chimneys. Townspeople were waking to a new morning, going about their early chores. "I can't imagine anyone being too proud to accept help when he's down."

Sky expected to find Cody flat on his back in the bed where she'd left him. What she found as she entered the rear bedroom made her stop short. Framed by the window, he stood with his long, naked back to her, leaning against two crutches. He was barefoot beneath a pair of loose-fitting red drawers riding low on his slim hips.

She stared, mesmerized. "Cody, what are you doing?"

Awkwardly, he turned around to face her. His tawny gold hair was rumpled and his skin a faded shade of tan. Sunlight splashed across his muscular shoulders and spilled over his curling chest hair. He reminded her of a wobbly injured lion.

Sending her a sleepy smile, he drawled, "Hello, Sky. Didn't know you'd be back so soon." He gazed at her with open admiration. "You look as bright and pretty as the wild flowers in the back yard."

She gazed wordlessly across at him, at the play of sunlight on his virile body, a new and unexpected heat surging through her. As their eyes met, she blurted out, "Thank you. I've come back to give you some help—but you shouldn't be getting out of bed yet."

"I need to build up my strength. Dad made these crutches for me so I can get back to work."

The preposterous idea made her spine stiffen. "You certainly cannot get back to work until that wound has healed."

Sudden determination flickered in his hazel eyes. "Ma'am, as soon as I get the hang of these critters, I'll be jumpin' in a rig and back on the job." He leveled his gaze at her. "That's the way it is."

He leaned into the crutches and hopped toward the door on

111

his good foot. His movements were unsteady as he maneuvered through the doorway and out into the hall.

She followed. "You might start bleeding again. Infection could set in."

"I gotta practice using these."

She was on his heels. "If Doc Potter finds out, he'll . . ."

He came to an unsteady halt midway into the front room. "Who is that man out front parading around with the rifle?"

"He's from the town's police force. Ned borrowed him to stand guard after I heard—"

"Hell," he blustered, forging ahead, "I don't need anyone to protect me. I can take care of myself."

As he lunged toward the front door at a reckless speed, he caught the edge of the Indian carpet beneath one of his crutches. It rippled in waves, tripping him. Both crutches shot out in opposite directions, clattered to the hardwood floor, and he catapulted sideways.

Sky let out a fearful screech and dived forward to stop his fall. She caught a flailing arm just as he fell, the force of his weight pulling her down as well.

"*Ahhhh!*" he yowled, his left leg pinned beneath him.

Sky rose up on one elbow, her senses spinning. "Oh, no! Your wound." Her skirt in disarray, she scrambled to her knees and helped him roll slowly over onto his back. His face had gone chalky-white and tensed with pain. "Oh, Cody." She could hardly breathe. What damage had he done? "We've got to get you back to bed."

He gritted his teeth, staring up at the beamed ceiling. "I can make it. Get my crutches."

The challenge seemed monumental. She thought of the guard outside. "Wait. I'll go get the officer to help us."

"*No!*" His powerful hand gripped her wrist. "Don't." He slid his tongue over his lips. "Just give me a minute."

She closed her eyes and took a deep breath. No, of course he didn't want anyone to help him, to see him like this—the town marshal laid out on the floor in helpless misery. All because of those cowardly skulking outlaws. Cody had his pride. She understood.

"All right." She placed her hand on his shoulder. "I'll get one of your crutches and we'll get you up."

Gathering her skirt above her ankles, she rose to her feet and retrieved a crutch. Fortunately, he'd fallen near an upholstered chair with wide sturdy arms. She propped the crutch next to the chair and took his right hand, its warmth penetrating her. "I'll help you sit up, then, you can inch over and grab the crutch for support."

He looked up at her and winked. "That'll be easy."

She shook her head and smiled, noticing his clean-shaven jaw and the slight red nick on his strong chin. She was tempted to tease him about it, that he'd been a little clumsy shaving himself, but it seemed trivial with him lying there like a fallen buffalo.

She took both of his hands, planted one foot on the floor between his legs and the other outside his knee, and firmly pulled him toward her until he was sitting up. The effort caused sweat to break out on his forehead, but at least some color returned to his pale cheeks. He scooted over to the side of the chair, his lips thinning, revealing his pain.

"Here, put this arm around me," she suggested as he took hold of the crutch with his right arm. "Think you can push up on your good leg?"

He nodded. "Yeah."

They both gulped a breath and Cody lifted himself upward awkwardly. But when he got halfway up, he attempted to put weight on his wounded leg, shuddered in acute agony, and slumped back to his rear. He released a string of curses. "Sorry. Damn!"

"It's all right. I know it must hurt like the devil," she said. "When we get you back in bed, I'll give you some laudanum."

"Hah!" He snorted. "How about a slug of whiskey right now!"

She turned her face toward his, only inches away, and almost replied, "This early in the morning?" Better judgment stopped her. "All right," she said instead, "I'll get you some."

She detached herself from him and hurried to the liquor cabinet in the dining room.

"Bring the whole bottle. I don't need a glass," he hollered.

After she'd brought some Scotch whiskey, and he'd taken two long swallows, they tried again. As they struggled, her cheek pressed to his bare muscular chest and she inhaled the fresh peppermint smell of shaving cream against the musk smell of man. This time, with Cody's shaky strength and her most focused determination, they managed to bring him to stand on one unsteady foot.

In order to get up, Cody was forced to lean heavily on Sky. A lesser woman would have folded like a tent, but she kept her back and shoulders taut and rose grandly by his side. Her steady hand grasped his naked waist. He took a firm hold of the crutch, and they started back down the hall. She was a tall woman, reaching his shoulder, and luckily surefooted. His glance caught the curling auburn tendril escaping from her braided coiled at the back of her porcelain neck. He was moved to thank her, but swore under his breath instead when the grinding pain hit him.

Damned bullet hole! Damn those vermin who'd shot him! He'd get them, round them all up—the yellow dogs.

He was sweating bullets by the time they reached the bedroom door and he hopped to the bed, dragging his bad leg. She propped his crutch against the wall as he fell back onto the sheet. His upper thigh pulsated with pain.

"That's enough of the crutches for today," she said, a scolding tone in her voice.

He closed his eyes for a moment, regretting his fall, and that she'd been there to see it. When he opened them, he saw her eyes widen in fear.

"Cody, you're bleeding again."

He looked down at his leg, saw the dark, wet stain spreading over his drawers, and cursed.

"I'll go boil some water and get some fresh cloths. Can you slide these off by yourself?"

He nodded. He knew she didn't want to embarrass him by having to remove the drawers, rendering him completely exposed. He tried to make light of it. "Won't take a minute. But don't let me catch you peeking."

Her face reddened. "This isn't funny, Cody." She pivoted toward the door and was gone.

When she returned, he'd removed his underwear and lay naked beneath the sheet, holding a compress against his thigh. She carried folded towels and a small laundry tub filled with steaming water, which she set on the side table. Above her forest-green skirt, the starched white cuffs of her blouse were rolled up to her elbows and her face was flushed. The form-fitting blouse emphasized her womanly figure; the high color in her cheeks only accented her beauty.

Damn! Why did he have to be laid up like this? He felt as helpless as a hog-tied heifer.

"That's a lot of water just to clean up my leg." He edged up to a sitting position.

"I thought you'd like a sponge bath after I tend to your wound."

His eyebrows jumped an inch. "A sponge bath?"

She started unfolding an oilcloth. "If you'll excuse my observation, you and this room are starting to smell pretty gamey."

"Well, I can take my own bath." He avoided her eyes, wishing

Gerta were here to see to his needs so he wouldn't suffer the uncomfortable arousal he experienced being in the same room with Sky.

A slight smile curved the corners of her lips as she slid the oilcloth underneath him. She smelled like summer roses. "It won't take long. You can help wash those parts you don't want me to."

He drew the top sheet self-consciously above his waist and scowled.

"Cody, really." She stepped back, her hands clamped to her narrow hips. "I've already seen everything you've got under there." Her gaze lit briefly on the rise at his groin.

For an instant, heat flooded his face and his ears burned. Should he allow himself to be embarrassed or just lie back and find some humor in this unavoidable situation? Then his leg started throbbing again and he felt foolish. Lifting the sheet away from his wound, but careful to leave his vitals covered, he groaned. "Just clean out that devil and bring on the suds."

It was a devil. She worked deftly, staunching the blood, then pouring on some disinfectant.

"Ahhh!" Cody winced at the sharp searing sensation and ground his teeth together. "That burns like witches' brew!"

"Well, I'm no witch." Her delicate hands moved quickly to apply a fresh poultice and gauze bandages. "If you weren't in such a hurry to gallop off on those crutches, your wound wouldn't be bleeding now."

He glanced up into her defiant blue gaze. This eastern miss had a way of curling his toes with just one look. "Sorry, Sky. No offense intended."

Leaning back against the pillows, he closed his eyes wearily. How could he be tired at this hour of the morning? He felt her lift his arm and start to scrub him with a soapy towel. From beneath lowered lids, he watched her glide the cloth from his shoulder to inside his elbow, and his arm went warm and tingly.

"Lift up, please."

He brought his arm up and crooked it behind his head as she washed his armpit and drew the towel over his neck and upper chest. Enjoying the tantalizing sensations from her warm hands and the lathered towel, he gazed at her directly. A sheen of moisture glazed her upper lip. He had an impulse to trace the outline of her generous lips, feel their softness with his fingertips.

As if reading his thoughts, she shied back a step, her face and slender neck coloring a rosy hue, and wrung out the towel in the heated water. "You won't mind rinsing yourself," she said in a businesslike tone.

Taking the wash towel, he rinsed his arm and chest while admiring the way her blouse conformed to her high, full breasts. He gave her a slow, lazy smile. "You're pretty good at nursing."

"I've had some practice with my uncle when he was sick."

He nodded. From the window, he saw the watchman walk by in the side yard. "Why is that officer posted here? Doesn't he have enough to do chasing street thugs in town?"

Continuing to wash downward over his hip, she gingerly approached the area around his wound. "I tried to tell you . . . the claim jumpers have put out a threat on your life."

He arched his chest and dug his head back into the pillow, sucking in a breath of pain.

"No matter what it feels like, your wound is beginning to heal." She patted his thigh gently with a dry towel.

"I don't need extra protection. I'll smoke out the cowards as soon as I'm back on my feet." He forced his head up and glared at her. "And that will be soon."

One of her auburn eyebrows quirked upward.

He sent her an impatient look. "When is Gerta coming back?"

"Not soon enough." She rinsed out the wash towel and tossed it at him. "Here, you can finish up yourself."

She picked up the tub. "I'll be back with more hot water."

"What for?"

"Your hair needs washing."

He scoffed. "I'd rather have lunch."

"All right. Lunch first, then we'll wash your hair."

He glared. "You're a stubborn woman."

She frowned. "You don't need to get scowly with me, Cody. I didn't shoot you." Her skirts disappeared in a flounce out into the hall.

He wiped the soap from his other arm, grousing under his breath. How would he avoid the close intimacy of a hair wash?

Lunch consisted of two slices of bread immersed in a bowl of milk, and one boiled egg.

"What is this?" Cody stared at the meager offering on a tray she plopped on his lap.

"It's milk toast and a coddled egg," she sniffed, unfolding the cloth napkin.

"*Milk toast and a coddled egg!* I'm starving and you bring me food for an old maid?"

She dropped the napkin across his chest. "Tonight, I'll fix something heavier. Doctor Potter said to keep you on a soft diet as long as possible."

He snorted. "Doc Potter knows all about a 'soft diet' . . . more like a liquid diet."

Her face screwed up at that. "Eat your toast before it gets cold."

Scooping up a chunk of the saturated bread with a large spoon, he slid it into his mouth. The bread was lukewarm and slimy. Grudgingly, he swallowed. "Blah!" he gagged. "Awful stuff!"

Her expression wilted, her gaze lowering briefly to the floor. Then without a word, she spun around and left the room.

He blew out an exasperated breath. He'd insulted the cook

and he didn't give a damn. The coddled egg was as tasteless as the slimy toast. He slammed the tray over onto the table.

"Bring me some real food!" he hollered.

Silence was his only answer.

His leg started thrumming again and he gripped the sides of the mattress. "Hey, nurse," he bellowed. "You got some more of that stuff for pain?"

She appeared at the door, her expression stiff. She was still in a snit over lunch. "If you'll lower your voice, I'll be glad to give you a dose of laudanum."

Contrite, he bobbed his head.

After she'd given him a good slug of the stuff, he lay back against the pillow. When she opened the window to let in some fresh air, he watched her, thinking he'd like to just float away on the mountain breeze.

When Sky brought in another tub of hot water, Cody had settled into a mellow mood. Washing his hair wasn't such a bad idea.

"Can you sit up," she asked, "with your legs over the side of the bed?" He grunted unhappily as she assisted him. Positioning herself, she instructed him to lean over the tub on the side table.

She pushed a wash towel at him. "Hold this over your eyes."

She scooped and lathered and he groaned as hot water sloshed into his ears. Briskly, she scrubbed his hair and scalp.

"Hey," he objected. "Take it easy."

"Your hair will be squeaky clean when I'm through. You'll feel so much better," she soothed.

But when she started scooping a mile a minute, the water poured down over his neck and into his eyes, and he raged, "Watch it. My eyes! The soap!"

"Sorry." She scooped faster.

His eyes burned like fire from the lye soap. More water

drenched his back. "Noooo." He caught her by the wrist to make her stop. The cup clattered to the floor, spilling its remains on the braid rug. He shook his head like a wet dog.

"Cody! Now look what you've done."

"Give me a towel!"

Flustered, she picked up a dry towel from the bureau. He grabbed it and reared back on the bed. Refusing to give up her end of the towel, she began vigorously drying his hair. "Hold still!"

Some of the hair on the top of his head got caught in the towel and he yelped. On impulse, he reached out and grasped her hips and yanked her down on the bed beside him. She cried out in surprise, trying to twist away from him, but only got tangled in the sheet.

They were nose to nose. "Your turn to be uncomfortable." He glared triumphantly into her eyes, eyes that shot fire-sparklers at him.

The towel slipped from her hands and he clamped onto them, pinning her arms over her head. She squirmed, insisting he let her go. He snorted with glee. "How do you like it—being pinned like a rabbit in a snare?"

She grimaced. "You've lost your mind. Let me up this instant!"

Their faces were so close. Her tempting mouth very near his. He ran his tongue enticingly over his lips. Her breath came in little pants, quick and warm. Before he could think or stop himself, Cody captured her lips with his, covered her body with his. She fought, but not that hard, and he easily held her arms pinned above them.

His tongue nudged between the softness of her lips and found its way into her mouth. When he found her tongue, he teased it, then stroked it. Beneath him, she ceased struggling and exhaled a barely audible whimper.

He moved his left knee somewhere between the folds of her skirts and felt his wound begin to throb, but it couldn't compare with the throbbing between his legs. God, how could he have wanted to strangle her a minute ago and now be exploding with desire?

Letting go of one of her hands, he traced the inside of her exposed wrist and forearm along her arm to her collarbone, following his fingers with small kisses to the shallow of her neck. She released a trembling breath into his hair. "Cody . . ."

His hand traveled lightly over the swell of her breast and cradled it. Leaning over, he kissed the tip of it, letting his mouth linger, breathing warmly through the thin fabric of her blouse.

Her eyes closed, she began shaking her head side to side. "Cody, no . . . You . . . We can't." With obvious effort, she pushed his hand away and edged off the bed.

Seductively his gaze slid downward over her, then back to her face. "Sky, don't tell me you didn't enjoy that kiss."

CHAPTER TWELVE

Sky gawked at Cody, who was reclining across the bed, looking like a cat that had swallowed the cream. "It . . . it wasn't supposed to happen."

"What wasn't supposed to happen?" A glint of mischief sparkled in his oh-so-distracting hazel eyes. "The kiss?"

She clenched and unclenched her hands into fists in the folds of her skirt, a fiery heat burning her neck and face. "You know exactly what I mean."

"Can't you say whether you liked it or not?" He lolled back, staring at her, his tanned muscular arms folded behind his head. A hint of a smile lifted his full mustache.

"I . . . can't say," she said, the impact of Cody's lips on her mouth and breast leaving her knees quaking beneath her skirt. She hated that he had her at a definite disadvantage. The sheet had fallen loosely down around his hips, barely disguising the swell of manhood rising below the slope of his abdomen. She swallowed. Thomas had never revealed such excitement over a mere kiss.

Tearing her gaze from the stimulating sight, she blurted, "The laudanum has certainly made you bold. You're ignoring your life threatening condition."

Her patient regarded her with amusement. He ran long fingers through his damp, wavy hair. She couldn't help wondering what it would feel like to slip her fingers through that golden mane, inhale its clean smell.

"But my condition is improving, thanks to your special care," he said, his voice teasing.

She knew the blush radiating up her neck was caused by something besides the warm summer breeze, and she wasn't about to lead him on. Ignoring his studied gaze, she gathered up the wet towels.

"When I'm back on my feet, I'll help you wash your hair, Sky." His tone was light, close to mocking.

The towels draped over one arm, she lifted the tub from the side table. "If you're recuperating this quickly, I should get back to Burtram's and my job."

Cody's sunny expression soured. "That fox hole." His brow furrowed. "It's no place for a lady. I'm surprised you've held on this long."

Starting to fume, she paused at the door. Without acknowledging the gambling hall's smoke and noise, she countered, "It's not that bad. I like my work there."

"It's no place for . . ."

Without letting him finish, she swept over the threshold on her way to the back porch. She'd be darned if she'd stay and listen to any more of Cody's disapproval. Why should she bother to defend her goals to him? He'd wanted her to leave Leadville from the first day she arrived.

On the porch, she nudged open the screen door and tossed the tub's dirty water into the back yard. Thoughts buzzed inside her head. A man always expected a woman to satisfy his needs, but when a woman wanted something . . . or to achieve a goal . . . that was a different matter.

Well, she was through trying to please a man. She didn't care if her ambitions displeased Cody. She'd helped him through a life-or-death challenge, and now it was time to return to the path she'd set for herself.

In the kitchen, Sky prepared elk stew for the evening meal.

As she peeled and sliced a bunch of wild onions, her eyes burning, she recalled the dinners she'd made for Thomas. How determined were her efforts, and how many times she'd failed to meet his expectations. One attempt stood out painfully in her mind.

On an evening when Thomas's boss, the bank president, and his wife were at their home for dinner, Thomas had reprimanded her on her improper placement of the silverware. Didn't she know that the forks went on the left side of the plate?

He'd sputtered out the affront just as she'd picked up the claret decanter. She'd been so mortified, she overshot the wife's goblet and poured the dark red wine into her ample lap. As the woman sent squeals of shock across the dining room table, Sky had rushed to the kitchen for a clean towel. Racing back, she'd tripped over the cat, fallen forward, and knocked the florid-faced woman halfway out of her chair.

Now, she wasn't sure if she felt like crying or laughing, remembering the poor woman's expression, her eyes nearly popping out of their sockets.

She knew she'd been a fumbling failure in her attempt to perform the social role of Thomas's late first wife. Later, as she wept in their bedroom, his verbal and physical abuse had escalated.

Placing the stew in a covered pot on the stove, she exhaled a long sigh. Thankfully she was over a thousand miles away from Thomas and Placerton, Ohio. Her divorce would soon be final.

When she served dinner to Cody, she forced herself to put their stimulating kiss out of her mind. He'd been her patient and he was improving rapidly. That was all there was to it.

As he wolfed down the large serving on his plate, licked his lips, and begged for more, Sky smiled. She could make a satisfying, hearty meal when she wanted to. In this town, nobody worried about what side of the plate the knife and fork went.

And, for the first time in her life, she was nearly an independent woman, free to make decisions that would affect her alone.

"Señorita Saunders!"

Sky looked up from the row of columns in her ledger book into Antonio's gleaming brown eyes. "The marshal—" Excitement radiated from the boy's small wiry body. "He is coming!"

Her mouth opened in surprise. "The marshal is here?"

"*Sí, sí!*" Antonio's usually sober countenance broke into a wide smile, then he disappeared around the corner into the hall.

Sky rose from her chair and smoothed errant wisps of hair behind her ears. She wished her palms weren't suddenly damp. Why did she have this racing pulse? It had only been a week since she'd seen Cody.

She heard him before she saw him. The thump of crutches across the hardwood floor, his timbred voice greeting the daytime bartender. Her heart did a quick somersault. Rounding the office door at a trot, she nearly bumped into him.

"*Buenos días,* Señorita Sky." He touched the brim of his white Stetson in a small salute.

Off to the side, young Antonio hovered, staring up at the marshal with open admiration.

Beneath his tilted brim, Cody's hazel eyes twinkled like sunlight shimmering off rain-tipped pine boughs. Above his holster, he wore a close-fitting denim shirt, the open neck revealing just a hint of tawny chest hair. She couldn't help remembering their last kiss with only a tangled sheet separating her from his naked, muscular body.

"Hello, Cody," she managed, her body simmering with a discomforting heat.

He smiled in that playful way that made her tingle right down to her toes. "Thought I'd stop by to thank you for pulling me through when some had given me up for dead. Think I'll actually make it to my thirtieth birthday this weekend." In his extended hand he offered a large bouquet of columbine, wild roses, snow-white daisies, and mountain fern tied with blue-and-yellow gingham ribbons.

Genuinely surprised, she accepted the bouquet, her eyes misting. "No one's ever given me such a special gift." The wild flowers' pure, sweet fragrance surrounded her. "Thank you, Marshal."

"Hey, thought it was *Cody.*" He winked. "Guess I have to give some credit to Gerta; she helped pick most of the flowers over near the creek, since I don't get around well on two feet just yet."

She felt an eager affection coming from him, a tenderness in his gaze. It was too easy to get lost in the way he looked at her, and she shifted her gaze to his crutches. "You seem to be getting around well enough."

He grinned. "Ned brought me over in the buckboard."

"Oh, he did?" Why did she feel like some breathless girl of eighteen, switching from one foot to the other? "How's your wound? Does it give you much pain?"

"No. I haven't touched the laudanum for several days." His mustache lifted at the corners. "Well, I might have taken a nip or two of whiskey."

Before she could thank him again for the flowers, Ned's voice shouted over the din of the hall. "Marshal, come quick! Old Hoot Gibbs got in a row with the Gold Nugget bartender. He's gonna shoot up the place."

"Not again." Cody's expression revealed his reluctance. "Sorry, Sky. I gotta take care of this." He turned and made for the swinging doors.

"Be careful!" she called. As her heart fluttered unabashed, she saw that he maneuvered those crutches far better now than he had over his Navajo rug.

★ ★ ★ ★ ★

Relieved to hear an hour later that Hoot Gibbs had been restrained and that nobody had been shot; and, thank heavens, Cody in all likelihood would make it to his imminent birthday, Sky decided to bake him a cake.

Early Friday afternoon, she carried the one-layer spice cake over to the marshal's office. Having added extra spice and a half-inch-thick maple icing, Sky thought the cake the best she could create.

Now on her way toward Harrison Avenue, she caught sight of Antonio playing with a stray dog in a back alley. She called a greeting, but when he saw her, his eyes narrowed and he ducked behind the building. Such an odd little fellow, she thought, never playing with other boys. He could be so moody.

Not wanting the cake's fluffy icing to melt in the August heat, she hurried her pace. Above her, afternoon clouds rolled across the azure sky, promising rain.

Along Harrison Avenue, as she passed an alley behind State Street, a strange sound, like a wounded animal, caught her ear. At first glance, she saw a bundle of discarded clothing piled against the back of a clapboard building. But then she saw a face.

Halfway down the alley, a young woman huddled, her mournful sobs piercing the air. Sky froze. Her stomach knotted as she stared at the pitiful heap.

Compelled to help, she moved quickly toward her. "Miss, have you been hurt?"

The young woman seemed oblivious as she rocked back and forth, her head bent, her sobbing a thin lingering wail.

Sky stopped a few feet from the crumpled figure. Looking closer, she saw the woman held something wrapped in bloody rags, and her throat went dry. "Are you hurt?" she repeated.

Slowly the face slanted up to look at her through glazed, red-rimmed eyes. Why, this was a girl, not more than sixteen or seventeen! Could she be a prostitute renting one of the cribs along State Street? Sky blanched at the thought.

"Can I help you?"

The girl swiped her nose on the frayed sleeve of her wrapper, then pulled aside the bloodied rag, revealing miniature fingers fisted alongside a tiny, blue face. "Ain't nobody can help me." Her voice was flat, chilling.

Sky gaped in horror at the still, small form and dropped the cake pan to the ground. Shock stabbed her heart as the sudden image of her own loss only a year ago, flashed before her.

It was a hot summer day. The sun filtered through the lace curtains, stippled the bedroom hardwood floor with dancing lights. So bright, they hurt her eyes. Curled up on the bed, she wished the nausea would go away.

Once again, pain gripped her lower belly, moved in surges, washing over her . . . rushing like waves to the sea. Could her monthly have finally arrived? It had never been this late or this violent.

She clutched her belly and gasped for air. Terrified, she pushed herself off the bed. If she could just get to her pain powders on the bureau . . . Perspiration drenched her face, neck, and gown.

Then something tore like a knife through delicate tissue . . . forced its way out of her . . . slipped down her legs. She cried out, but no one heard.

Looking down between her bare feet, she saw a puddle of blood on the floor. Something lay in the center. So tiny. Only about an inch long.

Barely able to breathe, she slid onto her haunches and picked up the small, lifeless being. Still warm, it fit snuggly into the palm of her hand. Horrified, yet riveted, she stared.

Little nubbin head. Miniature webbed feet. Precious elfin thing. Would you have been a boy or a girl?

Tears blurred her eyes, tasted salty on her tongue. Fear gripped her. Don't let Thomas find it.

Still holding the small being, she lurched to the window. Her heart beating in a frantic rhythm, her gaze searched the back yard.

She felt so weak. But she dragged herself out to the garden gate and dug up the dirt behind the hollyhocks with her bare hands. Then she buried the tiny one, wrapped in a towel, and whispered a prayer.

Thomas had discovered her collapsed on the kitchen floor. She blamed her faint on the heat and never told him about the miscarriage. He wouldn't have wanted a baby, anyway. She had grieved alone.

Now the sound of moaning pulled her to the present. A few feet away, the girl continued to rock in a ceaseless, pathetic rhythm.

Sour bile bubbled to the back of Sky's throat, but she remained rooted to the ground. "Please. Let me—"

Ignoring her, the girl got to her feet and stumbled down the alley. Midway, she stopped and stuffed the lifeless bundle into an open woodbin, then disappeared around the far corner into the hubbub of State Street.

Disbelieving, Sky croaked, "No . . . You can't." The girl had just thrown away her dead baby without a thought of a decent Christian burial. Without a backward glance!

Almost immediately, a scrawny, rust-colored cat sniffed at the bin, then leaped to the top and peered over the edge.

"Get out of there! Get away!" Sky lunged at the cat, shooing it down the alley.

For a long moment, she stood transfixed, staring at the woodbin. Never before had she felt so helpless.

Yellowed newspapers blew in a sudden gust around her feet. Chills shivered down her spine. She whispered a silent blessing for the little soul, her throat constricting so that she could hardly speak.

With tears of loss streaming down her face, she turned and started back to the boardwalk, wishing desperately she'd never stopped. The tragic image of what she'd just witnessed would be seared forever into her memory.

The cake. Her heart heavy, she stooped and retrieved the joyful birthday surprise she'd prepared. The dishtowel covering the cake had fallen onto the ground, but the cake was still intact. She replaced the towel and continued on her way.

As if weeping with her, the clouds opened and raindrops spattered her sagging shoulders and stained the dusty boardwalk. Stumbling along, her vision blurred, she bumped into a grizzled miner, the blow knocking her sideways.

The collision jolted her and she blinked back fresh tears. *Cody!* Yes, Cody would know what to do. She nearly sprinted up the sidewalk, the cake pan bouncing against her bodice.

By the time she reached the marshal's office a few blocks away, she was breathless, a request burning inside her.

Cody stood near his desk, leaning against one crutch, as she burst through the front door.

"What's this?" His eyes widened. "You baked me a cake?"

"I've just seen a dead baby," she blurted. "You've got to help me bury it." Tears again brimmed in her eyes and spilled over her cheeks.

Intense astonishment flooded his features in the second before he came to her. "Calm down, now." His hand, strong and firm on her arm guided her into a back office. "You can tell me all about it."

He eased her into a chair across the room from an empty jail cell and took the cake pan from her, setting it on a nearby table. He sat down opposite her. "What happened?"

"I—I was bringing your birthday cake," she began raggedly, words tumbling from her mouth. "When I passed the alley—near State Street—I saw a girl holding something." She paused, gulping in a breath of air.

He winced and looked away for a moment when she described the young mother disposing of the dead baby in the woodbin.

"What you saw was a prostitute, Sky. You shouldn't have gone near her. There's disease . . ."

Oblivious to his explanation, she pleaded, "You've got to help me find the baby and then we'll bury it." She stared across at him, her heart pounding.

He shook his head, his eyes avoiding hers. But before Cody could deny her desperate request, she jumped to her feet and went to him. She clasped his arms, tried to shake him. Make him see the horror of what she'd seen and make things right. He was as immoveable as an ancient oak. Her own body shook with heated frustration.

"Now, hold on." Cody rose from the chair, towering over her, hard-muscle and sinew beneath her grasp. "I know you've had a terrible shock." His strong arms went around her and she wilted against his chest. "I'll find the baby, and Ned and I will bury it."

She tilted her chin, looking up at him. "Will you find a place by a creek . . . where wild flowers are blooming?"

He sighed, then gently stroked her hair away from her face. "Yeah, I'm sure we can find a place like that."

His smile kindled a warm glow deep inside her. Finally reassured, Sky rested her cheek against his shoulder, inhaling the clean smell of his shirt.

Jim Hacker, like a curious bear, peered around the office door. "Somebody cryin' in here?"

"Nah. Miss Saunders brought me a birthday cake and I guess she got kind of emotional about it." Cody looked down at her and winked.

She drew her handkerchief from her skirt pocket and blew her nose. "I dropped it on the way over here. I hope it's okay."

Hacker's bushy eyebrows lifted expectantly as he eyed the cake pan on the table. "I sure love birthday cake."

"Well, let's have some," Cody offered. "Put on a pot of your three-bean coffee, Jim."

Sky dabbed at her eyes and smiled in spite of herself.

The trio sat in the back office sharing the spice cake. Cody chewed quietly, never taking his gaze from her. She took small bites, not having much of an appetite. When she licked the frosting from her lips, he licked his too, causing a little thrill to follow the cake on its journey to her stomach.

Across the table, Jim Hacker swallowed the last of his huge wedge of cake and brushed crumbs from his chest-length beard. "Well, gosh durn," he said, glancing over at Cody. "If I found a lady who could cook this good, I'd marry her!"

Sky nearly choked. From the corner of her eye, she saw Cody flush noticeably. "It's a great cake," he added. "Any man would be lucky to have as good a cook as Sky."

When Ned entered the rear office, Cody pushed his chair back. "Join us for some birthday cake, and then we've got a favor to do for Sky."

Her cousin helped himself to the cake. "Sure, what's the—"

"I really have to be getting back to work." She rose from her chair, not wanting to repeat the sad story. "Thank you, Ned." She placed her hand on his shoulder, knowing Cody would explain everything after she left.

Cody walked her to the front door, more at ease now at managing one crutch. "Would you like to go to dinner tomorrow night?" He gave her arm a tender little squeeze that sent goose bumps skipping up to her shoulder. "The Tontine is a popular place."

"Yes, I'd like that." She smiled up into those shimmering hazel eyes and her knees nearly buckled. "Then you can tell me what happened," she added, anxiety returning as she thought of the discarded baby.

He nodded. "Don't worry. We'll take care of it." His lips brushed her brow before she turned to step outside.

Her heart felt almost light again as she hurried back to the hall. Tomorrow night she would have her first social engagement with Cody. The warmth of his tall presence still surrounded her. But more than that, she felt assured. The marshal was a man she could trust.

"Now, you watch out, Sky!" Granny Saunders's voice suddenly berated her. "Don't go off and do somethin' foolish. Remember, you're still a married woman—even if your embezzler husband is a worthless skunk!"

Sky sighed audibly. Wouldn't you know, just when her life was changing for the better, Granny had to interfere. *Oh, Gran. I won't do anything foolish. Besides, this man is different.*

"I'm so glad you found the baby," Sky said to Cody as they left Tontine's restaurant the following evening. Visible relief and gratitude encompassed her features.

"We buried it up near California Gulch." It hadn't been a pleasant task, but Cody had promised her he'd take care of it, and he'd wanted to ease her mind. He shook his head. "I can't believe you went near Stillborn Alley. It isn't a place for decent women."

"As I said, it happened by chance. The pathetic girl was sobbing just as I passed by."

"You mean, the wh—the prostitute?"

She stiffened, her eyes widening in disdain as they moved up Harrison Avenue. "I would hardly call a girl of maybe seventeen a prostitute."

"You haven't been here long, Sky. I've seen some younger."

Her face turned cherry red with anger. "The girl held a dead baby in her arms, Cody. Doesn't that upset you?"

"It happens all the time. That's why they call it Stillborn Alley." He glanced up the street, uncomfortable with the conversation. "I don't like what happens over there, but how can anyone stop it?"

"You're the marshal." A glint of desperation shone in her blue eyes. "Can't you do anything for these women?"

He cleared his throat abruptly, absorbing the sting of her criticism. His dinner was not sitting well. "Why would you care about them?"

She eyed him defensively. "Why wouldn't I care about them? I can imagine what it would feel like . . . to lose a baby."

Her answer baffled him. A young lady from a comfortable background could hardly feel kinship to these women. Damn! The evening threatened to disintegrate in a puff of smoke.

For an awkward moment, neither spoke as they moved along the sidewalk, heading in the direction of Burtram's Hall. He sniffed the scent of lilac water. Her scent. It made him light-headed. Almost catching the tip of his crutch in the uneven boardwalk planks, Cody measured his stride to hers.

"Wish I could take you for a ride, Sky. I know a place where the creek flows real smooth. You can hear the water rippling over the rocks."

She tipped her face up to his and he felt a quickening of his heartbeat.

"Maybe, when your leg mends . . ."

Was she remembering the night they'd ridden out to the gulch under a full moon? His gaze settled on her moist, parted lips and lingered there, an undeniable magnetism drawing him to her, a need growing in him, not only to be closer physically but to protect her from the wildness, the pain of this rough town.

They reached Burtram's, where the sound of raucous voices echoed from behind lighted windows. He escorted her around the building to the back door.

She'd been silent for the last few minutes as they weaved through milling pedestrians. Leaning his crutch against the building, Cody stepped toward her on his good right leg. "You sure are quiet for an eastern gal," he teased, hoping to veer her back into a lighter mood.

The twilight cast lavender shadows over her expectant features. "An idea just came to me about those State Street women." She moved closer to him, a new energy in her voice. "What if they had a chance to grubstake the miners? Make an investment in their own future?"

Her midnight-blue eyes searched his face as she reached out, her fingers twining around his upper arm.

He chuckled, not believing her naive question. "Are you joking? Leadville's hookers becoming mining partners?"

"I am not joking! Why shouldn't a woman—any woman— with a little nest egg be able to invest her money, the same as a man?" She stepped away from him and cocked her head. "She might even strike it rich, just like Horace Tabor."

He smothered the urge to laugh out loud. "Don't think Lieutenant Governor Tabor would appreciate Sallie Purple and her gals as his business partners."

She gathered up her skirts and turned toward the back door. "I don't know why he wouldn't. She may already share some of his business secrets."

He sighed, gazing at her. "Don't go in yet."

She made a slight motion to go, then stopped. Although the darkening shadows shielded her face, her voice seduced him. "Why not?"

Before he knew what he was doing, his hands gathered around her waist and pulled her up close. Once again the delicate fragrance of her lilac cologne filled his senses. "Sky, you're one special lady."

"Don't make fun of me, Cody."

"Never." Words were lost as he tilted her chin gently upward and covered her lips with his. But one kiss was not enough. He showered her forehead, her cheek, the tip of her nose.

She murmured something softly, her body easing, relaxing into his embrace. He drew her even closer, his body becoming hard with wanting. The touch of her fingers gliding through the hair at his nape set him aflame. Finding her mouth once more, he plunged his tongue deep within its warm, sweet depths.

The very air around them pulsed with electric currents. He caressed her back, and his hand slid longingly up her side to the fullness of her breast. She moaned a palpable response.

For the first time, Sky seemed to surrender herself to the passion of his kiss. With ease, he undid the tiny buttons at her bodice. She sighed in pleasure when his fingers slipped inside her camisole to caress and fondle her lush breast.

"Sky, Sky . . ." he implored, his voice hoarse with desire.

In response, her body arched into his, her aroused nipple becoming a taut bud in the palm of his hand. He ached to slide his tongue over the silken flesh beneath his fingers.

The back door swung open and a large bulky frame moved outside. Cody opened one eye and recognized the burly bouncer, Cougar Joe.

"Oh—sorry, folks," Cougar's voice grated. "Is that you, Marshal?"

Sky gasped and jumped in his arms.

Damn the fool! "It's me, Cougar." Cody grudgingly pulled back from Sky.

The bouncer snickered. "Just came out to roll me a cig. Sure is a pretty night, ain't it, Miss Sky?"

"It was," she replied crisply, fastening the top buttons on her bodice. "Goodnight, Marshal." Her expression was unreadable in the darkness. "I'd better be getting inside."

With a flounce of her skirt and a few steps, she opened the door. Before she entered the dreadful place, Sky turned back to him. "Thank you for what you did . . . and happy birthday."

Yeah, a great birthday. He was left standing in the cool, empty night, his desire still burning and unfulfilled. Several feet away, the bouncer lit his cigarette and took a long, slow drag.

Cody cursed under his breath. How was he ever going to get Sky Saunders alone when she still lived in this coyote's lair?

CHAPTER THIRTEEN

Sky sighed in her half-sleep, on the edge of the dream. Cody's face hovered over hers, drawing nearer. His lips would be warm, she knew, his arms strong. He wore no shirt. She was stark naked and her body tingled all over. Especially in her most feminine parts.

A whistling sound made her stir on her rumpled cot. Fighting to hold onto the sensual dream, she pulled the sheet over her head and licked her dry lips, anticipating the kiss.

A staccato animal noise punctured the silence, jarring her awake. Her eyelids grated open and she stared at the partially opened window. Morning sunlight spilled between the drawn shade and the windowsill. Again, a disjointed braying brought her to her elbows. Someone's mule had gotten loose and it had decided to serenade the neighborhood. Why did the wretched beast have to stop right below *her* window?

Groaning, Sky threw her legs over the side of the cot and padded across the floor on bare feet. She was just about to close the window when a gravelly voice reached her ears. "Miss Saunders!"

Still groggy from sleep, she pushed the window up instead of down and stuck her head over the sill. Directly beneath her stood a splay-legged mule shaking its mangy head. Seated on the mule was a gray-bearded man wearing a slouch hat and dusty clothes. He gave a low but spirited whistle.

Sky's mouth dropped open. "Mr. Gunther?"

The man tipped his grimy hat. "It's me, miss, yes it is." He looked up at her, a crooked smile spreading over his weathered face.

"Shut yer yaps down there!" a bawdy woman hollered from an upper window of the saloon next door. Her advice was followed by an empty beer bottle tossed precariously close to the old miner's head. The bottle cracked against the ground and splintered into several pieces. The mule let out another ragged bray.

"Shush, Miss Fanny. Yor makin' too much noise."

Sky gathered her nightgown together modestly in the front. "What do you want, Mr. Gunther?"

"I need to talk to you, miss. 'Bout our partnership."

"Oh . . . yes." The reason for his unexpected visit became instantly clear. "I'll get dressed and come down. Please wait at the back door."

Stumbling over to the makeshift chest, she poured water from a pitcher into the small basin and splashed some on her face. There was no time for her routine ablutions. Her mind raced as she hurriedly pulled on a plain brown work dress and crammed her feet into high-topped shoes. Dan Gunther was here and he wanted to talk to her about "their mining partnership." No matter that she hadn't heard from him in weeks; he must have good news or he wouldn't be here.

She went over to a far corner and knelt down. Working a loose floorboard free, she found her hidden purse, holding coins she'd saved from last month's pay inside a sewing box. With bated breath, she counted out a gold eagle and several smaller coins. Considering for a moment what she'd need to live on until next week's pay, she dropped the smaller coins back in the box and tucked the purse inside her skirt pocket.

Hurrying down the stairs, she almost tripped. Her palm

perspired so, it dragged along the railing.

Gunther was waiting outside the back door, having a smoke. Miss Fanny waited nearby, chewing on a mouthful of something unrecognizable.

"Come inside," Sky suggested to him. "It's more private."

He shouldered his way into the hall, his body reeking of tobacco smoke and untold other grime. Removing his hat, he gazed at her from behind crinkle-lined eyes and wasted no time getting to his mission. "I'm onto a true vein, Miss Saunders. Ol' Lady Luck is about to give up her treasures."

Despite the man's distasteful odor, a prickly thrill chased up her spine. "It looks promising, then, Mr. Gunther?"

He wagged his unkempt head. "Real promisin'. But I need some funds to keep goin'. I could get me a workin' partner, but I won't until I'm sure. Then, again, don't know 'bout that." His dark eyes narrowed to slits. "A man don't always know who to trust in this town."

"Oh, I agree. You should be very sure whom you choose to be a business partner." To show her good faith, Sky fished her purse from her pocket. Opening it, she said, "I've got a gold eagle. It's all I can spare right now."

A flicker of what she thought was disappointment skittered over his leathery features. "That's fine, miss. It'll help." Pulling a crumpled, dirty bandanna from his back pocket, he chuckled. "Here's my collateral. And they ain't no codfish balls." When he opened the bandanna, two silver-flecked nuggets the size of pearl onions twinkled up at Sky.

Excitement leaped in her chest. "You want me to keep these for you?"

"Yes, ma'am. They're jist a sample of what I'm gonna mine out of Lady Luck. She whispers her promises every night in my ear." He grinned, revealing uneven, tobacco-stained teeth. Extending his gnarled paw, the miner placed the wadded up cloth in her hand. "You keep 'em safe for me—till next time, partner."

"Yes, sir." Her breath welled up beneath her breastbone as she eased the precious bundle into her pocket.

A familiar braying came from outside. "That's Miss Fanny callin' me. She's a mighty jealous gal." He gave a throaty laugh. "I better not keep her waitin'."

She watched the old coot hop up on his mule and waved to him. Dan Gunther touched his stubby fingers to his slouch hat, let out a long whistle, and took off down the alley. The clatter of pots and camping gear banging against Miss Fanny's scrawny rump accompanied him.

Sky smiled to herself. If she were a writer of dime novels, "Whistlin' Dan" would definitely be one of her characters.

Jack Burtram came up behind her. "Who was that grizzly ghost?"

"Oh!" She jumped, surprised to see her employer so early in the morning. Lately he'd been spending nights with Winona, his new lady friend who ran a small theater on Chestnut Street. "That was a business friend of mine. Dan Gunther."

"Gunther!" Burtram scowled. "Why, that old fart's been begging money off gullible tinhorns for as long as I can remember." His droopy lids lifted suspiciously. "You're not giving him anything are you?"

Sky's blood simmered. "Really, Mr. Burtram, I don't see where that's any of your business."

Before he could lecture her further, she nipped up her skirt and swished past him. She didn't consider herself one of Mr. Gunther's "gullible tinhorns." After all, he'd given her the silver nuggets for safekeeping. And, she had the agreement.

Then again, she hadn't meant to be so bold as to sass her employer. This rebellious town must be rubbing off on her. By the time she reached her room at the top of the stairs, her pulse galloped faster than a racehorse.

After bolting her door, Sky lifted the secret floorboard. Inside her sewing box, she found the familiar folded paper. Opening it, she reviewed the agreement Ned had witnessed. For her three-hundred-dollar investment, Dan Gunther had agreed to share fifty percent of all profits from the Lady Luck Mine.

Reassured, she tucked the agreement and the wrapped nuggets back into her sewing box.

Covering the board with a rag rug, she rose and went to the window. Leadville's giant mountain peaks stretched out for miles. Staring at them, she crossed her fingers at her sides.

Find that silver, Dan Gunther! Keep your promise!

Trying to sleep that night was impossible. Sky lay awake, staring at the flickering shadows across the ceiling, thoughts of Whistlin' Dan loping through her mind. Excitement over the Lady Luck mine and its infinite possibilities hummed a siren song in her ears.

Finally, when her stomach growled, she gave up on sleep. A midnight morsel might calm her nerves. After pulling on a loose-fitting dress and slippers, she sneaked downstairs. Burtram, she'd noted, wasn't sleeping in the converted storage room down the hall. He was probably being entertained by his new lady friend. Thankfully she wouldn't have to bump into him on her venture to the kitchen.

The front hall was unusually quiet. Perhaps on this weeknight, most of the rowdy customers had taken their bottles to bed instead of trying their luck on gambling.

Fumbling for a match in the dark, Sky lit the oil lamp hanging on a hook near the kitchen door. This morning, she'd made some sugar cookies and, after serving some to her blustery employer, hid the rest in a chipped crockery pot behind a sack of coffee beans on the counter. She'd just lifted the lid on the pot and was about to reach inside it, when a discomforting sound escaped from behind the broom closet door.

She straightened, listening. What she heard sounded like a muffled sob, then an animal whining. Curiosity overtook her. She went to the oil lamp, lifted it off its hook and glided back to the broom closet door. Slowly she turned the knob, her heartbeat thudding in her throat.

The closet door creaked open. In the dim light from the lamp, she saw the shadowy figures of a boy and an animal crouched together on the floor. Two pairs of eyes stared up at her. She gasped and the lamp jiggled in her hand. "Antonio?"

The boy, cowering in the far corner, pulled a shaggy dog close to him. The dog growled protectively.

"*Sí*, it is Antonio."

She saw his tear-stained face and runny nose. Pain clutched her heart to think anyone might have harmed this child, who was always so eager to please. Drawing her handkerchief out of her pocket, she handed it to him. "What's wrong, Antonio? Who hurt you?"

He shook his head. "Nobody." He blew his nose loudly on her handkerchief.

The odor of unwashed boy and unwashed dog filled her nostrils. "Why aren't you home at this time of night?"

"This is my home." He turned forlorn eyes on her and exhaled a ragged sigh. "Señor Burtram lets me sleep here. I work for him and he gives me food."

Astonished, Sky pulled a three-legged stool from the corner and lowered herself onto it. She set the lamp beside her on the floor, its light creating a jack-o'-lantern effect on the boy's features. "But where are your mother and father?"

"My mama is gone to heaven." Antonio choked on a sob. "I don't know my father."

His revelation stunned her. So that was why she'd seen this

scraggly young boy at odd times working in the gambling hall. Her eyes misted. "I'm so sorry, Antonio. I didn't know."

He blew his nose again and handed the wet handkerchief back to her. Gingerly, she slid it into her pocket. In the close heat of the closet, the dog began to pant. Antonio petted him affectionately while the dog licked his cheek.

"Chico is my *amigo*. My only friend." Desperation flickered across his shadowed features. "Señor Burtram—he doesn't like Chico. He told me tonight to get rid of him."

She sighed, a cloak of sadness wilting her shoulders. "Maybe Mr. Burtram thinks there's no place for him here in the hall."

"But where will he go? Chico is my only friend." Fresh tears burst from Antonio's dark eyes and streamed down his face. His pain-filled gaze focused on her. "Will you ask Señor Burtram if I can keep Chico?"

Sniffling herself, Sky attempted a brave voice. "I will talk to Mr. Burtram. I will try to convince him to let you keep Chico." She stroked his thin arm, then ruffled his thick, dusty hair. "Are you hungry?"

He nodded quickly and wiped his drippy nose on his shirtsleeve.

"I put away some sugar cookies I made this morning. I'll see if there's something to drink," she said, wishing there was fresh milk.

"I like sarsaparilla."

She raised her eyebrows. "Sarsaparilla? Who gave you that drink?"

His dark eyes grew mischievous. "Cougar Joe—he says it will make me a man."

She smothered a smile. "I'll have to have a talk with Cougar Joe about that." She lifted the lamp and turned to go. "You and Chico can come with me but don't expect any sarsaparilla." *The idea,* she thought. Well, at least the sweetened sassafras drink wasn't liquor. But what would Joe be giving the boy next?

She found some bottled well water in the kitchen and set half a dozen cookies on a plate. After she'd poured two glasses for herself and Antonio, she discovered a tin bowl on a back shelf and poured some water in it for Chico. "Here's a treat for you, boy." She dropped a cookie next to the bowl.

The dog wolfed down the cookie and drank greedily, then sat at her feet, his scruffy tail banging from side to side.

When she and Antonio finished eating the cookies, he yawned, eyeing the closet with dread. How could she send him back to its miserable, cramped darkness?

"Antonio," she asked suddenly, "would you and Chico like to sleep in my room tonight?"

The boy's ebony eyes shone with interest. *"Sí, señorita."* He hesitated. "But what will Señor Burtram say?"

Sky lit the coal stove. "Señor Burtram is away for the evening." She took the lamp over to the closet door and peered inside.

"But *señorita*," Antonio asked, "you are not going to sleep in there?"

She smiled. "Certainly not. Would you please get me that water bucket on the floor. If you're going to share my room, you'll need to wash up, first."

A frown creased his forehead. "No."

"Yes! Now, hurry. I have to heat some water on the stove."

Antonio grudgingly obeyed. While she heated water and found some soap, he removed his ragged shirt but balked at taking off his pants.

"Don't be bashful," she scolded. "I've seen boy's underwear before."

"I don't want you to see me naked," he said firmly.

"Oh," she said, realizing he wore no drawers. "Well then, I'll help you wash above and you can wash yourself below."

She cleaned his face and ears and scrubbed his upper body amidst squeals of protest. How long it had been since Antonio's last bath, she wouldn't dare have guessed. Even in the shadowed light, the water in the bucket quickly turned a dirty gray.

After he'd finished washing himself, Sky surprised him by dunking his head in the second bucket of water, then lathered and rinsed his hair. He complained in a stream of Spanish she imagined must be most colorful. She was glad her understanding of the language was limited.

He tried to glare up at her as she toweled his thick hair. "I can do it." He grabbed the towel from her hands.

She laughed to herself, remembering how Cody had complained when she'd doused him during his hair-washing. Men and boys were much the same. But she sobered when she saw the boy yank back on his frayed, grimy shirt. He so definitely needed looking after.

"Too bad there isn't enough water to give Chico a bath." She winked at Antonio.

He set his mouth in a defiant line. "He don't need no bath."

Not much, he doesn't, she thought. "It's late, boys. Let's get some sleep." She lifted the lamp and guided them upstairs.

Once inside her small but cozy room, Antonio and the dog settled down on the rag rug beneath the solitary window. She placed an extra sheet over him and rolled up one of her shawls for a pillow, saying, "If you keep Chico quiet, Antonio, he can stay here tonight. But let him out early in the morning—before Mr. Burtram comes in."

The boy's eyelids drooped in the glow of the oil lamp. "*Sí, señorita. Grácias.*" He snuggled closer to his stray companion.

Sky blew out the lamp and crawled into her cot.

"Señorita Saunders?"

"Yes, Antonio?"

"Don't forget to ask Señor Burtram about Chico."

"I won't forget."

For some time she lay staring at the ceiling, listening to the steady breathing of the boy and his dog. A new ache hung on her heart. Poor Antonio . . . an orphan. She swallowed over a lump in her throat. These past weeks, he'd probably been crying himself to sleep in the broom closet just below her, and she'd had no inkling.

Antonio desperately needed help. But how could she help him?

She'd given her last golden eagle to Dan Gunther and set her hopes on a faraway dream, even though she knew dreams didn't always come true.

But she'd also given her promise to the half-breed boy. She had to think of something.

CHAPTER FOURTEEN

The familiar timbred voice coming from inside the office made Sky pause, a ripple of excitement racing through her. *Cody.* From the serious tone of his exchange with Jack Burtram, she sensed Cody's visit was more in the nature of business than a social call. Unable to resist, she listened outside in the hall.

"I think the claim jumping going on lately is part of a larger plan to chase out the small miners, Jack. These culprits have gotta be in a gang. They've got a ringleader."

"You think so?" From behind Burtram's desk, a chair scuffed along the floorboards.

"I'd bet on it. They seem to strike out of the blue. They hit a small claim near a bigger one and burn out or blow away the miner. Then, within a short time, another man moves in and just happens to be partners with the bigger claim owner."

"Damn!" Burtram snorted.

The sound of Cody's boots moved away toward the other side of the room. "That's why I'm making calls to several of the saloon and gambling hall owners I trust to ask their help."

"Sure, Marshal. What can I do?"

"Keep your ears open for any bragging going on. You know what I mean. Sometime, these rats are gonna have a slip of the tongue when they've had too much redeye. I'm looking for names."

"Yeah. I got yer meanin'."

"But keep it quiet that you're listening. I don't want their leader to get word I'm onto something."

"Nah. I'll keep it under my hat," Burtram vowed.

Sensing this was an opportune time to enter the conversation, Sky stepped across the threshold. Her concern for Antonio's well-being had been heightened earlier this morning after speaking with Burtram. She had a mission of her own, as well as the marshal.

Cody stood in the middle of the room, handsome in a green plaid shirt and well-fitting jeans, radiating a vitality that drew her like a magnet.

"Good afternoon, Marshal." She glanced up into his hazel eyes, sparked with mutual attraction. Was he reminded of their last moment together, when he'd kissed her in that most passionate embrace? Heat flared in her cheeks.

He removed his white Stetson and smiled. "Same to you, Miss Sky."

Fighting to retain her composure, she offered, "You're looking well—and you've given up your crutches."

He nodded. "Tossed 'em out in the toolshed. Sure feels good not to need 'em anymore."

Burtram's heavy-lidded gaze switched back and forth between them, his mouth drawing into an impatient line. "Guess the social hour's over. You got some work to do, Miss Saunders?"

You old crank, she thought. "Certainly, Mr. Burtram. Could I offer you two a cup of coffee?"

Her employer's expression brightened. "Well . . . I suppose I could drink a cup."

She turned to leave the room, smiling to herself. She could always placate the man with food or drink.

"Thanks. I've got to make some more calls. See you, Jack." Cody put on his hat as he followed her into the hall.

"I need to talk to you about something," she said when they were out of Burtram's earshot.

He looked at her with a lopsided grin. "Sounds good."

"About something important."

"Oh, sure. When?"

"Tomorrow's Saturday," she thought out loud. "Tomorrow afternoon?"

"I want to question a miner up near Stray Horse Gulch tomorrow. How about I pick you up in the rig and we can talk on the ride?"

"Thanks, Cody."

He tipped his hat. Despite an effort to keep a more business-like demeanor toward him, her smile softened. Her gaze lingered on the marshal's broad shoulders as he sauntered through the crowded hall to the front door.

An azure sky, a late summer breeze, the steady rhythm of the black gelding's hooves on the trail, and Sky Saunders sitting next to him. Cody breathed in the delicate fragrance of lavender, keenly aware of her trim hip moving against his, and thought he was the luckiest man in the state of Colorado.

He hummed a little folk tune, waiting for her to get to that "something important" she had in mind.

"I had a visit from my mining partner a few days ago," Sky stated, an air of confidence in her voice.

"Oh, you mean old Dan Gunther?" That crusty miner couldn't be what she'd wanted to talk to him about.

"Yes, Mr. Gunther." She tilted her head, glancing up at him from beneath the brim of her dainty straw hat. "He thinks he's on the brink of finding a major silver bonanza."

He cleared his throat, tamping the urge to chuckle out loud. "Is that right?" His gaze fell to the creamy expanse of her neck below her upswept auburn hair. Several stray tendrils fluttered in the breeze and he had the strange urge to reach over and touch them.

"Don't make fun, Cody," she reprimanded, her voice going serious.

"Wouldn't think of it, ma'am." He stared soberly at the road ahead. "Now, what was that important something you wanted to talk to me about?"

She sighed, as if carrying a heavy burden. "It's about Antonio."

"Antonio who?"

"I don't know his last name," she blurted. "You know him . . . young Antonio at the gambling hall."

"Oh, that kid." Completely baffled, he stared at her. "What about him?"

Her eyes glinted blue sparks from beneath long mahogany eyelashes. "I'll tell you, if you promise not to make a joke out of it."

Instantly, he was all ears. He slipped his hand over and touched her knee through the folds of her periwinkle cotton dress. "I promise. Tell me."

Politely removing his hand from her knee, she sat up straighter. "Antonio is an orphan. His mother died only six months ago, and his father disappeared several years before that." Her voice wavered. "He works for Burtram around the hall and he's been sleeping in a broom closet downstairs at night."

Cody shook his head. "Poor kid. That is tough. Doesn't he have any family around here?"

"Burtram said when Antonio's mother came to work for him as a cook, she never mentioned her family. She probably hadn't been in touch with them because of her shame. Antonio's father was a drunk and a drifter."

Cody glanced over at her pensive expression. "There must be quite a few stories like his in these mining towns."

Sky moved her fingers down the small buttons of her dress.

He forced himself to look ahead, wishing his hands were there instead of hers. "Now, Antonio has latched onto a stray dog he wants to keep," she said, "and it's only a matter of time till Burtram makes him get rid of it.

"I hate to see him growing up in a gambling hall, Cody, with no guidance or direction." Her voice trailed away for a moment. "If it hadn't been for my Grandma Saunders, and my aunt and uncle, I don't know where I would have ended up."

"Sounds like he wouldn't have had a much better life if his old man had stuck around."

She expelled an exasperated breath. "But now he'll just grow up crude and wild."

Cody shrugged. "Sometimes it's better to let wild things stay wild."

"No. I'll never accept that."

"Think of yourself first, Sky." He leaned into her shoulder. "I know of a boarding house opening up on the east side of town. Mrs. Henson's a new widow and she'll run a clean, respectable place. Why don't you get out of that hornet's nest you're in and move into her house? As for Antonio—drop him off with the Catholic sisters."

"Well, I'll consider the boarding house."

Cody hoped she would consider his advice. But by the way she gazed off toward the mountains, he knew she only had that half-breed kid on her mind.

Cody pulled the horse to a stop in front of a ramshackle building on the edge of a mine yard. "Wait here," he instructed. "I've got to talk to Abe Fitch for a couple minutes."

Sky watched him stride up the sloping yard, looking none the worse for wear. No one would guess he'd been hobbling around on crutches only a few weeks before. A man in grime-covered overalls appeared at the door to the shack and invited him inside.

The odor of smelted ore hung thick on the air, invading her sensitive nostrils. Remembering the first time she'd visited a mine site and twisted her ankle kept Sky content to stay seated in the rig.

She scanned the horizon, dotted with various mining claims, and wondered where Dan Gunther's mine was on Stray Horse Gulch. Why hadn't she pressed him earlier to draw her a map? Damn it all.

Not long afterward, Cody returned to the rig. His lips were set in a straight line as he took up the leather traces and urged the horse forward.

"Wasn't Mr. Fitch of any help?" she asked after they'd ridden a ways in silence.

"Nope. He was about as talkative as a fence post."

"But you thought he had some information."

"That's what I'd hoped. One of his neighbors got chased off his claim the other night, and I thought Abe might have seen something." Gazing over the rock-strewn hillside, Cody frowned. "He wasn't much like himself. I think he's afraid."

"You think someone's frightened him?"

"Yeah. Abe probably thinks he's gonna be next."

Chills skittered down Sky's spine. She thought of Dan Gunther and her stomach went queasy. "Have you heard of the Lucky Lady mine up here, Cody?"

"Can't say that I have."

"The Lucky Lady is Dan Gunther's mine. I'd appreciate it if you'd keep your eyes and ears open, in case he might need some protection."

He nodded and winked at her. "I'll sure do that."

They rocked along the rutted trail, winding downhill until they approached a grove of tall spruce and Douglas fir. The mid-afternoon sun emerged from between scattered clouds, beating down on her back and arms. She licked her dry lips.

"I brought some apple cider and fresh butter pound cake. Would you like to stop and have some?"

The corners of Cody's mustache lifted. "Yes, ma'am. There's a little creek that runs along these trees. This'll be a good place."

She spread out the gingham cloth over a large flat rock where she set the pound cake, the bottled cider, and two tin cups. They leaned back on the mossy ground and drank deeply of the quenching cider. The portions of cake she laid out disappeared quickly.

"I love it here." She removed her straw hat and looked up through the trees, inhaling the tangy scent of pinesap.

"It's great to get away for a while." From beneath his white Stetson, Cody's gaze roamed lazily over her bodice and flowing skirt. His rapt attention did not escape her. She knew her cheeks flared with self-conscious color.

He glanced over at the creek, sparkling in the sunlight. "Tempting, isn't it?"

"What do you mean?" She smiled, puzzled. "It's not deep enough to swim in."

"Deep enough to get your feet wet."

"Oh, I guess it is." She stretched one high-topped shoe from beneath her skirt, thinking how cool the water would feel on her hot, bare feet.

Cody yanked off his boots, smirking like a kid playing hooky from school.

She giggled and started unbuttoning her shoes. By the time she'd removed both of them, he was kneeling beside her.

"Here. Let me help."

Before she could stop him, he'd reached up and was teasing her black cotton stocking down over her calf. The touch of his warm fingers sent pleasant tingles skipping up to the very pit of her stomach.

"Cody!" She tried to retrieve her leg, but he held her foot

firmly in his hand. "You are bold!"

He laughed from deep in his throat, obviously enjoying her dismay, and slipped the stocking from her toes.

She wrenched away and rolled down her other stocking.

"Come on in, Miss Priss!" he called, hopping into the creek.

Tiptoeing over pinecones and smaller rocks, Sky made her way to the creek bank. The sight of the tall marshal, his jeans rolled midway up his muscular calves, grinning from ear to ear, made her almost gleeful.

She lifted her skirts to her knees, higher than a lady should, rushed forward down the bank and into the gurgling water. "Ohhhh, yikes! This is c-o-l-d!"

"You'll get used to it." He reached down and scooped up a small handful and playfully sprayed it at her.

"Don't do that, Cody. My dress."

Laughing, he turned and waded farther up the creek.

She followed, keeping her skirts hoisted above the current. The water was refreshing, she had to admit. The sun caressing her shoulders left her nearly lethargic.

But several yards ahead, Sky stepped on a moss-covered rock and lost her footing. She let out a shriek and fell sideways onto one knee.

Cody whirled. "What happened?" He hurried downstream to help her.

"Oh, no!" she sputtered. "Look at my dress!"

"Don't worry about that." He whisked her up in his strong arms. His closeness sent her pulse spinning and her mind whirling. Did he think she was the clumsiest female he'd ever met?

He set her down on the bank in the shade of the trees. "Think you'll survive?"

"Yes, thank you." She blotted her wet legs and feet with her damp petticoats. "Of course, my dress is half-soaked."

"The sun will take care of that on the way home." Mischief

brewed in the sparkle of his eyes. He picked up one of her stockings she'd left on a nearby rock. "But first, let's put your stockings back on."

Very properly, she said, "I can do that myself."

Her words barely escaped her lips when Cody began edging the stocking over her toes.

"Stop, now."

Too late. He'd slipped the thing up to her ankle and was about to slide it further up her leg. She jerked her bent knee toward her chest.

"You don't want any assistance?" His hazel eyes held untold tomfoolery. With a firm hold of her heel, he slid his fingers inside the cotton fabric and began to trace circles with his fingertips. Ever so lightly. On the bottom of her bare foot!

Her surprised hoot echoed through the woods.

A broad smile split his face. "The lady is ticklish."

"No! No!" she cried, trying to slither away from him.

A futile attempt. His powerful frame engulfed her, those large hands roaming to places she never realized were so sensitive. Peals of laughter, her laughter, rose to the treetops. "Someone will hear us. Stop!" she choked out, gasping for breath, fighting away his maddening fingertips.

"All right. I'll stop." His face hovered inches above hers. "If you give me something."

She knew what he wanted. How would she get out of it—even if she wanted to? "What?" she asked, biting her lower lip.

His sultry smile was her answer. Her heart pounding like a sledgehammer, Sky squinched her eyes closed. She was doomed.

His warm breath caressed her cheek before she felt his mustache, then his lips. Feather-light. Then, his tongue. Moist and hot and seeking, it circled her lips. Mesmerized, she parted her lips and he nudged it inside her mouth. Like a torch, his wanting tongue probed until she longingly touched its tip with her own. Felt a spark erupt inside her.

She smelled his clean, masculine heat, felt his broad chest crushing hers, and knew a passion totally unknown before this moment. His fingers caressed her bare leg and explored their way upward along her silken drawers to the curve of her buttock. She could only whimper in growing ecstasy as he gently squeezed and fondled her there. "Oh, Cody . . ."

Her fingers weaved through the soft wave of hair at his nape, and he moaned with pleasure. "Sky. There's so much I'd like to do for you. Do *to you* . . . "

Then her dress was billowing out around her hips, and she felt his warm hands spread her legs so that they straddled his. "We shouldn't be . . ." But the delicate touch of his fingers slipping inside the opening of her underwear and brushing softly along her inner thigh left her breathless.

She should stop him, stop this—before every shred of her willpower was gone. But how could she?

His willing lips covered hers again, his tongue once more seducing hers. His fingers found her feminine curls and gently, urgently stroked her. Blood rushed to her face and moistness filled her most secret parts. Now his thumb teased her. *There!* Teased and stroked until all reason fled and only wanting remained. Arching her back, she gave way to his coaxing touch.

Her passionate cry soared above the trees as she exploded in an erotic convulsion.

Her body saturated with the heated rush, she sighed against Cody's shoulder. He kissed her forehead, eyelids, and the side of her mouth.

"I wanted to pleasure you, Sky," he murmured. "Did I?"

Her voice was a whisper. "Like no other."

Dizzying currents ran through her as she lay in his embrace. Her eyelids fluttered open and she was nearly blinded by sunlight shimmering through the trees. What had just happened?

What might happen next?

Her dilemma whirled before her. Knocking Cody over onto one elbow, she sat straight up, gulping breaths of air. "This shouldn't have happened. I'm still . . ." The words tottered on her tongue. *I'm still a married woman.* Could she blurt them out? Give this sensual, admirable man a reason to throw her away like second-hand merchandise?

He blinked at her sudden change in demeanor. "You're what?"

"I'm—late." She snatched up her other stocking and yanked it on, relieved that she at least was still fully dressed. "I'll be . . . missed." Scrambling over to her forgotten shoes, she hurriedly pulled them on, bothering only to fasten the top few buttons.

Cody stared at her, obviously annoyed. "You're thinking about that kid, aren't you?"

Without waiting for an answer, he retrieved his hat from a bush down the bank and crammed it on his head. "Come on, then. We'd better get back."

Dismay welled in her breast as she watched him charge, like an angered buffalo, up the slope to the rig. She wanted to call out, *It's not what you think!* An errant breeze ruffled her hair, pressed her still wet skirt against her legs. Where Cody's lips and hands had warmed her, the sudden gust left chilling waves of gooseflesh.

CHAPTER FIFTEEN

By the time they returned from the gulch, fading sunlight splashed buildings a golden tint, reflecting a glare from windows that burned the eyes. Long shadows stretched over rooftops and roadways.

Instead of basking in the day's warm glow, relishing the fresh memory of their intimate creek-side encounter, Sky felt a sense of disquiet. The closeness shared with Cody earlier in the afternoon had ended in uncomfortable silence between them. He'd hardly uttered a word all the way back.

She knew her sudden attack of conscience had caused his somber withdrawal. No man liked rejection. Yet her reaction to his sensual foreplay had been inevitable. What else could a not-yet divorced woman have done? She should have come right out and told him. But what would he think of her then? She sighed. Possibly she'd find a way to tell him, after the final divorce papers arrived. Then she'd be truly free.

Now traffic along Leadville streets threatened to drown out any conversation she might have encouraged. Pedestrians and horse-drawn wagons clogged Harrison Avenue, causing Cody to grumble when their progress slowed to a crawl.

"Every danged miner in the territory must be in town tonight. They're lookin' for some whiskey to wash away that smelter dust."

She glanced over at the cynical expression on Cody's face beneath his slanted brim. *Whiskey's not all they're looking for,* she thought. Might Cody seek out female comfort in a parlor house later tonight? The idea was repulsive, causing a surge of heat to well up inside her.

After they reached the gambling hall, he assisted her from the rig. "Thank you for taking me on the scenic ride," she said as they walked between buildings to the rear entrance.

"I enjoyed the company." His voice sounded indifferent, and her heart sank.

As they rounded the corner, a shaggy brown and white dog bounded up to them, its tail wagging. "Chico!" Sky petted the stray's dusty head, looking down into his expectant face.

"I'd be careful of these alley dogs. They carry diseases."

She smiled up at Cody. "This is Antonio's dog. He's been taking good care of him."

"Oh, well, if it's Antonio's mutt."

"Look." She gestured toward Chico. "One of his eyes is brown and one is pale blue."

"Yeah. That's different." Taking her elbow, he ushered her to the back door. "Time we both got home. Didn't you say you'd be late?"

Avoiding a reply, she watched Chico romp beside them. He suddenly trotted several yards away and crawled under the far corner of the building. "It looks like Antonio's found a hiding place for his new friend." She gazed up the alley. "I wonder where the boy went?"

Cody moved closer to her, his expression concerned. "I wish you'd stop worrying about that kid. He's only going to cause you trouble." He raised his hand and brushed the callused knuckles gently along her cheek.

Standing so close to him and feeling his touch made her almost giddy, but she couldn't prevent voicing her thoughts. "Someone has to care about Antonio and what happens to him."

Cody opened the door for her, then abruptly stepped back.

"Goodnight, Miss Saunders," he said, his tone as cool as a mountain creek.

"Cody . . ." she called to his retreating powerful frame, a shiver of fear rippling through her limbs. Even if he'd heard her, she knew he wouldn't turn around and come back.

Swallowing disappointment in their less-than-affectionate parting, Sky slipped inside the hall and went to look for Antonio. She wondered why he hadn't been outside playing with Chico and if he'd had any dinner. Checking the kitchen and not finding him there, she moved up the hall to the swinging doors and peered into the noisy front room. The pervasive odor of cigar smoke and grimy bodies assailed her. Through the hazy light, she scanned the early evening crowd and saw a circle of men near the end of the bar. They were making great sport of jostling a youth amongst them.

It didn't take a second glance to recognize Antonio as the object of their amusement.

Pushing through the swinging doors, she made a beeline for the revelers. Instinct told her whatever the men were up to, it had to be no good.

As she approached, a grisly miner with a beard as rough-edged as a scouring brush grabbed Antonio by the arm and held a beer bottle to his mouth. "Drink up, you little spic." The man tipped the bottle, forcing its contents down the boy's throat. Antonio's dark eyes stared defiantly up at the brute. Some of the beer dribbled down his chin onto his ragged shirt, and he gagged.

"Stop this right now!" Sky shoved into the raucous group and put a protective arm about Antonio's thin shoulders. "How dare you attempt to intoxicate this child?" Her eyes blazed into the miner's jeering face.

He spat a stream of tobacco juice on the floor near her feet. "We was only funnin' with him, ma'am." An echo of snickering erupted around the circle.

"If you or any of your vermin friends come near this boy again, I'll—" Sky searched the crowd for Cougar Joe, but couldn't see him. Where was Jack Burtram?

The grisly miner squinted at her, a devilish smirk splitting his weathered face. "You'll do what, ma'am?"

"I'll have you all thrown out of here," she said through clenched teeth, her blood roaring in her ears.

Antonio trembled, his body perspiring beneath her hand. He looked imploringly from the sniggering men back to her.

Spinning around, Sky started to guide the boy through the gathering crowd, her angered gaze fixed straight ahead.

"That's not a very nice way to say goodbye, sugar." Someone grabbed her around her hips, knocking her against the end of the bar. Another groped for her buttocks through the folds of her skirt.

She let out a shocked gasp. Then she saw the glint of a gun butt sticking out from a shelf beneath the bar. The bartender's protection. Well, right now, she needed it more than the bartender did.

Sky lunged and grabbed the gun. Its unfamiliar cold metal weighed heavily in the palm of her hand, but she swung the barrel upward, pointing it crazily at the men.

Bleary eyes stared at her in disbelief.

"Watch out, honey. Looks like that pistol's cocked!" one scowling miner rasped.

"I'm warning you—Leave us alone!" She met his gaze straight on, her heart thumping madly.

From the corner of her eye, she saw some wild-haired ruffian jump up on a chair. What would they do next? Lasso her? Humiliate her further in front of the boy?

In panic, Sky jerked backward. The gun went off, exploding in her hands. She heard the shattering of glass and saw a multitude of dust-covered backsides dive under nearby tables. A black hole appeared in the floorboard not four feet in front of her. Acrid gun smoke stung her nostrils. Loud whoops bellowed from the front of the hall, and several men raced for the swinging doors.

Cowards! Beasts! They were lucky she hadn't winged one of them.

Holding the gun at her side, Sky reached for Antonio, who was watching her admiringly from behind a bar stool, and hustled him toward the rear of the hall.

He tottered along beside her, reeking of alcohol. "You showed them dirty *gringos,*" he slurred, his eyes wide.

When they got to the kitchen, she laid the pistol on a counter, her hands shaking, her heart still banging like a sledgehammer. "What did those men make you drink?"

"Some whiskey." He hiccupped. "And a beer."

Sky pinned him with a stare. "How much whiskey?"

"Only this much." He measured about two inches with his short fingers. "They wanted me to drink it like a man."

She shook her head. "I wish I were a man." She clenched her fists at her sides.

Antonio's black eyes widened. "Do you think you could drink more than them?"

"No," she replied, ladling water into a metal pan and lighting the stove. The boy desperately needed washing again. "I wouldn't have to drink alcoholic spirits to prove I was a *real* man."

His gaze dropped to the floor and he rubbed his arm.

"Did they hurt you?"

"A little. They twisted my arm. They laughed at me." His chin lifted defiantly but his eyes misted with pain. "I don't care if they call me bad names—I don't listen to them."

Sky's heart lurched with compassion. She'd known the physical and mental wounds a man's cruelty could inflict. She remembered the bruises and the painful admonitions. Now, this innocent had been mistreated by the adults who should have protected him.

Her arms went around him and she instinctively ruffled his mop of unkempt hair. "Most of the men who come to this hall are crude and rough, Antonio. Their ways are not like all men. Not like the marshal," she added, her thoughts drifting to Cody.

Antonio leaned against her, allowing her the brief moment of affection, and Sky wondered if hers was the first warm embrace he'd known since his mother's death many months before.

Then he hiccupped. *"Sí, señorita."* He drew away, looking up into her face. "The marshal is a good *gringo*. I watch him ride on his big horse. He makes bad people listen to him." His narrow shoulders lifted and a smile brightened his dusky features. "When I grow up, I want to be just like him."

Sky's breath caught over a sudden lump in the back of her throat. "Well, I'm sure the marshal would be proud to know that," she said, wishing Cody was here to hear the boy's admiring words. She definitely planned to tell him.

While Antonio washed his hands and face, she heated beans and baking powder biscuits made earlier, and they shared the light supper. After their meal, the glazed expression cleared from Antonio's eyes.

"Here, let's take off your dirty shirt and I'll wash it for you," Sky suggested, helping him tug it over his head. "You can put on a clean shirt while this one dries overnight."

His forehead wrinkled. "I don't have no other shirt."

"You only have this shirt?"

He nodded and looked down at his badly scuffed shoes.

"Oh, dear." She dunked the soiled garment in a pan of heated water and began to scrub it with lye soap. "I guess we'll have to get you a new one."

Slipping the pistol into her skirt pocket and carrying the clean wet shirt, she led Antonio up the back stairs. "You can sleep in my room again tonight."

She didn't know how long she could share her room with the boy until Burtram discovered it. The arrangement must be resolved; a broom closet was definitely not decent sleeping quarters for anyone, let alone an eight-year-old boy.

Leaving Antonio sitting outside her door in the hall, she undressed and prepared for bed. When she went to get him, he'd curled up into a ball and fallen fast asleep.

At the end of a late August day, the heat in the hall was oppressive.

"Antonio," she whispered, shaking him gently. "Come to bed, now." She helped him to his feet, and he shuffled alongside her into her room.

She knelt over his makeshift bed beneath the window and draped a sheet over him. He gazed up at her, still half-asleep. "You are brave . . . You shot at the dirty *gringos*." His dark lashes fluttered, then closed.

Smiling down at his intense young face, Sky dropped a kiss on his warm cheek. "Sleep well, Antonio."

A fitful breeze, accompanied by noise from the saloon next door, rushed through the open window. She glanced over at the row of lighted upstairs windows where naked silhouettes moved behind drawn shades and hugged herself protectively. Was Cody being entertained tonight by one of Leadville's finest? After all, he was a man with human needs—needs that she couldn't meet.

Frustrated, she shook her head and moved away from the window. After the ecstasy of his embrace this afternoon, how tempting it would be to release her goal of independence and chase wantonly after the town marshal. Principles be damned. But then, she didn't want to be beholden to any man. Or be owned by another husband.

165

Not even Cody.

She sat down on her cot and felt the cool steel of the pistol lying on the rag rug where she'd left it. Her gaze fell to the sleeping boy. Tonight, her earlier fears for Antonio had been realized. His youth and innocence had been threatened. How long could she protect him here? He had no guardian. The child possessed no more dignity than his abandoned stray dog that wandered the streets fending for itself.

A fearful little tremor washed over her. She must act soon or Antonio would continue to be mistreated—would likely grow up as wild and abusive as the majority of drunken miners passing through Burtram's front doors.

Sky's heels tapped along the rough boardwalk early the following morning. The address Cody had given her of the new boarding house on Alder Street was two blocks ahead. Her mind whirled with the possibilities of a new shelter for her and Antonio.

Even the necessary nuisance of the squirt wagon, pulled along by a vocal, dilapidated donkey, didn't faze her optimism. The operator, a young, robust man wearing baggy overalls, splashed water from large wooden barrels onto the wide road in an effort to keep the dust down.

"Good morning, Miss Saunders," a familiar masculine voice rang out behind her.

She glanced over her shoulder to see Cody astride his buckskin move up alongside the boardwalk. The mere sight of him sitting tanned and tall in the saddle, his white hat brim slanted at a jaunty angle, took her breath away. His alert expression didn't reveal any signs of a night of overindulgence.

"A good morning it is, Marshal," she replied, feeling a blush color her cheeks. How could he address her as *Miss Saunders* after their intimate encounter on the creek-bank yesterday?

"You're out early enjoying the sights of Leadville." He cocked one tawny brow over a curious gaze.

Caught in her tracks.

She paused, tilting her chin in his direction. "Well, I am on a mission. I'm looking for new living quarters."

The corners of his mustache lifted. "Oh, so you're lookin' for a new room?"

She adjusted the brim of her straw hat to shield her eyes from the sun, and his curious gaze. "I'm on my way to the boarding house you mentioned yesterday."

He smiled with obvious satisfaction. "I'll bet Mrs. Henson can oblige your needs. She runs the only decent place in town." He gave a smart little salute and guided his horse back into the moving thoroughfare.

Observing the way Cody's light blue shirt fitted across his broad shoulders and the sway of his hips in the saddle almost made Sky forget her urgency. Guilt, like a mouse, nibbled at her for not revealing her complete quest. But her intuition told her Cody wouldn't like what she was about.

Arriving at the front door of a newly painted clapboard, two-story house, she knocked at the screen door. Mrs. Henson, a straitlaced woman of middle age, answered and invited her inside.

Their conversation proved to be much shorter than Sky had anticipated.

"I do not accept children," the woman said, her plump jowls quivering. "And definitely—no animals."

Sky retraced her steps back over the uneven boardwalk, choking on the stubborn dust kicked up from oxen's hooves, her shoulders sagging with discouragement.

Oh, Antonio. Where will you go from here?

By the time she neared the gambling hall, the suggestion

Cody had made on their way up Stray Horse Gulch surfaced in her mind. Now it seemed the only alternative for Antonio.

Chapter Sixteen

The spire of the new Church of the Ascension pricked the smoke-clouds drifting overhead. Shifting winds had pushed smelter smoke down over the town from nearby mines, spreading the landscape with a gauze-like haze.

From across the street, the sound of pounding hammers echoed in Sky's ears.

Next to her, Antonio dug in his heels. "But, *señorita,* this is a church. I can't live here."

"The sisters live behind the rectory." She attempted a positive tone, avoiding his dubious dark gaze. "And it will be a good opportunity for you to get some schooling."

At that moment, she heard a canine whimper and glanced around to see Chico bound into Antonio's arms. A length of rope trailed from around his neck. The dog must have chewed through it after they'd tied him to a hitching post in front of the gambling hall.

"*Chico!*" Antonio's glum expression instantly changed to joy as the straggly mutt licked his face. "You followed me."

"Oh, Chico," Sky murmured, much less enthusiastic.

"Will they let me keep him?" Antonio's eyes widened with expectation.

The dog's dwelling place had not been her immediate concern. She doubted Father Patrick or the nuns would readily welcome his presence. Another mouth to feed.

She shook her head. "I don't know, Antonio. We'll see what they say."

At least Jack Burtram had approved Antonio's departure when she'd asked if she could place him with the sisters. "Sure, go ahead. I can't keep track of the kid half the time." He'd run his big hands through his thinning black hair. "It doesn't pay me to keep him."

She shuddered to think what would become of the boy if she didn't find him a decent place to live. She smoothed a lock of dark hair from his forehead. Even after her painstaking efforts at cutting his thick mane, undisciplined waves rebelled. At least he smelled clean after a bath last night, and his new white, store-bought shirt made him presentable to his possible future guardians.

"Now, let's hurry. We don't want to keep Father Patrick waiting."

With hope and a fast-tripping heart, she grasped Antonio's warm perspiring palm and hustled him toward the church rectory. But he wrenched his hand free of hers as she plunged the metal knocker against the arched door. "I don't like this place."

"Don't worry," she reassured him. "It will be an exciting new adventure for you." She held onto his arm as she spoke for fear he'd escape with Chico in a flash if she didn't.

Finally, after several bangs of the knocker, the wide door swung open and a petite nun with a round, friendly face greeted them.

"Good morning, Sister." Sky made a little curtsy. "I'm Miss Saunders and this is Antonio Pérez." She used Antonio's mother's last name, as Burtram hadn't known his father's. "We have an appointment with Father Patrick."

"Oh, yes. Oh, yes." The nun raised a pudgy finger to her dimpled cheek, her brown eyes lighting on Antonio. "Come in. Follow me, please."

Sky coaxed Antonio over the threshold before Chico could follow, and they tagged behind the small nun who scurried ahead, her black robes swaying.

"I'm Sister Mary Angeline," she said, smiling over her shoulder. "Father Patrick is talking with the workmen. They're behind schedule," she confided, the noise of hammer and saw nearly drowning out her soft voice.

Her plump hands rose on the air in front of her as if she were about to sprinkle fairy dust. "But I'll find him."

The only dust Sky could see wherever she looked about the unfinished church was sawdust, which floated on sunlit streams from the windowless windows and tickled her nose.

"Please wait while I tell Father you're here." Sister Mary Angeline gestured to a plain wooden bench in the narrow hall and disappeared around a corner to the sanctuary.

Once they were seated, Sky smiled over at Antonio, who looked worried and anxious. She placed her arm around his wiry shoulders and swallowed over the nervous lump in her own throat. She'd been raised a Methodist by her aunt and uncle, and this was her first time inside a Catholic church.

Hurry, Father. Be kind, Father.

When she'd met the parish priest a few days before, it had been only for a short time and he'd obviously been preoccupied with the ongoing clamor of construction. She hoped he remembered the reason for their appointment today.

"Ah, Miss Saunders," an Irish voice boomed, bringing her abruptly to her feet. "And how are ye this busy mornin'?"

Sky's breath caught in her dry mouth. She stood face to face with the square-built priest, recognizing his ruddy complexion and graying red hair. Standing slightly behind him, another nun, tall and purposeful, observed her.

"Good morning, Father Patrick." She half-turned. "This is Antonio, the boy I mentioned to you the other day." She motioned for Antonio to stand in front of the priest and he did.

The father's gray eyes behind wire-rimmed spectacles considered the boy. "Aye. So it is." His lips settled into a noncommittal line. "Let us go into my office, Miss Saunders, where we can talk more plainly. The lad can wait for ye out in the hall."

Sky opened her mouth to object. Antonio should know what his future held. But the priest and the tall nun swished past her and she had no choice but to follow. She smiled back into Antonio's anxious face. "I won't be too long."

"Would you please keep your eye on him, Sister Mary?" She addressed the short nun standing off to the side.

The nun cocked her head, reminding Sky of a little bird. "Yes, miss. He may come watch the workmen in the sanctuary."

Once inside the crowded office, Father Patrick announced, "This is Sister Prunella Agnes, me able assistant."

Prunella. Good Lord. What dreary soul had given her that name? "Hello, Sister Prunella," Sky managed.

The nun stared at her from close-set, piercing eyes. Her thin lips drew upward awkwardly as if smiling were a task she rarely attempted.

Father Patrick gestured for Sky to sit in the high-backed chair in front of his desk. The sister stood ramrod-straight next to the adjacent wall.

"Now then, Miss Saunders," the priest began after settling himself in his chair opposite her. "If I remember correctly, the lad is an orphan and ye need to find a place for him to stay."

Sky cleared her throat. "Yes, Father. And, I was hoping—"

"Would ye say he is a good worker?"

"Oh, yes. Antonio is a strong boy, even though he's not exactly robust. He's used to doing many household chores."

The priest nodded appreciatively. " 'Tis a good thing. We could sure use some cleanin' up around here."

"I would hope," Sky forged on, "that in exchange for his work, and my contribution to the church, Antonio could receive some schooling."

Father Patrick's pale eyebrows lifted. "Hmmm." He tapped a pencil on some papers in front of him on the desk. "Sister Prunella, do ye think ye might give the lad a few lessons?"

Sister Prunella's lips puckered in her long sallow face. "Does the boy know his alphabet?"

Sky sat up straighter on the uncomfortable hard-backed chair. "I'm teaching him."

"Well, I suppose I could give him some instruction with his English," she replied crisply.

"I know Antonio would be grateful."

"Ye realize, miss, that this is not a permanent situation," Father Patrick emphasized. "We'll keep our eyes open for a family that might be willin' to take him."

An uncomfortable pause filled the stuffy room. Perspiration gathered beneath Sky's camisole and dampened her dress beneath her arms.

"Bein' the lad's background is . . . well, ye know 'tis question-able . . . some folks might think he'll be difficult to raise."

Sky bristled beneath her Sunday straw hat, indignation rising angrily in her chest. "Antonio may come from an unfortunate beginning, Father, but I know he has the potential to be a lov-ing and responsible addition to any family."

"Of course, m'dear." The priest rose from his chair. "We'll give it a try. Sister Prunella will show ye where the lad will stay."

"Oh, I almost forgot. There's one more thing." Sky shot to her feet. "His dog, Chico."

Father Patrick and Sister Prunella exchanged surprised glances.

"A dog?" Sister Prunella's nostrils flared as if she'd smelled something distasteful.

Father Patrick's eyes grew larger behind his wire-rimmed spectacles. "Where?"

Sky smiled sheepishly. "He's waiting outside the front door."

Frowning, Father Patrick moved past her. "Come, then. Let's be havin' a look at him."

Sister Prunella, tall and brittle as a quill, followed the priest, her habit skirts brushing soundlessly along the dusty floor.

Seeing Antonio's curious expression as he and the plump Sister Mary Angeline returned from the sanctuary, Sky paused to explain. "Father Patrick wants to look at Chico."

Antonio grinned and scampered to catch up with the priest's long strides. Sister Mary Angeline tagged along behind Sky. For a fleeting moment, Sky saw the humor in this urgent race to the front entrance. It would seem they were hurrying to greet a visiting dignitary, rather than a bedraggled stray mutt.

With one strong push, Father Patrick swung the arched door wide and all eyes peered out onto the boardwalk. To the side, lying next to a workman's wheelbarrow, lay Chico. When he spied the group of humans clogging the doorway, he jumped to his oversized paws and trotted up to them, his matted tail wagging furiously.

"Chico!" Antonio called.

"So, this is yer dog, lad?" Father Patrick gazed upon the friendly stray, a strained smile working his square jaw.

Cocking his unkempt head, Chico gazed up at the parish priest out of his one brown and one pale blue eye.

Sky smothered a chuckle. "He'd be a good guard dog . . . and he could chase away other strays." She hoped she sounded convincing.

"*Sí*. And he don't need much food," Antonio added.

Father Patrick's brow furrowed in concentration. His gaze darted between Antonio and Chico as the fingers of his square hands intertwined. A man caught in a dilemma.

While Antonio stooped beside Chico and spoke a language only the two of them understood, Sky chewed on the inside of her lip, waiting for the father's decision.

Sister Mary Angeline's voice behind them broke the awkward silence, and couldn't have come at a more opportune time. "The workmen need your advice on where to place the baptismal font, Father. Shall I tell them?"

With a wave of his hand, Father Patrick half-turned. "Tell them I'll be right there."

Sister Prunella lifted her haughty chin. "About the dog, Father."

"Aye, I haven't forgotten the dog."

Antonio gazed imploringly up at the stocky priest.

"He can stay with ye, lad, if he behaves himself. Sister Prunella will show ye where ye can keep him in the back yard."

Sky's sigh of relief was audible. "Thank you, Father."

Antonio chimed in. *"Grácias. Grácias, Padre."*

After tying Chico to a tree behind the church, Antonio returned to the front entrance. A solemn-faced Sister Prunella commanded, "Follow me." She led him and Sky down a long hallway to the nuns' quarters at the rear of the church.

Off a darkened room furnished sparsely with two cots, an oblong plywood table, and two chairs, she opened the door to a small, windowless chamber. "We'll make a bed for the boy here," she said in a flat voice. "He can take his meals in the rear courtyard."

"This will be fine, Sister. Thank you." Sky avoided Antonio's eyes as she couldn't help thinking the room was hardly bigger than his current broom closet. But Granny Saunders had always told her beggars couldn't be choosers. She drew out a parcel from her handbag.

"I brought his things," she said, her voice catching in her

throat. "An extra shirt, a pair of socks, some soap, and a comb." It seemed such a small parcel; the boy's possessions should have amounted to more than this. At least a photograph of his mother. Tears welled in her eyes and she quickly handed the parcel to Antonio. "Now, obey the sisters, Antonio. They will take good care of you."

Giving him a light hug, she smiled reassuringly down into his dusky, anxious face and forced herself to make her exit. Without further comment, Sister Prunella, tall and purposeful, marched into the outer room ahead of her.

"Señorita Sky."

She looked back over her shoulder. "Yes?"

"Will you come visit me?"

"Of course, Antonio . . . Next week."

He stood in the middle of the small chamber holding his parcel close to his chest, holding his tears at bay, his black eyes fixed on her. The tears, Sky knew, would come later, in the shadows of the night when he lay upon his strange new bed.

It was all she could do to turn away and continue up the hall to the front door.

Outside on the street, she hurried her pace, filling her lungs with the gusty September air. She had done her duty, done the best she could for Antonio. Although the nun's demeanor held little warmth, Sky felt relief just knowing he would have living quarters away from his demeaning life at the gambling hall. Food and shelter. An opportunity for some education.

Yes, she reassured herself, she'd done the best she could for Antonio.

By the end of the week, Sky could wait no longer. She missed Antonio, his sometimes shy, sometimes defiant little face. Chico. It was strange, but she even missed Antonio's lop-eared, clumsy mutt. She decided to make a surprise visit to the boy so when she saw Cody again, which she hoped would be soon, she'd be able to tell him everything was going well for Antonio in his new residence with the sisters.

Friday afternoon, she set out for the Ascension Church, a hamper of freshly baked sugar cookies on her arm. A light rain spattered the boardwalk as she reached the block before the church, scenting the air with the ever-present dust from the street. She tugged her hat brim over her forehead and quickened her pace.

No one answered her repeated knocks at the front door, and rather than wait in the now-steady rain, Sky moved quickly to the rear of the church. She opened an unlocked iron gate, saw a walkway leading to the courtyard, and entered. Plaintive Spanish words reached her ears. She recognized Antonio's childish voice. Was he crying? Hurrying, she rounded a vine-covered stucco wall.

Several yards away, crouching down on his knees in the now pelting rain, the boy scrubbed large flagstones with a brush twice the size of his hand. Next to him sat a wooden tub filled with gray water.

The sight before her was so unexpected, she halted abruptly. "Antonio?"

His tousled head lifted and he stared at her for a moment. Locks of dark wet hair clung to his face and moisture from his nose trickled down into the corner of his mouth. His red-rimmed eyes blinked. "Señorita Sky?"

Setting the hamper over near the wall, she rushed to him. "Why are you out here working in the rain?"

He slipped into a seated position and rubbed his knees. "It is my punishment." His voice held shame. "I can't say the English words."

With her handkerchief, Sky patted rain from his face, embers of anger glowing in her belly. "How long have you been out

177

here scrubbing?"

Antonio shrugged. "Since this morning. Sister Prunella says I have to finish all the stones before I can go in."

His words felt like icy daggers piercing her chest. Burtram had *never* made the boy work this hard.

Antonio swiped his runny nose on his shirtsleeve. "I hate it here, *señorita*. Sister sent Chico away. He . . ."

"Here, here! What is this?" Sky turned to see the tall, black-enshrouded Sister Prunella making long-legged strides toward them. "Miss Saunders, this is highly irregular." She sneered down her long nose at Sky. "We would expect you to at least inquire when you may visit the boy." Her mouth pulled into a sour pucker.

"Having a child do a man's work in this cold rain is highly irregular," Sky responded, her spine stiffening. "And I knocked at the front door, but no one answered."

Sister Prunella sniffed. "Get back to your work, young man," she called with disdain. Antonio grudgingly stuck the brush into the dirty water and resumed his arduous task.

"Sister, I don't understand why you have Antonio working so long in these conditions."

The nun's close-set eyes bore into hers. "Come out of the rain, Miss Saunders, and I will explain it to you."

She stepped under a nearby sheltered walkway. Sky remained beside Antonio. "First of all, the boy doesn't show proper respect. He is belligerent. He doesn't know his alphabet beyond the letter M."

Sky recoiled at the nun's accusing tone. "He's only been here a week. That's hardly enough time . . ."

"He must work to find redemption," Sister continued, her beady eyes shining with holiness, "and say his rosary beads. Why, he doesn't even know the Hail Mary!"

"He's a bright child," Sky defended. "He shouldn't have to

learn on his knees."

The nun scoffed. "The boy won't try to learn or mind."

Ignoring her, Sky looked about the courtyard. "Where is Chico?"

"That dreadful dog killed two of our chickens!" Sister Prunella's voice rose to a thin bleat. "He chased them to death. We ran the mongrel off."

Sky felt a churning in the pit of her stomach. "Where is he now?"

The sister's dark brows leaped up like hawk's wings. "I have no idea. He barked out in the alley most of last night. Sister Mary and I didn't get a wink of sleep."

Her head throbbing, Sky glanced over at Antonio bent over the courtyard stones, his arm barely moving the scrub brush. She opened her mouth to demand that he come in from the rain and rest, when he sat back on his haunches.

His black hair plastered to his haggard face, he said, "Sister, I have to go pee."

The nun's pencil-slim fingers flew to her flat breast. "Well, you see how dreadful his language is. Then, what can one expect from a child living in brothels all of his life?"

A vise tightened around Sky's forehead. "I don't think your judgment is necessary," she bit out.

"I have to pee now!" Antonio demanded.

Sister Prunella waved him away impatiently. "Oh, go then. But get back here immediately and finish your work or no dinner."

Bursting with pity, Sky watched Antonio push himself up like a wounded animal and move stiffly away. She would not allow him to suffer further insult. Conviction steadied her voice. "Sister Prunella, Antonio is not an indentured servant. And I did not agree to have him treated as such."

The towering nun stared at her in disbelief.

"I'll get his things and we'll leave."

"This is very irregular," the sister muttered, but turned and walked like a ramrod to the other side of the courtyard. "You'll find his belongings in his bedchamber." She pointed through the nun's quarters to the tiny room Sky remembered from her earlier visit.

"Thank you. I'll find them." She went inside while Sister Prunella stood at the doorway to the courtyard, standing straight and purposeful, keeping watch.

Entering the stale, dark chamber, she found Antonio's parcel beside a makeshift bed of what appeared to be wood shavings in the corner. Wood shavings covered by a single thin sheet. A lump gathered in Sky's throat as she picked up the parcel and checked to see all of his possessions were there. Yes, just as when he'd arrived.

Leaving the dank chamber, she was struck by intense guilt. Why had she ever brought him here? It had been a disheartening mistake.

As she met Antonio in the rear yard, she embraced him. "You don't have to stay here anymore. We're going back to Mr. Burtram's."

Antonio's red-rimmed eyes lit up like stars. *"Grácias, señorita!"*

A barking dog chorused Antonio's response. Frantic scratching sounds punctuated canine whining at the courtyard gate.

"That's Chico!" Before Sky could stop Antonio, he ran stiff-legged to the back gate and let the dog inside.

Brittle Sister Prunella lurched forward to object, her fingers splayed like steel prongs. "No, no! Don't let that filthy animal in here."

An enthusiastic Chico, his coat matted from the rain, bounded into the stone yard, his large muddy paws leaving telltale prints on the scrubbed stones. Seeing the tall sister, her hands raised in front of her chest, he loped over to her and pounced forcefully on her immaculate black habit.

"*Ohhhh!*" The gangly nun tipped backward, tripping over her cumbersome skirts, and landed unceremoniously in the large tub, splashing dirty water everywhere. There she stuck like a giant black cork, her stocking-encased stick legs flailing, unable to do more than squeal in protest.

Sky covered her mouth, stifling laughter. She could only imagine what the cold, scummy water must feel like seeping through layers of holy skirts and invading those saintly drawers.

Gathering her proper concern, Sky rushed toward the floundering nun. "Sister, let me help you." She yanked the drenched woman up by her sharp elbows, releasing her from the grimy tub.

"Go! Just go!" came Sister Prunella's commanding cry.

Antonio, grabbing the disheveled Chico, sent Sky a victorious glance and herded the dog up the inside hallway.

"Oh, dear. Oh, dear." Plump Sister Mary Angeline, holding a large towel, swished past Antonio and scuttled out to her upright blustering sister.

"Where have you been?" Prunella asked harshly.

Avoiding Sister's mean gaze, Mary Angeline wrapped the towel around the dampened nun. "I was cleaning Father's room when I heard all this commotion."

Wanting only to make a quick exit, Sky hurried after Antonio. Now was not the time to thank the sisters for all their caring efforts toward him. She would leave the hamper of soggy cookies. And maybe she'd send them a few chickens at Thanksgiving.

In the front hall, just as Antonio was attempting to open the large arched door, she bumped into Father Patrick, knocking his spectacles slightly askew. "We're making an early departure," Sky blurted, nearly out of breath.

The priest frowned, adjusting his spectacles. "You're leavin'

. . . with the boy?"

"Father, this just isn't what I'd hoped for Antonio."

"Did Sister Prunella tell ye about the chickens? We can't have the dog runnin' amuck, you know."

"Yes, I know. And Antonio needs a closer relationship with his . . . guardians." She ruffled Antonio's wet hair and faced the priest with renewed determination. "Somehow, I'll find a loving home for him."

CHAPTER SEVENTEEN

The rain had subsided but somber clouds still hovered overhead as Sky, Antonio, and Chico left the Church of the Ascension. Holding up her sodden skirts, Sky picked her way across the muddy street, her thoughts in turmoil. Almost a week had passed since she'd left her young charge at the church, believing he had a real chance at finding a home. Now she was right back to her starting place. Alone, and with no idea what to do next.

Antonio romped ahead with Chico, his clothes still clinging to his slight frame, his hair a mass of slick dark waves. The humiliation he'd suffered from Sister Prunella seemed all but a scrap of memory in his young mind. Where he would sleep tonight, or tomorrow night, was not a concern. Señorita Sky was here now; she'd take care of everything.

Sky sighed miserably. How would she explain Antonio's sudden return to Jack Burtram? Could she continue to smuggle Antonio into her room at night without his knowledge? If Burtram found out, would he send the boy back to the musty broom closet?

Now that she felt responsible for Antonio, her goal of personal independence would have to be set aside.

Material gain seemed as far from her reach as it had ever been. She hadn't seen Dan Gunther in several weeks and only knew he was somewhere up on Stray Horse Gulch. If he'd struck rich ore in his mine or gone belly up, she would probably be the last to know. A cloud of hopelessness drifted over her.

She couldn't even go to Cody. He'd warned her not to get involved with either Whistlin' Dan or Antonio. Enough of her Saunders's pride still existed to keep her from asking for his sympathy or assistance.

"I'm hungry, *señorita*. I didn't eat nothing since this morning." Antonio interrupted her brooding reverie, his jet eyes plaintive.

Remembering the sugar cookies she'd left with the nuns, Sky looked down at him with regret. But she forced a smile. "I'm hungry, too. Let's get something at Harding's General Store." He grinned and ambled ahead.

Since the post office was located at the rear of the store, and she hadn't checked her mail in several days, she decided to wait in line at the general delivery window.

"While I'm waiting, you go pick out your favorite kind of jam, Antonio." He scampered over to a side wall.

She was disappointed when again no letter postmarked Placerton, Ohio, awaited her. When would her divorce papers finally arrive? Mr. Backston, her attorney, appeared to be in no hurry to pass along anything newsworthy. The thought of Thomas buying off the man, learning her new address, and harassing her left her slightly nauseated.

A desire to race back to her room, get herself and Antonio into dry clothes, fix a cup of mint tea and fire off a letter to her attorney propelled her through the store.

She rounded up Antonio and brought her purchases to the front counter. Mrs. Harding, a stooped-shouldered woman of middle-age, rang up her bill while finishing a conversation with another customer.

"You hear of anybody wantin' to rent that cabin, Silas, let me know. I don't want it standin' empty come winter."

"Yes, ma'am." The man hoisted his bundle of merchandise and left, the front door banging after him.

Her attention diverted from the letter, Sky snagged a handful of coins from her purse. "You have a cabin for rent?" she inquired of the woman.

"Sure do, miss. My no-account brother-in-law was rentin' it, and he run out of money diggin' in one of those mines. He up and moved back to Kansas." Mrs. Harding swept a lock of gray hair back into her untidy bun. "My husband and I don't have time to fool with it."

"Where is the cabin located?"

"Just west of town. You know someone who might be interested?"

"How much are you asking?"

"Not much. Twenty-five dollars a month."

Sky raised her brows. "Twenty-five?"

"It's a sturdy little place. Got its own well."

Sky did some quick figuring. The boarding house would have cost more just for herself. She made about a hundred dollars a month at Burtram's. Renting a place of her own would remove her from the chaos and danger of the gambling hall, although it could present dangers of its own.

Paying rent would also wipe out much of the grubstake she could put into the Lucky Lady mine. But a cabin would be more of a home for Antonio than he'd ever known. And available property went fast in this growing town.

Summoning her courage, Sky leaped on the opportunity. "I'd like to take a look at that cabin, Mrs. Harding. As soon as possible."

Toward dusk, Cody and Ned rode up Stray Horse Gulch to pay another call on Abe Fitch. The first visit had proved futile, but Cody sensed the miner knew something and was holding it back. Hell, it seemed everyone he talked to lately was either deaf, dumb, or blind. He itched to get just one piece of information he could tie into the rash of recent claim jumping.

He hadn't signed on as Leadville's marshal to sit back and let men get their mines stolen out from under them.

They passed the grove of evergreens where he and Sky had stopped that afternoon not long ago. Flashes of memory danced before his eyes. Sky falling into the icy creek. The surprised look on her face as he scooped her up and carried her to the bank. Teasing her black stocking down over her bare calf. Sunlight streaking her auburn hair as she lay beneath him. Her sweet lips parting when he touched her . . .

His body hardened uncomfortably. Damn! He had business to take care of; he didn't need thoughts of her distracting him.

As if in agreement, a lone blackbird cawed high in a pine overhead. A tree limb cracked somewhere in the distance.

His buckskin snorted and shook its thick black mane, and a chill skittered down Cody's spine. He'd been ambushed not far from here. With a shrug, he shook off the disquieting memory.

Riding next to him on his smaller pinto, Ned remarked, "Think Fitch will be in a better mood for talkin'?"

"He's had almost two weeks to chew on what he knows."

Ned looked doubtful. "Yeah, but I'll bet he's scared to tell us anything. Scared those devils will come back and get even."

Cody scoffed. "How can we protect him, or any of these miners, if we don't know who their enemies are?"

A sudden gust of wind brought with it the smell of wood smoke. Lifting his gaze above the tree line around the curve, Cody saw an ominous swirl of smoke.

He shot a glance back at Ned, who was staring in the same direction.

"Smells like trouble." Cody dug in his heels, urging the buckskin ahead. "Could be Abe's place."

With Ned's pinto following close behind, they galloped up the rutted road and off through a scattering of ragged pines.

His hunch was right. Through the clearing, he spotted Abe Fitch's shack, orange flames licking the lower edge of its only window.

Entering the mine yard, he abruptly drew in his horse. Up the hill, behind some tall firs, he thought he saw a flicker of movement. "Abe!" he hollered. "Abe, you out there?"

Ned jerked his pinto to a halt nearby and dismounted.

Cody leaped to the ground and raced to the shack's open door. "Abe might be in there."

"That shack could go up fast!" Ned called, his voice rising an octave. "Don't risk it, Marshal!"

Ned's warning faded as Cody yanked his bandana from his neck up over his nose. He peered into the smoky shack. In the middle of the room, he made out an overturned lantern and Abe Fitch lying next to it. "I see him."

"Cody, wait!"

His nostrils filling with suffocating fumes, Cody crawled belly-flat across the rough plywood floor. Smoldering planks burned his palms, seared his fingertips. A silent scream of pain darted from his hands up his forearms.

Got to get to him fast! There. There's his foot.

Inching forward, his throat sandpaper-raw, his eyes burning, he reached out and clamped onto Abe Fitch's booted ankle. Then he caught hold of the man's other boot and pulled hard.

Faster than a singed jackrabbit, Cody hauled Fitch to the open door. Ned, his lower face also wrapped in a neckerchief, grabbed onto the miner's limp body and they dragged him out into the yard. Abe's arm was badly burned, but the rest of him seemed intact.

Seconds later, billows of black smoke engulfed the small shack, turning it into a pile of crackling tinder.

Bathed in his own grimy sweat, Cody ripped off his bandana. Gagging and coughing, he gulped deep breaths of mountain air, then bent over Fitch, desperately searching below his jaw for a pulse.

Ned squatted down next to him. "Is he dead?"

"His hair's all matted . . ." When he found no pulse, Cody turned the man's head, examining further. His fingers came away blood-smeared. "Damn!" He sat back on his haunches. "They shot him. I felt the bullet hole in the back of his head."

His deputy grimaced. "Those dirty bastards. Abe never hurt nobody."

In the purple twilight, Cody scanned the surrounding hillside. "They beat us to him, the yellow dogs. Set his place on fire to cover up the murder."

"Who do you think's behind all this?"

Cody wiped the sweat from his forehead. "I got a gut feeling it's somebody we know. Lower than skunk shit and right under our noses."

"Poor Abe. He never had a chance."

Cody felt the muscles tense in his jaw. "We'll get them," he ground out.

Coughing again from the smoke fumes permeating his clothes, he lifted the dead man's shoulders. "C'mon. Let's take him back to town for a proper burial."

Ned picked up Fitch by his boots and they started over the sloped yard to Cody's buckskin. "Hey, is that Abe's hat? There, by your foot?"

"Don't know. Wait a minute."

They set the body down and Cody scooped up a slouch hat. In the firelight, he could just make out the shape of the black hat, feel its greasy inner band.

Holding it up to his nose, he sniffed. "It reeks of cheap hair oil. I never saw Abe wear a hat like this." He scowled into the darkness. "It's got to belong to somebody else."

★ ★ ★ ★ ★

Sky finished rinsing the lunch dishes in the tin washbasin and picked out a clean towel from one of her trunks. She began drying the blue crockery plates as she surveyed the one-story log cabin that she, Antonio, and Chico had moved into the day before. Thanks be to the new landlords, the Hardings, who'd helped them move their meager possessions.

Admittedly the cabin was rustic, and except for the gambling hall, not to be compared with any of her former residences. The walls were papered with various newspapers, she guessed to keep the wind from seeping through the cracks. On closer inspection, she found the former tenant had a wide reading interest: *Harper's Weekly, Frank Leslie's Illustrated, The Cincinnati Gazette,* and *The Rocky Mountain News.*

The focal point of the twelve-by-fourteen-foot room was a small stone fireplace where she would cook in a large Dutch oven, one among many new challenges. The fireplace would provide their heat until she could find an inexpensive pot-bellied stove. Mrs. Harding had loaned her a circular rag rug in varying shades of blue. It added a feminine touch to the room, furnished only with two spindly chairs and a few upended wood crates she'd use for temporary tables. Her bed consisted of a straw mattress on a rope-tied wood frame in a corner. She'd found it only a smidgeon more comfortable than her cot at Burtram's. It would do for now.

There was still much work to be done before Leadville's long winter approached. Curtains needed to be hung over the two cabin windows and the larder stocked with food supplies.

When the cabin was presentable, she'd invite Cody over for dinner. Just thinking about him caused her pulse to beat faster. She missed him, more than she wanted to admit: his twinkling hazel eyes, his cocky grin, his large-boned hands. Hands that had touched her and left her breathless. A sultry glow rose from deep inside her. Embarrassed at the sudden revelation of her own vulnerability, Sky tamped down her emotions and shooed them away.

Even if she was now a free spirit, she should keep her wits about her.

Glancing out the window she'd cleaned this morning, she saw Antonio and Chico playing tag in the side yard and her heart gladdened. She knew she'd made the right decision. Antonio had actually welcomed his humble new sleeping quarters in the attached storage shed behind the fireplace, which ran the length of the cabin.

If he could have Chico near him, he was satisfied.

A mass of clouds rolling in over California Gulch promised afternoon showers. But her attention to the graying sky switched to a lone rider on a buckskin kicking up its own cloud of trail dust. Her heart caught in her throat as the tall man in the saddle guided his horse off the road and up into her front yard. She recognized the white Stetson and unmistakable broad shoulders. *Cody.*

Slipping out of her dusty apron, Sky pinched her cheeks and hurried to open the door. Her joyful anticipation diminished as she stepped onto the front stoop.

She sensed his mood in the way he dismounted, his long leg abruptly swinging over the saddle, his brisk stride to within inches of her. She saw the anger in his eyes, barely concealed, as his gaze swept over her.

"Burtram told me you moved out here with the kid. Why?"

She stiffened, abashed at the blunt question flung at her like a bucket of ice water.

"Is this a social call, Marshal?" she asked, returning his question with a cool stare. "Or did you come here to arrest me for something?"

He stared back with obvious concern. "I want to talk to you."

"Oh, well then." She stepped back inside the cabin, holding the door open. "Please, come in."

The top of the doorframe was so short, he had to bend forward, removing his hat as he shouldered his way inside. His height and breadth dwarfed the room, and the space between them. He made no effort to take off his yellow rain slicker.

"Welcome to my—our home," she said, suddenly breathless standing so close to him.

His gaze took in the papered walls, then focused on her. "Why'd you move in such a dang hurry?"

Cody's reproachful tone made her feel obliged to explain. "Burtram's isn't the most preferable residence for a single woman, or a boy." She moved over to the washstand and folded the dishtowel. "You said so yourself."

"This place is a mile from town. How're you going to get to work every day?"

She frowned, becoming annoyed at his probing. "I'm sure Ned has an extra horse he'll loan me. I can walk, if I have to."

"That'll be some walk, when it snows three feet."

The door opened and Antonio burst inside, his cheeks flushed from chasing Chico. He looked up at Cody with youthful admiration.

"The marshal and I are talking, Antonio," Sky explained. "If you want to play outside for a while longer, you'd better put on your jacket."

The boy looked curiously from her to Cody, then grabbed a wool jacket from a wall peg near the door. He took his time shrugging into it.

"I can teach Antonio right here, so he will be ready when the new school opens in the spring."

"Why couldn't the nuns keep him at the rectory and teach him there?"

Sky saw Antonio's features crumple at Cody's tactless question. His black eyes glinted defiantly as he turned and banged out the door.

She bristled at the intrusion on her private domain. "Is this why you're paying me a call, Cody? To question my caring for Antonio?" Her hands curled into fists at her sides. "It just so happened, the saintly sisters felt it their duty to punish and humiliate Antonio because he couldn't recite the entire alphabet."

Cody clamped his jaw, vexed at the direction the conversation had taken. He hadn't intended to rile Sky, but to alert her to the dangers of her impulsive actions. But there she stood, ready to blow her top at him, her rich auburn hair wispy around her cameo face, her blue eyes shimmering. His gaze traced the creamy length of her throat down to the fullness of her high breasts and small waist, small enough for his hands to encircle. How he wished he could crush her to him this second, feel her inviting breasts warm against his chest.

"I'm not questioning your good intentions toward the boy," he said, quelling his sensual attraction. "I just came from Abe Fitch's funeral this morning. He was shot dead and his place burned to the ground last night."

Her forehead converged in a frown. "I don't see what that has to do with me."

Exasperated, he sighed. "This gang of claim jumpers is ruthless and unpredictable. It isn't safe for a young woman to live out here alone."

Sky waved him away and stepped over to a window, gazing out at the sleet tapping on the windowpane. "I can't worry about a bunch of outlaws up in the hills."

He closed the space between them, his towering frame so near she felt his body heat radiating toward her. "Do you have a gun here?"

"Well, no . . ."

"That's what I thought," he said, his voice tinged with sarcasm.

She whirled and glared up at him. "I'll get a gun, if I think I need one."

He gave a short cynical laugh. "What good is a gun if you don't know how to shoot it?" Without waiting for her answer, he ordered, "Move back to town!"

She huffed indignantly and crossed her arms in front of her.

His face coloring a deep red, he half-turned toward the door. "I can't promise I can protect you out here."

Her temper flared at his assumption. "I don't recall ever asking you to."

He grabbed the door handle. "Have it your way, then." He shook his head. "I can't remember a woman any more mule-headed than you."

"Oh, I bet you've known a lot of them!"

He slammed out the door and mounted his horse before she could catch her breath, her heart hammering mightily in her chest.

A part of her wanted to run outside and tell him never to come onto her property again. She could manage her life just as well without him. Instead, she raced out to the front stoop, hoping he would look back and at least wave. But Cody sat straight in the saddle, heading onto the road back to town.

Sleet spattered the ground, the chill air surrounding her. She glanced around the yard. "Antonio! Chico!" She stepped to the side of the cabin. He and Chico were nowhere to be seen. She recalled Antonio's dark expression at Cody's remark about him staying with the nuns when he'd rushed out the door.

Had Antonio run away?

Fetching her wool shawl from inside the cabin, Sky threw it over her shoulders and started up the town road. "Antonio!" she hollered, peering into the scattered trees and hearing no response. It wasn't like him or Chico not to come when she called. Fear chased at her heels as she picked up her pace.

Ahead, she could still see Cody's yellow slicker. Even if he was the last one she wanted to turn to right now, she needed Cody's help. If she ran fast enough, maybe she could catch up with him.

With the sky roiling above her, the wet wind in her face, Sky hiked up her skirts and sprinted down the road.

CHAPTER EIGHTEEN

Making her way along the deep ruts in the road, the sleet stinging her cheeks and hands, Sky continued calling for Antonio. An eerie silence was her only answer. The usually busy thoroughfare into town was strangely untraveled, as if the oncoming storm had chased wayfarers inside to their warm hearths.

She dashed ahead, trying to catch up with Cody. Her chest heaved with exertion, her breath chafing her lungs.

"Cody!" she called, straining her voice to reach his ears.

Faster! she willed her legs. Her pumping thigh muscles burned in response.

"Cody, stop!"

Through the blur of ice-arrows, she saw him slowly turn his horse and angle his head back toward her. Raising her arm, she waved frantically. Her shawl slipped from around one shoulder and trailed out behind her as she raced ahead.

"Wait, please!"

To her relief, Cody's buckskin cantered toward her, eating up the space between them, its nostrils flaring.

Sky shivered beneath her sodden dress as she met horse and rider in the middle of the road. "I can't find Antonio," she rasped, her throat raw, her heart hammering. "He's run off."

A frown creased Cody's brow beneath his dripping hat brim. For a moment, she panicked, feeling like a fool, fearing he wouldn't care enough to help her.

But he quickly removed his boot from the stirrup and leaned over, extending a hand. "I'll help you up."

With a sense of urgency, she put her right foot in the stirrup.

Lifting her into the saddle, he asked, "Why would Antonio run away?"

"I'm not sure, but I don't like the looks of this storm. We've got to find him!"

"We will."

Cody's reassuring voice close to her ear eased the tightness in her breast, if only for a moment. Then he opened his rain slicker and wrapped it around her. She rested back against his muscular chest absorbing his body heat, welcoming it.

He urged the buckskin forward and it bolted down the road. Cody's embrace surrounded her like a protective shield, yet a layer of apprehension would still cling to her until they found Antonio and Chico.

Halfway back to the cabin, he asked, "Has Antonio been this far out of town before?"

"No," she answered, fear chilling her like the oncoming storm. "He only knows the streets around the saloon." She grasped the saddle horn as the horse carried them headlong into the gray, pummeling sleet.

Behind Sky, Cody tipped his hat against the wind, a myriad of emotions swamping his mind. What had he gotten himself into? Just a short time ago, she'd shown him the door when he tried to give her genuine advice. Now she desperately sought his aid. He was headed on a wild chase, looking for that half-breed kid when he should be riding back to town to help Ned and Jim search for Abe Fitch's killer.

The steady rhythm of Sky's hip and thigh as she rode sidesaddle moved against him seductively, making his body hard and muddling his mind beyond coherent thought.

Yet, he reminded himself, no matter his strong physical attraction to Sky, he owed her. She'd saved his life when she could have walked away and let him bleed to death from his bullet wound. His job, his sworn duty, was to serve and protect.

Her head swiveled as she scanned the area on either side of the road. "I don't see any sign of them," she said, her tone bleak.

"They're probably not far away." Cody's thoughts were not as positive as his words. He squinted into the curtain of fog, cursing the oncoming storm.

At the cabin, he reined in his horse. "I'm gonna leave you here and I'll keep looking." He slid one hand up her arm, ready to help her down.

"Oh, no you won't." She twisted around in the saddle, her eyes shooting blue blazes from under long, frosted eyelashes. "I want to go—"

"Sky, I know every nook and cranny from here to California Gulch. You're soaking wet and you need to get inside."

"But, I . . ."

He clasped her upper arm, a silky-wet lock of auburn hair falling in a curl around his fingers. Its lavender fragrance caressed his senses. Clearing his throat, he said, "Besides, Antonio will need to take your seat when I find him."

She exhaled deeply, grudgingly. "I guess you're right."

He assisted her to the ground. "You got enough wood to make a good-sized fire?"

She nodded and wiped away a tendril of hair slicked against her cheek. Her eyes, shadowed with concern, gazed up at him, causing a strange tightening in his chest.

"Get that fire goin' and we'll be back in no time." He offered her a quick smile, then dug his heels into the buckskin and tore off toward the gulch.

Sleet turned to snow. Large, sticking flakes. They blinded his vision so that he could see only about ten feet in any direction.

He knew the potential of an autumn mountain storm. It could come on almost without warning at dusk and build to snowdrifts of half a dozen feet before daybreak. And, from the looks of it, this one could be trouble.

He had to find Antonio soon, before he got lost in this rugged terrain. He shook off snow clinging to his hat brim and peered out into the blurry white.

Where are you, kid?

Looking down at the road, he cursed under his breath. If the boy and his dog had come this way, their tracks were now covered.

"Antonio!" he shouted. *"Antonio!"*

The only response was the sound of his horse's hooves thudding over the snowy trail and the wind whistling through scattered pine.

Gotta find you, kid.

Through the veil of snow, he envisioned Sky's deep blue gaze when he'd left her standing at her front door. Imploring. Trusting. A spark of heat, like an ember, burned in his chest. He couldn't fail her. He had to find the kid, and find him soon. His deputies would have to hold the fort until he got back.

Up ahead, he spotted a wad of coarse dark hair snagged on a low scrub oak and knew they must have headed this way. He thought of places that might attract a young explorer. A hunch grabbed him. Abandoned mines. He knew of one near the gulch.

Tugging the collar of his rain slicker up higher around his neck, he leaned against the wind. "C'mon, fella," he encouraged the buckskin. "We're almost there."

Minutes later, Cody approached the ramshackle buildings on Ole Gunderson's abandoned claim. Ole had headed down to South Park last spring after injuring his back loading ore.

He squinted through falling drifts, his jaw tensed, hoping to God the kid hadn't met up with an accident.

"Antonio!" he hollered, urging his horse up toward Gunderson's log shack.

A sharp, resounding bark made him glance to the left. A multi-colored dog with one brown and one pale blue eye greeted him with frenzied barking. "It's all right, Chico," he said with a calm he didn't feel. "Where's your partner?"

The dog cocked one brow and came over to him, his tail wagging tentatively.

"Help me, Chico!" a plaintive voice cried out.

His horse's ears twitched and Cody jerked forward in the saddle. "Antonio? Where are you?"

"Down here."

Cody's gaze darted several yards towards the sound of the voice. The mineshaft! He slid to the ground and scrambled over snow-covered smelter slag to the uncovered opening.

About ten feet down into the dank black hole, he could barely see Antonio huddled inside an ore bucket. The bucket was attached by a rope to a pulley atop the shaft. As the bucket swung precariously, the kid's dark eyes glinted wide in fright. Cody sucked in a breath. Only luck was keeping the bucket from crashing to the bottom of the shaft under the kid's weight.

Don't scare him more than he already is.

"Hey, Antonio," he called, taking hold of the pulley handle. "It's Marshal Cassidy. What are you doin' down there? Miss Saunders is mighty worried about you."

"I slipped—and fell in."

That was obvious. "Are you hurt?"

"No, but I want to get out!"

"Well, kid, that's just what we're gonna do." Cody started cranking the rusted pulley. "Hold still, now."

Antonio gave no reply.

Snow blowing at his back, Cody turned the handle. Long unused, the pulley whined, making him fight for every inch. He

199

stared down the shaft into Antonio's small, ghostly, shadowed face. Even from here, he saw the boy's frame shake from the cold.

Overhead, the clotted sky darkened. Nightfall was not far away. He had to work faster.

Clamping his jaw against the wind, he gave the handle a mighty shove. His hold slipped. With unexpected force, the pulley handle flipped backward, glancing a blow to Cody's shoulder. He fell to one knee. The bucket knocked against the side of the shaft making a grating sound.

"Ahhh! Marshal!"

"I'm here, kid." Cody blew out an obstinate breath, shrugged off the minor pain, and pulled himself to his feet. "Hang on."

His hands had gone stiff inside his gloves, and he worked one at a time as he held the handle. With renewed effort, he began again. "Think of that hot supper Miss Sky is fixing for us," he called into the shaft. He focused on the supper and Miss Sky as he fought the rusted pulley until his arms ached.

Inch by inch, the bucket with Antonio inside creaked upward. Most kids his age would be blubbering for their mamas by now, but then, Antonio didn't have a ma. He only made occasional whimpering sounds. He was a brave kid; the streets of Leadville had made sure of that.

Finally, Cody saw the top of Antonio's head reach the opening of the shaft. "Grab onto me. Now." The boy raised his arms and Cody caught him around the chest and hoisted him from the dangling bucket.

"*Caramba!*" Antonio exclaimed and stumbled to his feet.

Cody brushed the snow off Antonio's hair and jacket, then clapped his own gloved hands together, attempting to get the blood flowing.

When he started to guide the boy over to the buckskin, Antonio pulled his jacket together, his mouth set in a tight line.

"You want to take me back to live with those bad sisters. I don't go back."

Cody stared at Antonio, realizing he must have overheard his comment to Sky about the nuns. After all he'd been through, the kid sure was stubborn. He had balls. "No, Antonio." He shook his head. "I want to take you back to Miss Saunders. She's waiting for us now."

Black eyelashes flickered. He thought the kid was about to cry. "Com'on, partner." Cody extended his hand. "I bet she's got a hot supper waitin' for us."

"You promise? I don't go back to the church?"

He smiled at Antonio through the oncoming snow, hoping he'd see he was sincere. "I promise. You're not going back there."

His small frame quivering in the cold, the kid stared at Chico, hovering nearby. Then he nodded slowly. "Okay. I want to live with Miss Sky!"

"I know she'll take care of you." Cody took Antonio's hand. "Now, let's go. I'm about to freeze my butt off out here."

Sky watched Cody and his horse disappear down the gulch road, savoring the memory of his brief reassuring smile, the warmth of his hard body surrounding her. She whispered a prayer that he'd find Antonio safe, and soon. Then, shivering, she bounded inside the cabin in search of dry clothes.

After changing into a soft, rose-colored wool dress and sweeping her hair back with a tortoise shell comb, she brought kindling from the attached woodshed in to the fireplace. In no time, a fire crackled on the hearth.

Glad to feel warmth in her fingers and toes again, she made a fresh pot of coffee and rolled out a batch of baking powder biscuits to go with the venison stew she'd started this morning. Cooking in a Dutch oven over an open fire was a challenge, even after using the rustic coal stove at Burtram's.

She glanced over at the side window, now shuttered for the winter, and wished she could see into the yard. Going to the door, she opened it and looked out at the falling snow. Through the sparse trees, the road was barely visible. Twin strips leading nowhere. Worry following her, she ducked back inside.

Fearful, unwanted thoughts began to chase through her mind. Cody, after searching the rocky gulch, heading back without finding Antonio. Cody going down a steep ravine, falling off his horse and breaking his leg. Antonio and Chico attacked by wild, ravenous cougars . . .

Dear Lord. Sky pressed her hand to her thumping heart and wandered restlessly around the room. She'd lost the first seed of life within her when she'd suffered her miscarriage. She could not lose Antonio.

Time dragged. All she could do was worry and wait. She lit the oil lamp and watched the stew burn. Angrily, she poured water into the pot and stirred the gummy concoction, then hung it higher above the fire. The biscuits, at first nicely raised and golden brown, shriveled. She set them in a covered basket, knowing they would be hard and cold by the time Cody and Antonio returned. She prayed it would be soon.

Miserable, she lay down on the narrow bed and drew the quilt over her.

What seemed like hours later, the sound of a muted bark roused her. Swinging her legs over the bedside, she pulled herself up and stumbled to the front door. Through the heavy snowfall, she made out the blur of a man wearing a yellow slicker, riding a dusky horse. A dog bounded alongside. Cody and Chico. But where was Antonio? Icy fear twisted around her heart. For a moment her thoughts raced, a crazy mixture of hope and dread.

Surely Cody wouldn't come back without the boy?

As the horse and rider neared, Cody waved and then another,

smaller hand also waved. She caught the black thatch of Antonio's hair and saw him safely tucked inside Cody's protective arms, just as he had protected her. Of course, she should have known. Emitting a cry of joy, she hopped up and down on the front stoop.

A surge of affection for Cody rose up within her along with a mass of goose bumps. She retreated inside just long enough to stir the over-cooked stew and snatch her damp shawl off a wall peg. A horse's nicker and Cody's whoop as they entered the yard almost knocked her off her feet.

Bursting with expectation, she once again emerged from the cabin and peered into the snowy night.

Larger than life, Cody reined in his horse a few feet away. His and Antonio's smiling, frosted faces greeted her. Their breath formed little puffs of steam in the chill air as Cody dismounted and eased his charge to the ground.

"You found them," she croaked happily, rushing to Antonio and embracing him. Chico loped up to her and rested his grimy paws on her apron. Ordinarily she would have scolded him, but tonight she didn't care; relief and gratitude at seeing them safe filled her.

"Antonio got stuck in a mineshaft near the gulch." Cody answered her question before it left her lips. "Chico and I helped pull him out."

"Oh, Antonio! You could have broken your leg—or your neck!" she admonished. "Come inside, right now. You both must be frozen stiff."

Cody winked, sending a jolt of heat down to her toes. "I'll be there soon as I unsaddle Buck and put him in your pole shed."

Once inside by the fire, Antonio rambled on about how he and Chico ran away because they didn't want to go back to live with the nuns.

"You must *never* run off like that again, Antonio," she scolded.

"You made me very worried."

"I want to stay with you, Miss Sky," he said, his gaze intense as she poured heated water into the washbasin.

She smiled and handed him a bar of soap and a towel. While he scrubbed his face and hands, she said reassuringly, "Yes, we made an agreement about that, didn't we? As long as you study your lessons and help me with the chores."

"Sounds like a bargain to me," Cody offered, entering the cabin. His cheeks flushed red from the cold, he closed the door, shutting out the frigid wind, and removed his dripping hat and rain slicker.

Aware of his presence filling the room, Sky gestured to a wall peg beside the door. "You can hang your things over there."

She saw that his shirt was soaked through beneath his leather vest. "You really should change into something dry, but I'm afraid I don't have any men's clothes." Grabbing a blanket from the top of a chest, she added, "At least this will take away the chill."

His mustache lifted in an easy grin. "Thanks." When he accepted the blanket, his long fingers brushed hers.

His touch caused a funny little twinge at the base of her stomach. "You can hang your shirt and vest on the chair while Antonio puts on his bedclothes." She went to the doorway to the shed where Antonio slept. "After he changes, we'll have supper."

Cody stood tall in the middle of the room, unbuttoning his wet shirt to his waist. His bicep muscles rippled as he shrugged out of the sleeves. Light from the fire played across his golden chest hair. "Whatever you're cookin' sure smells good."

Sky swallowed hard, the sight of his magnificent physique making her almost forget what she was cooking. "It's venison stew."

"I'm ready. Let's eat!" Antonio announced, having jumped

into his nightshirt while she lingered, cow-eyed on the threshold.

Man and boy wolfed down the over-cooked stew and hard biscuits as fast as she heaped their plates. Chico gulped every scrap Antonio gave him under the table and begged for more.

"Great stew," Cody mumbled.

"*Sí.*" Antonio licked his lips.

"Great biscuits."

"*Sí.*"

Sky looked from one grateful face to the other, satisfaction permeating a place inside her that had been empty before. "Thank you." She poured more coffee in Cody's mug and finished her own supper. The view of Cody's exposed chest despite the blanket made her avert her eyes, but didn't stop a warm glow from washing over her.

When collecting and stacking the dishes in the basin, she saw Antonio yawn expansively. "Time for bed, young man."

The boy willingly straggled toward his makeshift bedroom. Chico followed, his tail drooping. Sky went ahead, carrying the oil lamp, but Antonio stopped at the doorway, his wind-burned features openly curious. "Is the marshal going to sleep here tonight?"

Momentarily abashed at the mention of the obvious, Sky glanced at Cody. She could hardly ask him to go back into the worsening storm. He would have to stay the night. She forced a calm smile over the rush of heat flooding her face.

"Marshal Cassidy is welcome to stay, since we don't want him to go back into this bad storm. He can sleep by the fire."

"*Sí. Buenas noches.*" Antonio's sleepy gaze lingered on Cody's face, then he went off to bed.

By the time Sky pulled the heavy bed covers up to Antonio's chin, he was slipping away into a faraway slumber. Chico curled up beneath the foot of the narrow bed and, after watching her move to the door, his eyelids closed.

Drawing a long curtain across the doorway, she said quietly, "They're both near dead to the world."

His blanket left behind on the chair, Cody tossed more logs on the fire, the glow from the hearth emphasizing the muscular planes of his broad chest. She could only stare at him, dimly recalling that she'd never seen Thomas stripped to his waist.

Cody looked over at her, a slow smile lighting his eyes. "After the ground they covered today, they'll probably sleep till Sunday."

"No doubt they will. Thank you for rescuing him," she said with sincere gratitude. "Antonio admires you a great deal."

A wistful expression stole across his face. "I was glad to do it. He's a good kid. Determined, like you."

"Yes," she whispered, hesitating, wondering what she should do with her hands and whether she should sit or stand. What was the matter with her? Why was the room suddenly too small for the two of them?

Steady, driving snow tapped against the cabin walls. With renewed purpose, she finished cleaning up the dinner dishes. "Doesn't seem like it'll stop anytime soon." Her voice sounded odd, like it belonged to someone else.

He moved behind her, his face just above her shoulder. The heat from his body permeated the length of her. Quivering inside, she braced herself.

"Hmm." His breath tickled the back of her neck. "Lucky we've got enough firewood to last the night," he murmured.

She wished Cody wouldn't stand so close. His naked chest nearly brushing her back was disturbing. Even if she'd nursed him and seen just about all of him—this was different.

He put his hand on her arm and her skin responded beneath her sleeve as if it were a hot coal. She closed her eyes, a dizzying current racing through her limbs.

"That was a wonderful supper, Sky. You know, I thought

about you waiting here, all the way back."

His lips were very near her ear.

"You're welcome," she said in a voice tinged with emotion. "I'm so glad you both came back safely."

"Come over by the fire. It's warmer there."

She didn't need to be warmer. Moisture dampened her upper lip and she would have liked to unbutton her dress.

Cody draped his long frame over the seat of the chair, resting his muscular forearms on the back. "Guess these wood crates aren't too comfortable. Maybe you'd rather sit on the bed." Did his hazel eyes twinkle with a certain mischief?

No, she didn't want to sit on the bed. Or the flimsy wood crates. But where else was there? The floor?

Cody sensed her unease, aware of the sensual sparks passing between them. He was having trouble keeping his gaze from wandering over the rise and fall of her inviting breasts beneath her well-fitting bodice. His mind kept going back to the day they waded in the creek up on Stray Horse Gulch. The day he'd teased her, and touched her. His body felt like a hot poker as he thought about it.

He couldn't just sit there. So, he stood abruptly. "Here, you take the chair. I'll sit on the bed."

She broke into a little grin. "This is ridiculous." She plopped down on the edge of her bed next to the wall.

Lowering himself back into the chair, he inclined his head toward her. "Did I ever tell you what a fine job you did nursing me?"

Color flooded her high cheekbones. "You were a perfect patient, most of the time."

"I owe you so much, Sky."

The way he spoke the words, the glimmer of emotion in his eyes, started that same commotion at the base of her stomach. Sky wished he would stop looking at her so intensely, drawing her in like a magnet. Yet a part of her thrilled to the tingly sensations he aroused.

"You don't owe me anything. I just didn't want to see Leadville lose its marshal," she said too quickly. She stared past him at the fire, unable to meet his steady gaze.

"I doubt if any of the gals at Sallie Purple's would have done as much."

"Sallie Purple's? That house of prostitution?" She stiffened with moral indignation. How could he admit even knowing women who lived there?

Swiftly, Cody rose from the chair like a golden giant and came to her. "Sky, I didn't mean I'd let one of them . . ." His fingers caressed her cheek, his touch nearly unbearable in its tenderness.

She released a ragged sigh.

His hands slipped up her arms, bringing her closer. "You're the only woman I'd want by my bedside," he whispered into her hair. "Or in my bed."

Stunned, she lifted her chin to study his face, the strong features she'd come to admire, dare she admit: to love?

His eyes shone with green-gold lights of desire as he pulled her to him, her breasts flush against his chest. Like the touch of a lighted candle, his body heat shimmered through her.

She could not tear her eyes away from his ardent gaze. Could not keep her knees from wobbling beneath her gown.

Warm and gentle, his lips brushed hers. So tempting. So giving.

At every crack and crevice, the night wind continued its persistent howl.

She couldn't make the wind go away any more than she could stop herself from rising on tiptoe to return Cody's kiss. Feel the pressure of his growing desire.

In the recesses of her mind, she knew where this was leading.

Before the night was over, she would make love with Cody. She was powerless to stop it. Didn't want to stop it. In her heart, she was no longer a married woman, tethered to a man who'd shown her neither respect nor passion.

She clung to Cody with fierce anticipation.

Chapter Nineteen

The kiss lingered. At first gentle, sweet, like their first kiss that summer night overlooking the gulch. Sky sensed a momentary shyness about Cody—the way he held her—almost as if she were made of delicate porcelain china.

But when their bodies blended together, his lips coaxed hers to part and the tip of his tongue, hot and moist, entered her mouth. She touched it with the tip of her tongue and felt a tiny explosion inside her body. A delightful shiver of wanting ran through her.

One of his large hands cradled her face and tilted it up so he could look deeply into her eyes.

"If you want me to stop, tell me now, Sky," he said in a husky whisper. "Or there's no telling where this will lead us."

Yes, she knew without his warning where their longings would take them. The devilish spark in his sensual gaze revealed his desire, and certainly reflected her own. It wasn't a decision they could discuss objectively. Not when his other hand moved up the side of her bodice to her breast and caressed it wantonly.

Sky gasped, her eyes half closing, while the immediate sensation seared from her breast down to the ache between her thighs. Once again, her lips parted, welcoming his mouth and searching tongue.

Purposefully, he unbuttoned her gown and lifted it over her head. The gown drifted to the floor followed by her silk camisole, leaving her naked above her lace drawers.

She stood before him, her body tingling. Yet she felt no shame, only excitement welling up within her.

As long as it had been since she'd let Thomas near her, she could not recall his desire to undress her. They had disrobed separately, avoiding looking at each other's bodies. She'd come to think all couples approached the sexual act in this indifferent way. Now she realized this was a pleasuring between a man and a woman. She wanted to share it with Cody. Breathlessly, she undid her drawers and slid them over her hips.

His sharp intake of breath was audible. "You're beautiful, Sky."

She looked up at him through a veil of dark lashes, his hungry gaze igniting her. "You make me feel beautiful."

Seconds later, they lay on the quilt before a crackling fire. When Cody scattered kisses from her neck down over her breast, sparks flickered through her veins. This must be a dream, she thought. But no, she'd never felt so alive in a dream.

Suddenly he raised himself up on one elbow and gazed at her in the glow of firelight. "What is this?" He traced a finger over the swell of her upper breast. "A birthmark?"

Slightly embarrassed, she glanced down at the familiar dark mark. "Yes, it is."

"Looks like a little bird spreading its wings."

Deciding to share a childhood memory, she raised up to face him. "When I was small, Granny Saunders would undress me at bedtime and say, 'That's your little bird. Make it fly . . . ' I would climb up on my bed and cry out, 'Up in the sky!' Then I'd fly into her arms."

Cody's mustache lifted into a smile. He nuzzled her neck. "Bet that's how you got to be called Sky, isn't it?"

She nodded. "I liked Sky better than Marguerite, my given name."

Capturing her breast in his warm hand, he circled the small

bird with his thumb. His voice came low and urgent next to her ear. "Come fly with me, Sky."

Her nipple hardened against his palm and she sucked in her breath, feeling speechless and lightheaded.

Hot and seeking, his lips found hers once more. She moaned beneath him as his hand glided down over her belly.

Dear Lord. She'd fly wherever he would take her.

Cody watched her with an inner eye, taking measure of her response to his every touch of her silken skin. Certainly she was a virgin, and he wanted to take time to explore, to arouse, and to give her pleasure. Inhaling her womanly scent of lilac water mixed with wood smoke as his fingers reached her mound of curls made him harden with desire. He knew his erection was large when he was aroused, and he did not want to cause Sky undue pain.

But how he wanted her. More than any other woman he'd met. He would not allow himself to think of how long he had wanted her.

She moved against him, returning his kiss with a sweet eagerness. He groaned with tormented desire.

When, finally, Cody lowered his body over hers and stroked her inner thighs with his enlarged member, she moaned. Her hands clasped his upper arms. "Cody . . . I'm afraid."

"Don't be, my love," he whispered, sensing her unease the first time. "We'll go slow. Oh, Sky. I want to make love to you."

She lingered on a sigh, her legs parting slightly, and he nudged closer to her moist silken portal. He would die if she stopped him now.

Beneath him, Sky fought the sudden panic that caused her heart and lungs nearly to explode inside her chest. She felt the heat of his body course down the entire length of her, felt his swollen erection press between her legs.

This is Cody, an inner voice confirmed. She squeezed her eyes shut and exhaled deeply. Why did she need to remind herself? Everything about him was different from Thomas.

This is Cody. And I want him.

"Come with me, Sky." His mustache brushed her cheeks, her eyelids. Softly. Coaxing. "Only a small pain. I promise. Then we'll fly."

She looked up into his eyes, so close, sparked with gold. She trusted him, needed him. His arousal gently grazed her, begging entry not only to her body, but her soul. Desire overcoming conscious thought, Sky linked her fingers behind his neck and pulled him to her. "Yes. Yes!"

As he lifted her hips and entered her, ecstasy spiraled in an upward wave. Moving slowly, he eased inside her, every inch of her inner core pulsing, accepting him with liquid fire.

Together they found the tempo that bound their bodies, soaring faster and higher until Sky cried out for release. It came in an explosion of fiery sensations. She shattered into a million glowing stars. Stars that floated down around her, bathing her with a golden sheen.

Her body melted into Cody's and the world was filled with him.

"Sky . . . sweet Sky." Cody held her close for a long moment before slowly withdrawing from her.

She clung to him, her hands still woven through his damp waving hair, wanting him to fill her once more. Gazing deeply into his eyes, she said, "You gave me passion I've never known before."

His face still flushed with excitement, Cody sent her a charming, wicked wink. Then his gaze grew more serious. "There's never been anyone like you."

Her throat filled with sudden emotion and she fought back the sting of tears behind her eyelids. She buried her face in the crook of his warm neck, inhaling the comforting smell of the piney outdoors and his masculinity. Hiding the vulnerable expression she knew covered her face. Not wanting to yield to the burning need that lay captive within her.

From the shed came a muffled sound and Sky turned her head, listening. "I hope we didn't waken Antonio. I'd better go check on him."

Cody caressed a lock of her hair tumbling around his fingers. "Okay, but come right back."

She scooted up from the quilt, aware of his gaze following her, and grabbed her nightgown from the foot of the bed. Slipping it over her head, she went to the drawn curtain and peeked into the darkness. To her relief, both Antonio and Chico were still heavily asleep, the small room warm from the heated stone fireplace.

"They're fine," she whispered, sliding back inside the heavy quilt and snuggling next to Cody's warmth.

"You really care about that kid."

"Well, he has no mother. Someone needs to care about him."

"He could be more trouble than you think. Maybe some family in town—"

"We're not moving back to town," she said firmly. "Antonio needs someone he can trust right now. He needs to learn English and mathematics. I promised I would teach him. At least until the new school opens and he is accepted." She paused, realizing her voice had taken on the tone of a schoolmarm. "When the time is right, I'll try to find him a qualified family."

A slow smile lifted Cody's lips. "You're quite a woman, Sky. I only wish my mother . . ." His voice trailed off and he gazed into a far corner of the room.

Compassion filled her. She remembered he'd started to tell her something about his mother the night they rode out to

California Gulch. "You haven't seen your mother in a long time?"

He shook his head, his expression turning cold. "She ran out on my brother Will and me, and Dad, when I was around Antonio's age. Another miner caught her eye. Dad just wasn't quite as . . . appealing, I guess."

Gooseflesh scampered down her arms beneath her gown. "Oh, Cody. I'm sorry." What more could she say? She placed her fingers gently alongside his cheek.

He shrugged his shoulder. "We made out okay. Dad stopped mining and became a wheelwright. It brought in a better living." He glanced over at her with a forced smile that told her things hadn't always been "okay."

She listened intently, wondering about the many nights Cody and his brother must have gone to bed with an ache in their young hearts, an emptiness and yearning for a mother's arms. She was reminded of her own growing-up years, after Gran, with no mother to talk to or share laughter and tears. Her aunt had been far too busy with a houseful of children to bother caring about Sky's youthful dreams.

Stroking her arm, he said softly, "I forgot, you lost your folks when you were very young, didn't you?"

"Yes, they drowned when I was two. I was so lucky to live with Gran until her heart gave out . . . when I was thirteen."

"And then you went to live with Ned and his folks?"

"That's when I was sent to live with Ned's family. There were three boys and two girls." Glancing at the flickering orange flames on the hearth, Sky tensed at the memory. "I came to love Ned, but I never got over the feeling of being their 'poor relation.'

"I wore the older girls' hand-me-down dresses to school and some of my classmates would whisper in the schoolyard, 'Whose dress are you wearing today, Sky? That flour sack doesn't fit you very well.' "

Cody snorted. "What did you care? I bet you were the prettiest girl there, and they were probably jealous."

His toes rubbed up against hers beneath the quilt. She smiled unexpectedly. "I didn't let them bother me. I started wearing Ned's trousers to school in spite of the other girls' remarks. Let them taunt me, I thought. I was always ready with a well-packed mud ball or a quick shove."

A chuckle escaped from deep in Cody's chest. "You sound like me when some bully joked about my mother behind my back. Just loud enough so I could hear." He cuffed her chin. "You must have been some kind of tomboy." He grinned, gazing at her, a sparkle in his eyes. "Wish I could have known you then."

The night wind whistled at the door and the next thing she knew, Cody was kissing her again. Over her cheeks and lips, down her neck to the hollow at the base of her throat. They weren't passionate kisses like before, but tender, loving. The kind you give someone when you want to let them know you care. She found lying in his strong arms, nuzzling like two young bear cubs, was the dearest thing she'd ever done with a man.

Passion was exciting. Exhilarating! She definitely wanted to indulge in it again. But this was . . . almost peaceful. A sleepy, gentle holding and touching. The fire shimmered far away and she drifted in a cocoon, warm and protected. There was nowhere else she wanted to be but here, in the middle of a snowy night, with this wonderful, wonderful man.

A clinking sound woke her. Her eyes grated open. She stretched lazily and rubbed sleep from them, focusing on Cody bending over a rekindled fire on the hearth.

He wore a pair of red long johns she'd failed to notice the

night before. He'd removed them so quickly. The drawers looked nearly new and revealed his firm behind and muscular thighs.

"Got the coffee started." A smile glimmered in his eyes as they traveled from her face over her reclining figure beneath the quilt.

The way he looked at her and the way his lion-blond hair, ruffled from sleep, framed his angular face in the firelight, made her heart do a double somersault. "Ummm. I can smell it already." She propped herself up on her elbows and watched him work.

After banking the fire, he wiped his hands on a towel and hunkered back under the quilt.

"You're cold," she pretended to complain when his bare foot bumped hers.

But his lips were warm—and his tongue. She whimpered when it slowly rimmed her ear, teasing. "Cody . . ."

Somehow, her gown came unbuttoned and Cody's lips found her breast and suckled her taut nipple. She gasped at the sweet ache.

"Sky," he murmured, his voice raw with need. "You've turned my damn world upside down."

Then his hands—oh, his hands—came up the back of her thighs. Cupped her bare buttocks under her gown and pressed her body to his.

She absorbed the heat of his growing arousal, her own excitement pounding within her chest.

He began to rock against her. "I want you."

Within Sky a struggle ensued. She'd already given herself to him once as a married woman. Yet in her heart she had not committed a sin. His strong arms around her made her feel safe.

Surely he would understand when she told him.

She slid her hand between them and touched him, thrilling

to the length of his velvet-hard sheath in her palm. Boldly, she guided him to her.

The tip of his arousal caressed her inner thighs and molten liquid gathered inside her.

"Yes," she whispered, beyond conscious thought. "I'm nearly free . . . free of him."

Cody's eyelids flickered. He looked at her through a passionate haze. "What . . . what did you say?"

She stiffened with the horror that he'd heard her careless words. "It was nothing."

As suddenly as if he'd stepped into a frigid creek, Cody froze and pulled back. "You're nearly free? Who are you talking about?"

The bird outside in the yard ceased its chirping, the coffee stopped boiling. The world she knew paused and waited on a sheer cliff—waited for her response.

Sky forced herself to look into the eyes of this handsome, virile man lying only inches from her. The man she had come to love. An unstoppable fire burned up her neck and scalded her face. Words caught in her throat, but she choked them out.

"My . . . husband."

Cody gaped at her. "You're married?"

She winced and took a deep breath. "Yes. But . . . I'm getting a divorce."

His features twisted into an incredulous stare. "Why didn't you tell me?"

A chill draft blew over her from the chasm below. "I wanted to. I just couldn't find the right time."

He wrenched away from her and threw off the quilt.

Miserable, she shook her head. "I was waiting until the divorce became final."

"You could have told me a long time ago." Getting to his feet, he yanked his shirt and vest from the back of the chair and shrugged into them.

"I didn't want you to think badly of me." She gathered her nightgown around her and rose to her knees, realizing her mistake in not telling him sooner. Unbidden tears stung her eyelids. "He was cruel . . . and he cheated people."

Cody was already pulling on his pants, then his boots, his back turned to her. He didn't want to hear what she had to say. "I've got to check the snow damage and saddle up Buck."

"I want to explain . . ." Disbelieving, Sky watched Cody stride over to the wall peg and remove his rain slicker and hat.

The room whirled around her. How could this be happening? Only seconds ago, they were wrapped in each other's arms, about to make passionate love again. Now he was stomping out of her life like a wounded bull.

He pulled the door ajar, then stopped. Half turning, he looked over his shoulder, pinning her with his gaze. "I'd thought you were . . . innocent." A muscle worked in his jaw. "Well, I guess after you've made your fortune here, it won't matter to other men."

Moisture blurred her vision and her throat tightened. Other men? There could be no other man but him. "Cody, please!"

He opened the door and closed it, leaving her trembling in a gust of chill morning air.

Frantically she dressed, splashing her face with water from a crockery pitcher and crammed her bare feet into a pair of men's overshoes the previous tenant had left behind. Her feet swam in them, but she was mindless, thinking only to reason with Cody before he rode off. Flinging her woolen shawl over her shoulders, she threw open the front door.

On the stoop, snow reached her shins. The air was still beneath a clouded gray sky. She jumped off the stoop, sinking into a snow bank up to her knees, and plowed to the side yard where Cody saddled his buckskin.

"Please don't leave now. We can have coffee—and talk," she called, trudging over to him, icy crystals falling inside her loose boots.

"I'll get some coffee in town," he answered, his voice flat. He angled his head over toward the well. "I dug you a path; the water should thaw out pretty quick."

"Cody, you have to listen to me—" She wiped her nose with the back of her sleeve, her stomach churning with despair. What could she say to make him stay?

Smoothly, he mounted his horse and glanced down at her, his eyes unreadable. "I'll have Ned check in on you." He touched two fingers to his hat brim, turned the buckskin, and headed off toward the road.

Grief ripping through her, Sky plodded back through the knee-deep snow. A thousand needles could have pierced her flesh and she would not have felt more stricken. Unchecked tears streamed down her face and dripped from her chin.

"Señorita Sky! Where is the marshal going?" Antonio hovered in the open cabin doorway in his nightshirt, his small face puffy from sleep. With a sharp bark, Chico bounded out into the yard.

"Get back inside, Antonio! You'll catch pneumonia." Wiping her eyes with her shawl, she climbed up on the stoop, and pushed the boy back into the warmth of the cabin.

"But will Marshal Cody come back?"

"I . . . don't think so . . ."

Shivering, Sky turned and stared into the distance. Further down the road, a man in a yellow slicker rode away into the light gray dawn, a man who was respected and who'd shown her respect.

A man who had made love to her and changed her life.

She put her hand to her face and wept.

CHAPTER TWENTY

Cody urged the buckskin along the road, the animal's hooves punching tracks in the two-foot layer of snow. Clenching his jaw hard, he leaned into the brisk chill of dawn, muttering condemnations under his clouded breath.

Dang woman! Deceiving woman!

He had allowed his attraction to Sky to carry him beyond the point of common sense. He'd courted her, fallen for her, and finally taken her to bed. After holding her in his arms all night, reveling in the lush mysteries of her warm and generous body, he'd even fantasized about combining his future with hers. Despite his efforts in the past not to come this close to any woman, he'd been blindsided.

She had not rewarded him with similar fantasies, but with a lie. A lie she'd held like a dark secret inside her.

Sky was a married woman.

He cursed himself for being such a fool. A lame-brained jackass! Even a half-witted rabbit would have more sense than to leap into a trap like that.

He clamped his jaw until it ached. As did the lump in his throat. He could hardly swallow, it hurt so bad.

Sky, why didn't you tell me?

What would he have thought of her if she had? Cody knew he was prone to quick judgment of women, especially since his father revealed that his mother deserted them for a drifter. He'd mistrusted most women from that day forward.

Until Sky.

She was different from the others.

He snorted a cynical laugh. Different all right. She was married.

He thought of the first day she'd arrived in Leadville, when he met her at the train station. Tall and prim, auburn hair and a blush on her cheek like a summer rose. He'd seen the admiration reflected in those vivid blue eyes when he introduced himself.

Naturally, he'd assumed she was a maiden lady coming west in search of a new life. How could he have known she'd left a husband behind?

Cody had to admit his surprise when they'd made love last night. Although reserved at first, Sky had responded to him as though she were familiar with the intimate act. She was not a virgin.

Well, hell, he didn't think he'd ever bedded a virgin.

He could have overlooked an indiscretion on her part. Believing he would never marry, he'd participated in several indiscretions himself. But she'd loved another man. And, damned if he could stop it, jealousy burned through his veins.

He had to sort things out, shake off the nagging pain that burrowed deep inside his chest. It wasn't the kind of pain a man could drink away, like the pain from a mule's kick. He sensed this pain would still hang on even if he slugged down all the whiskey in Leadville.

A loud grumbling in his gut made him remember Sky's last words: "Please don't leave now. We can have coffee and talk."

Maybe he should have caged his bruised pride and gone back into the cabin with her for that coffee. Forced himself to listen. But would she have just spun more tales?

How could he ever trust her again?

Cursing to the wind, Cody urged the buckskin into a canter.

The time for listening had passed.

As town marshal he was expected to stick with chasing the criminals out of Leadville. Not go crowing like a dizzy rooster after some strutting red hen.

Abe Fitch's killer was still running loose. He needed to get back on his trail. Track the devil down.

Vowing that was what he would do, Cody gave the buckskin free rein and rode hell-bent toward town.

"Where the devil have you been, Marshal?" Resembling a grumpy bear, deputy Jim Hacker greeted Cody with a scowl that quickly eased into a grin above his black, chest-length beard. "We was about to send out half the police force—thought maybe you got buried in a snowdrift."

"Not exactly a snowdrift." Cody removed his Stetson and rain slicker and hung them on a wall peg behind his desk. "I dug in and waited out the storm up near California Gulch."

He wasn't about to reveal where he'd slept last night. Even after a decent breakfast at a café up the street, his mood was not good. A nagging headache throbbed at his temples.

Hacker chuckled. "Know what you mean. I settled in with half a bottle of redeye. That and my coon dog kept the chilblains at bay."

Ordinarily Cody would have come back with a companionable retort, but not today. He dropped into the chair behind his desk and raked his fingers through his matted hair. "You and Ned come up with anything on Abe's murder?"

Hacker's broad shoulders sagged. "We been askin' around town—some of the saloons. Folks feel bad about ol' Abe, but nobody knows nothin'."

Cody blew out a long disgusted breath. "We've gotta do better than that, Jim. My badge and yours will be on the line if we don't."

Hacker bobbed his bushy head. "Sure, boss. I know."

Rising from his chair, Cody strode over to the dust-streaked window. "It's personal now. I want to find that stinking coward, for Abe and for myself."

Hacker nodded with grim understanding.

Outside, men trudged by along the boardwalk, their hatted heads lowered against the brisk autumn day, their boots making paths in the crusted snow.

A sudden memory of the murder scene stiffened his spine. "Hey, where's that bowler hat I found up at Abe's place?"

"Over there on that shelf." The deputy ambled over to a far corner and grabbed a faded black bowler from the top shelf. He tossed it to Cody, who examined it with revulsion.

"Greasy, ain't it?" Hacker's lower lip curled up beneath his handlebar mustache.

"Yeah." Cody took a whiff of the inside of the hat. "It still smells like cheap hair oil."

"Didn't belong to no swell, that's fer sure."

Cody grinned. "Nope. It belonged to a skunk. We've got to smoke him out."

Hacker chortled. "Can't say I seen too many bowlers like that around town."

Past images scrolled across Cody's mind. "I've got a hunch, Jim." He pulled a sheep-lined jacket off another peg and threw it on.

"Where you goin'?"

"Think I'll order some wanted flyers printed up. Offer a reward to anyone having information about the owner of that putrid black hat. Money always brings stoolies out of the woodwork."

"Where you gonna get reward money?"

"From some of these business owners and irate miners." He crammed on his Stetson and opened the front door. "I'm heading over to Lovell's Print Shop."

"Okay, Marshal." Hacker stroked his beard. "When will you be back?"

"Soon as I follow up on my hunch, Jim."

Walking toward the print shop, Cody realized his headache had finally subsided, but not the memory of Sky in his arms.

Keeping focused on his work was the only way to keep her off his mind. Keep his sanity. A tightening in his chest convinced him he must.

An hour later, a sheaf of reward posters in hand, Cody strode into the county clerk's office. When he saw no one in the sparsely furnished front office, he called out to a dark-haired clerk leaning over a large map in the back room.

"Mr. Templeton here?"

The man's head swiveled in his direction. Sparse black eyebrows arched beneath a high, slanted forehead. Wide-set murky eyes stared at him with a mix of surprise and intense curiosity. A twinge of derision rippled through Cody's limbs, causing his muscles to tense.

"No, he ain't. He went to a meeting," the man answered, his voice sandpaper-rough.

When Cody remained where he stood, returning the murky-eyed stare with one of his own, the clerk drew himself up to a slightly stooped position of near six feet and ambled to the doorway.

"Something I can do for you, Marshal?" The shifty green eyes bulged, the protruding lips curled upward in an elongated, otherwise humorless face.

A hot poker prodded Cody's gut. His hunch had to be right. He'd seen this reptile of a man the day he'd taken Sky up to the mines, poking around where he didn't belong. He'd heard talk about him. But where?

"And you are?"

The man stepped across the threshold in a lanky stride. "Boris Wickham. I'm chief clerk and recorder for Mr. Templeton."

A bell rang inside Cody's head. Now he remembered. He'd heard men in card games refer to "that strange fella that works for the county clerk." Wickham was the brunt of drinking men's jokes. With his wide bulging eyes and lips, and gangly physique, they called him "Frog" behind his back.

Cody held up his reward poster headlined in bold print.

FIND THE OWNER OF THE BLACK BOWLER
IN THE MARSHAL'S OFFICE AND YOU'LL PEG
ABE FITCH'S KILLER.
$ REWARD OFFERED $

The date of the murder and an account of the fire followed.

Grinning determinedly he said, "I'd like to tack one of these next to your front door."

Jutting out his black spiky-haired head, Wickham gawked at the headlines. "Tack 'em wherever you want." His features twisted into an accommodating smirk.

The smirk wasn't as offensive as the man's hair oil. Cheap and repugnant. Familiar.

"Good," Cody said through clenched teeth. "I'll put one up on my way out." He moved toward the door, then turned, pinning Wickham with a steady eye. "Thanks for your help. We think these ought to flush out the yellow cowards who shot Abe Fitch in cold blood."

Apprehension flickered across the clerk's face, immediately replaced by an icy stare. "Good luck, Marshal. Sounds like it could be a tough job."

Cody didn't dignify Wickham's comment with an answer. He swung out the door, feeling the man's frog eyes pierce him, and his skin crawled. For less than two cents, he would have grabbed the bastard and pounded the truth out of him.

Wickham had to be his man, all right. Cody felt it deep in his gut. He'd watch him, catch him in the act one night.

Then, he'd watch him hang!

Sky wrapped her shawl snuggly around her shoulders, and tried to focus ahead on her day's work at Burtram's as the mare Ned had loaned her plodded over into town. She didn't need to remind herself to stop first at the postal counter at the hardware store to see if any mail had arrived from Ohio. The prospect made her fume. Her attorney seemed to have forgotten her. Who knew what tricks Thomas had pulled to delay her divorce papers.

At least Antonio was a joy, with his ready smile and eagerness to please. She'd left Antonio with Mrs. Hemmings, a neighbor woman with three children who'd agreed to look after the boy. In exchange, Sky taught the Hemmingses' children, along with Antonio, basic English grammar and mathematics four evenings a week.

It was not the most ideal arrangement. The youngsters tended to be lazy after supper and didn't always pay attention. On Saturday mornings, she made Antonio study for at least an hour before his chores. His reward was a dessert of his choice. His favorite was Granny Saunders's spice cake. Which pleased her. Not much had pleased her since the day several weeks ago when Cody rode out of her life.

Thinking about him only brought her pain. Tears welled up in her eyes and she brushed them away. For the thousandth time, she berated herself for not telling him of her marital position right from the start. Perhaps then he would have tried to understand. She swallowed over her tears.

This wasn't supposed to happen, this undeniable overpowering attraction. She'd promised herself, after the abuse she'd taken from Thomas, not to feel anything for any man again. Never in her most daring dreams could she have imagined such physical upheaval over a man, such sensual longing, as she felt for Cody.

"Oh, Gran. If you were here now, you'd give me a good swift kick," she muttered. Impatiently she dug her heels into the little mare, urging her ahead, then felt guilty. Of course, Gran wouldn't have kicked her. Just sat her down and given her a loving dose of good advice along with a hot cup of peppermint tea.

Tears pricked her eyelids again. How she missed Gran. How she loved and missed Cody. Foolish young woman.

Later, as Sky concentrated on monthly bills at her desk, she felt cool, masculine fingers slip over her eyes. "Oh, Ned!" she blustered, tearing his hands away and wheeling around in her chair. "You always do that. Can't you see I'm working?"

Her cousin chuckled. "Thought you'd like to get away from this drudgery for a minute and have a cup of coffee."

She looked up into Ned's amiable light brown eyes and realized her good fortune to have a cousin as close as a brother who'd stood by her in her latest time of need. Grinning, she replied, "Better watch your talk about drudgery around here." She lowered her voice. "Burtram could be just around the corner. But, yes, let's sneak a cup of Cookie's wake-up coffee."

In the kitchen, Ned took a sip from his mug and asked, "Have you seen ol' Dan Gunther lately?"

Sky thought back to the last time she'd seen Whistlin' Dan. "It's been quite a while, since before Antonio and I moved to the cabin. Haven't you heard anything from him?"

"Not since the end of summer."

"That makes me wonder . . ." Sky knitted her brows together. "With all this claim jumping, anything could have happened."

"Yeah, but we'd hear through the town grapevine."

"Something isn't right, Ned." Sky set her coffee mug down

next to the tin sink. "I'm going to pay a call on the marshal."

"What?" Ned reared back, gaping at her. "He's been snarly as a stray dog with a tic for the last few weeks. Guess you know why."

Sky sent him a withering look. "I don't care. I haven't been in a magnificent mood myself." It had been yet another day with no mail awaiting her from Placerton. "And this is important."

Ned cocked one eyebrow and gazed at her as if she were crazy. "Go ahead. It's your funeral."

A brazen west wind tossed up Sky's skirt as she walked with Ned back to the marshal's office. He hadn't been too enthusiastic about her coming with him, in light of Cody's owlish mood in recent days. She refused to dwell on the marshal's temperament. Her main concern was Dan Gunther's well-being. In a strange way, she'd come to think of the reclusive miner as a friend.

"I can't promise the marshal will get too excited over one stray miner," Ned said as they leaned into the wind.

"He will if I have anything to say about it." She tightened the forest-green bow of her brimmed hat beneath her chin and focused ahead. "We've invested our grubstake in Mr. Gunther's mine and we want to know if he's in any danger."

A glance westward to the snow-capped Rockies sent an icy quiver through her. Despite her outer bravado, inside she wasn't so sure how to approach Cody Cassidy. His callous stare that morning before he'd ridden away had left her wondering if he would ever listen to her again.

They turned the corner onto Front Street and came to the marshal's office. Ned opened the door and Sky entered, girding herself with resolve.

In the far corner, Cody and his deputy Jim Hacker were in a discussion. Cody, leaning back in his chair, had one foot propped up on his desk. When his gaze shifted to her, a look of surprise swept over his features and his voice broke off in mid-sentence.

"Good morning, Marshal."

He shot to his feet, looking directly at her. "Morning, Mrs. Saunders, isn't it? What can we do for you?"

"I'll soon be 'Miss.' " As their eyes met, a thrill ran through her, but at his reminder of her marital status, she drew a deep breath and forbade herself to falter. "I need to talk to you about Dan Gunther. He hasn't been seen for months now, and Ned and I are concerned."

Cody stroked his full mustache, which was so distracting, she averted her gaze to the papers on his desk. "Nobody's seen ol' Dan around town?"

Ned shook his head. "He hasn't been down for supplies as far as anybody knows."

"With all the claim jumping going on, we thought—"

Cody came around the side of the desk. "You want to ride up there and see if he's okay, Ned?"

"If you can spare me for an hour or two."

"Sure, if it'll ease your mind." Cody glanced at Sky. "And Mrs. Saunders."

An uncomfortable heat started under her lace collar at his words and the way he looked at her. "I'm going, too," she affirmed abruptly.

Cody's jaw dropped. "Sky, you don't want to go up there. It's no place for a lady."

She clamped one hand on her hip, responding with easy defiance. "I do, too. Dan's a friend as well as a business partner."

The flicker of amusement in those hazel eyes only bolstered her determination. She pivoted and headed for the door. "Good day, Marshal. Deputy. Com'on, Ned, let's go."

To her surprise, Cody grabbed his hat and coat from a wall

peg and followed her to the door. "I've got to call on a couple of miners up on Stray Horse. I'll ride along with you. Hold the fort for a while, Jim," he called over his shoulder.

Jim Hacker stared after them, his bushy eyebrows converging like a puzzled black bear. "Okay, boss."

On the way up to the gulch, they rode in a long silence, Cody and Ned exchanging only a few words as the trail climbed higher. Sky's mare fell behind several times and she coaxed her to catch up.

Mrs. Saunders, she repeated under her breath several times. Thank God, he didn't know her married name. She didn't want anyone in Leadville to ever know it.

Not for a minute did she believe Cody planned to check on any miners up here. But she was glad he'd come along. For their protection. Not for any other reason. Her eyes and her fast-tripping heart betrayed her now and then. She couldn't resist staring at Cody's broad shoulders and the way he rode in the saddle, a towering presence on his powerful buckskin.

After what seemed an interminable amount of time, Ned recognized a fork in the road and they veered left up another slanted trail.

"How far is it, Ned?" Sky hated to sound impatient. After all, she'd insisted on coming, but her backside had been in constant discomfort for the last mile.

Ned pointed. "As I remember, just over this hill."

They crested the hill and looked down on a small mine yard surrounded by an outcropping of scraggly pine. A ramshackle hut leaned against the side of a ridge. A mineshaft nearby.

Sky sensed the quiet isolation of the place, the loneliness only a miner could understand and live with day after day.

"Hey, Dan!" Ned called.

Only the sigh of the wind greeted their ears.

"Dan Gunther!" Cody hollered.

Sky guessed the men wanted to announce themselves before riding onto the miner's property. Gunther was a solitary man, probably not given to surprise visitors.

Then, a forlorn braying sounded from a cluster of trees at the far end of the ridge and a gray mule ambled into the yard.

"Miss Fanny," Sky and Ned chorused.

Cody pulled a rifle from its sheath and laid it over his lap. With a solemn glance over his shoulder, he gave instructions. "You wait here for us, Sky. I'll signal for you to come down after we check around the place."

A twinge of apprehension grazed her nerve endings. She nodded quickly and licked her dry lips.

"Come on, Ned." Cody snapped his reins and the two men started down the scree slope.

Sky scanned the yard, wishing in the next instant she'd hear an ear-splitting whistle and the eccentric old miner would emerge from the small mineshaft like a genie out of a bottle. She recalled with gentle amusement how he'd sprung from the rowdy gambling hall crowd the night they'd first met.

"Whistlin' Dan Gunther, where are you?" she whispered nervously.

Below her, she saw Cody, rifle in hand, and Ned approach the hut. The door appeared ajar and they ducked their heads and entered cautiously. Could thieves have ransacked the place? She dared not allow her imagination to run amuck as to what might have happened to Dan.

A few minutes later, Cody's tall frame filled the low doorway. He waved her down, his features immobile.

With fear in her heart, she gave the mare a little kick and urged the animal down the slope.

When she reached the hut Ned came out, muffling his face with a kerchief, and helped her dismount. "I think you should wait out here, Sky," he said in a voice unusually firm. "We found Dan in there. He's dead."

"Oh, no." Her knees threatened to buckle beneath her. "How did he die?"

"We think he just laid down to take a nap and died in his sleep. Real peaceful."

"Oh, I'm glad he didn't suffer." She fought back tears burning against her eyelids. "I want to see him. At least say good-bye."

"I wouldn't do that. He's been gone for a week maybe. It don't smell too good in there."

She moved past Ned to the open door. "That won't bother me."

"Don't come in here, Sky," Cody called from next to a cot.

She saw him cover Dan's body with a shabby blanket just as she inhaled the repulsive odor. Gagging, she snatched a handkerchief from her skirt pocket and rushed back into the yard.

"You see what I mean," Ned said, taking her elbow.

She nodded, coughing and gulping the fresh mountain air.

Cody emerged from the hut, also inhaling deeply. He handed Sky a folded piece of paper. "I found a note in Dan's shirt pocket that you two should find interesting."

Her vision blurred as she read the miner's scrawled words across the dog-eared page, and her hand trembled.

Ned tried to peer over her shoulder. "What does it say?"

"Good Lord, Ned," Sky announced, her eyes wide. "We've just inherited a silver mine!"

CHAPTER TWENTY-ONE

Sunlight shimmered on newly fallen snow. So bright it made Cody's eyes tear beneath his brimmed hat as he rode Buck out to the town cemetery.

A small group had gathered at the crest of a hill near Dan Gunther's wooden coffin: Pastor Sherrod and his wife, Ned and Cindy Saunders, a few grizzled miners who'd known Gunther by way of their saloon card games and mutual hard lives. The men huddled uncomfortably, sending occasional somber-eyed glances at the open grave and coffin several yards away.

"Guess ol' Dan's luck run out before he struck that rich vein he was always flappin' about," Cody heard one codger mutter to another.

"Yep," replied the other. "Heard he left his deed to some local gal, works over at Burtram's Hall."

That brought a snort from a third. "Don't know what good it's gonna do her. 'Lessen she tends to move up there with a pick and shovel." They all snickered at the last miner's jest.

Pulling up near a stand of pine, Cody dismounted and tethered the buckskin to one of the trees.

"Mornin', Marshal." They nodded as he strode their way.

"Morning, boys. Not a bad day to lay a man to rest." He smiled toward the parson and the others. "Good day, Pastor. Mrs. Sherrod."

A mournful braying jarred the still November air. Cody turned to squint against the sun and saw the silhouette of a young woman riding a dark gray mule and behind her a small boy atop a chestnut horse. He immediately recognized Sky and Antonio.

The slanted brim of her black hat covered Sky's glorious auburn hair, the skirt of her proper mourning dress draped softly over her long legs. Pink-tinged cheeks belied a sadness touching the corners of her sensitive mouth.

A bittersweet ache pierced his heart as he watched her rein in the scrawny mule she'd inherited from Dan Gunther. Drawn to her side, Cody offered his hand and she placed gloved fingers across his palm. Her body heat radiated from his hand up his arm like a lightning current.

For the first time in his life, words didn't come easy.

"Thank you, Marshal." She dismounted the mule, its headpiece decorated with bows of black ribbon, as though the animal were a prized Arabian.

Antonio hopped down from the mare and ran over to them. *"Buenos días, Marshal Cody."* His enthusiastic greeting stirred a warmth inside Cody's chest.

He gave the boy's wool cap a tug. *"Buenos días."*

Beneath her veil, Sky's violet blue eyes smiled at him briefly before she slid her arm around Antonio's shoulders and they went to greet Ned and the others.

Standing on the ridge of the hill, gazing after them, Cody felt a sudden loneliness seep into the marrow of his bones. His attraction to this married woman was shameless. Even as she'd stepped down beside him, the enticing fragrance of her filling his senses, he'd wanted to crush her to him. No matter that they were here to pay mutual respect to a dead man.

The fact that Sky was a married woman, that she belonged to another man, still rankled. She'd claimed to be seeking a divorce, but could he believe her?

Somewhere near, a tree branch cracked and like second

nature, Cody reached for his Colt. His fingers curving around the gun's cold wood butt, he scanned the trees, listening. Would anyone be fool enough to try an ambush at a funeral, in broad daylight? Seeing nothing, he released a brief sigh and noticed Sky look at him with apparent concern, then glance away.

He wondered what she was thinking. Under her veiled black hat, her hair was drawn into a sleek bun at her nape. He stared at her longer than he wanted to.

The parson motioned to the small group. "Folks, let us gather 'round and say a few words for the departed Mr. Gunther."

After the Bible had been quoted and blessings spoken over a man who'd probably never stepped inside a church, the men replaced their hats and got to work lowering Dan Gunther's pine coffin into the ground. Cody noticed Sky and the parson's wife dab their eyes with lace hankies, and he thought old Gunther would have hooted out loud. No, whistled out loud. He could imagine the grizzly cuss up there somewhere, still in his frayed red flannels, ambling off toward the golden streets, his pickaxe slung over his shoulder.

Cody watched Ned and Cindy walk Sky to her new mule. Ned helped Sky mount and then Antonio. She sat straight in the saddle, a beautiful woman. If things were different, he couldn't help think how proud a man he would be to have her as his wife. She'd saved his life once. What kind of a fool would let her get away? Had she said her husband was cruel? How could any man mistreat Sky? His blood simmered.

If she were his, he'd only want to cherish her. Make love to her every minute she was near.

Disheartened, Cody forced a smile and waved at the group. He urged his buckskin past them and headed back to town.

That night, he roamed through several saloons, seeking any tips he could find about Abe Fitch's murder. Sniffing out possible takers for the two-thousand-dollar reward. The effort at least made him feel like he was trying. It helped get his mind off Sky. But Abe's killers' trail, he feared, had about grown cold. A group of Dan Gunther's cronies at the Silver Bucket begged him to stay and join them. With regret, he declined. A cold drink would taste good right now. Maybe after his night shift ended, he'd reconsider.

He left the bar and walked in the direction of his office. As he passed an alleyway, shadowed figures caught his eye. He pulled his Colt and moved toward one drunk leaning over another, rifling through the man's pockets.

"Hey, mister," he called. "Raise those hands nice and slow."

"I ain't done nothin'," the would-be thief grunted.

"But you were about to." Cody holstered his gun, grabbed the man's arms behind him and snapped on a pair of handcuffs.

He yanked the other drunk to his wobbly feet and ushered both men out of the alley. After sending the one on his weaving way, Cody hustled the other up the street to his office. Unwashed hair hung over the man's downcast eyes and he smelled like a yard dog that'd sneaked in from the rain.

With distaste, Cody removed the cuffs and shoved the drunk into a cell. "Consider yourself lucky, mister. You've got a clean cot to sleep it off tonight. If you got to throw up, use the bucket."

"Hey, Marshal. That reward money still good?" the prisoner mumbled as Cody locked him in.

"What?"

"If that money's still good, I got a tale to tell 'bout that miner up on Stray Horse."

Narrowing his gaze, Cody grabbed the cell bars. "You know who killed Abe Fitch?"

The drunk swiped the mop of hair from his red-rimmed eyes. He looked familiar. No doubt he was one of Boris Wickham's cohorts. "I might know plenty," he boasted, reeling closer.

Cody's gut lurched with disgust at the man's stink, but his

ears burned with curiosity. "Spill it, then."

The reddened eyes leered at him. "You pay me the money up front and let me outta here and I'll spill what I saw."

Anticipation coursed through Cody's veins. "Tell me now and I'll consider it."

The prisoner's thin lips quirked up into a slanted grin, revealing a missing front tooth. "Frog Wickham shot that poor devil. I saw him."

Cody leveled his gaze, a muscle tensing in his jaw. "What did you say your name was?"

"It's Ratcliff," came the slurred reply.

"Well, Ratcliff, you sober up and we'll talk more in the morning." Whether or not the thug had anything believable to tell would be much clearer then. Ned could act as a witness.

But when Ned brought Ratcliff out of his cell the next morning, he was shifty as a cornered coyote. Even after Ned offered him a cup of coffee.

"Does this look familiar?" Cody asked, holding up the dusty bowler hat in front of the man.

Ratcliff swung his gaze from the bowler to the window. "Just like any other old hat." He shambled toward the door. "You got any charges against me?"

Cody knew he couldn't hold the man. Without a witness's testimony, there would be no trial. He tried persuasion. "Thought you were interested in that two-thousand-dollar reward."

Ratcliff shifted uneasily from one foot to the other. "What good's a reward if you don't live to spend it?"

Cody itched to leap across the room and shake the coward's balls loose, but what good would it do? Ratcliff's mouth had shut tighter than bark stuck to a tree. "Get out of here, Ratcliff. But keep looking over your shoulder, 'cause we'll be watching every move you make."

He didn't have to say it twice. The door banged shut.

"Damn!" Cody slammed the grimy bowler across the room.

Three days after Dan Gunther's funeral, Sky rode Miss Fanny to work. Adapting to the well-worn saddle she'd inherited along with the mule was going to be a challenge. The dried out leather creaked with the slightest motion. But the saddle was not nearly as uncomfortable as the thoughts of Cody Cassidy that kept swirling around in her head.

The memory of him at the funeral, looking up at her as she dismounted, made her insides turn to jelly. His intent hazel eyes and luxurious mustache beneath the tan Stetson, the fit of his sheep-lined jacket across the sweep of his broad shoulders, had nearly caused her to lose her footing as she stepped to the ground. He'd said nothing. But his eyes had said everything, triggering the memory of their night of lovemaking.

Just thinking about Cody made butterflies collide in her stomach. How she wanted him . . . still.

She blinked and realized she was already on the outskirts of town. As Miss Fanny loped up Harrison Avenue, Sky noticed several fish-eyed miners elbowing each other, gawking at her astride the mule. Lifting her chin, she looked straight ahead as she passed them, aware that a lady riding a mule on Leadville streets was a rare sight.

"Would ya look at that sweet little ass," one called out.

"Which one?" hollered another. "The lady's or the mule's?"

"Well, it sure ain't the mule's!"

Randy guffaws erupted behind her.

"Wonder what favors she did for ol' Gunther to make him give her that mine?" The last punctuated by hoots and snorts.

Sky's face and ears burned. Crude gossipmongers, she thought. If old Dan were still alive, he would have greeted them with an ear-splitting whistle, a punch to the jaw, and left the good-for-nothings choking on Miss Fanny's dust!

Ever since she'd started riding the mule to work, she'd endured the snickering and ridicule of both miners and the more respectable townspeople. Which of the insults bothered her more, she couldn't say—the miners traveling along the road or the few fashionably dressed men and women along the boardwalk. Sometimes a cold, judgmental stare from them was more humiliating.

Up the avenue, Sky recognized a young blond woman, about her own age, on the arm of Leadville's wealthy former mayor, H. W. Tabor. Wrapped snuggly in an ermine cape, the woman, nicknamed Baby Doe by the much older Mr. Tabor, approached a fancy black carriage. She smiled briefly at Sky atop Miss Fanny as they passed, calling out, "Honey, don't let those louts bother you." The supportive twinkle in Baby Doe's blue eyes eased the sting of the miners' slurs.

Sky liked her spunk, and waved. Never mind that the pampered beauty was a recent divorcée, strongly rumored to be the cause of Tabor's disintegrating marriage.

Another divorcée, Sky thought and winced. How would she ever convince Cody that she wasn't that kind of woman? That her circumstances had been beyond her control? And when would those damned divorce papers finally arrive?

Jostled between two wagons, Miss Fanny lurched, then brayed indignantly. The worn and cracked saddle creaked beneath Sky, giving rise to renewed humiliation. A new saddle would make her daily ride much more agreeable to her backside. But she couldn't afford one. The silver ingots Dan left her as collateral had already been spent on books and winter boots, food for them and the animals.

Regrets assailed her. Not only had she lost whatever chance she had with Cody, she'd lost Dan Gunther, her investment in a likely secure future.

After the deed on their claim was recorded, she had no idea what she and Ned would do with the Lucky Lady mine.

At dusk, Sky and Antonio rode down the trail to the cabin. Just behind her, on the poky mare, Antonio chattered about his day at the Hemmingses's. Chico rambled alongside, darting off to investigate an occasional straggly bush.

"If we finish our lessons early tomorrow, Mrs. Hemmings says Jerry and me can go hunt rabbits."

Sky sighed, her head aching from poring over balance sheets all day at Burtram's. "You're too young to go hunting."

"Jerry's gonna teach me how to shoot his gun."

Drawing her woolen shawl closer around her shoulders, Sky glanced back at him. "Oh, no, he's not. You're not ready to shoot anything until you're at least—twelve." Twelve seemed a good number since it was a long way away from eight.

An impatient whine tinged Antonio's voice. "I'm old enough. I'm ready now."

Sky shook her head, noticing a horse-drawn buggy moving toward them at a steady clip. As the rig approached, the driver stared intently at her, then cracked a short whip over the horse's flank. With a sharp whinny, the black horse bolted into a dead run.

Her heartbeat pulsing in her throat, Sky gawked in fascinated horror at the oncoming horse and rig.

Antonio's voice came from far away, but she made no sense of it. The sound of steel-shod hooves pounding the hard ground, the rise and fall of the jet mane above flared nostrils held her a captive of disbelief.

The horse and driver bore down upon them. "Get off the road!" Sky screamed to Antonio. She jerked Miss Fanny's reins to the right in an effort to block Antonio and the mare from the speeding demon rig.

"H'yah!" rasped the driver.

A lightning crack of whip and frantic snort of the beast resounded in her ears. The stench of horse sweat and her own fear singed her senses.

But the awkward mule couldn't move fast enough. A deafening rumble of wheels and a slashing whip stung her cheek. She shrieked and the mule beneath her, eyes rolled back in fright, stumbled sideways. Sky thought she'd be thrown into the roadside ditch, but hung desperately to the saddle horn.

"Miss Sky!" Antonio cried. "Are you all right?" He reached out to her, terror in his dark eyes.

Choking back the dust from the departing rig and her own threatening tears, she righted herself in the saddle. "I'm fine." She focused on him in the waning light, so young and vulnerable. "Are you hurt?"

"No." His small chin quivered even as he sat up straighter on the mare. "Why did that man try to kill us?"

She patted blood from her face with her handkerchief and stared after the phantom rig. "I wish I knew."

A snatch of memory flared before her. Hooded eyes. Murky. Like cesspools. Where had she seen them before?

Spine-tingling fear gripped her.

Shivering, she peered down the road stretching ahead in the twilight. A quarter-mile to their cabin and no other vehicles in sight.

"Let's go home now, Antonio. As fast as we can."

Sky dug her heels into Miss Fanny's barreled ribs, urging her ahead, wishing she'd heeded Cody's advice about learning how to shoot a gun. If only she had one now.

CHAPTER TWENTY-TWO

A brisk wind nipped at Sky's heels, compelling her to lift the collar of her woolen cape higher around her neck and speed up her steps toward Harding's general store. Uncertainty hung like a cloud over her as she hoped against hope that her divorce papers from Ohio had finally arrived.

Contributing to her malaise was last night's horrifying incident. Should she report it to Cody?

Tossing without sleep through the night, she'd remembered the driver of the rig and his deep-set sinister eyes. The same man who stared at her in town that day last summer when she'd hitched a ride out to Ned's place to talk to Dan Gunther.

If she did tell Cody, what would he do about it? Or, what *could* he do? Even if he found the demon driver and questioned him, it would be her word against his. Antonio was too young to be a credible witness. And he didn't seem to recall anything but being scared.

Sky released a frustrated sigh and glanced ahead at oncoming pedestrians. To her surprise, she saw Cody tying his horse to the hitching post in front of Harding's. His gaze penetrated hers. To her dismay, her heart hammered foolishly.

He stepped onto the boardwalk and tipped his hat as she approached. "Morning, Mrs. Saunders."

Mrs. Saunders. How ridiculous.

"Good morning, Marshal," she replied coolly and attempted to move past him.

His eyes narrowed as he stared at her cheek. Her gloved hand flew to her face, but not fast enough to hide the whiplash she knew was still a bright scarlet.

Removing a leather glove, he gently touched the sensitive area with warm fingertips. "What happened here?"

Slivers of pain and excitement darted through her. Despite her flimsy coat of emotional armor, she wanted to nestle in his protective arms, have him hold her like he did the night they'd made love. Then she reproached herself, not wishing to reveal her lingering attraction.

"Antonio and I were nearly run down on the road going home last night. The driver cut me with the end of his whip."

His chiseled features reflected alarm. "Did you see who it was?"

As she described the phantom driver, Cody moved closer. Even on this chilly day, his body heat penetrated her right down to her toes.

He reached out and grasped her arm, a flash of raw anger in his eyes. "I'll bet I know the driver of that rig. I'm going to go talk to him right now," he said, his voice edged with a steely tone she'd not heard before.

"But I . . ." She started to say she didn't know if she wanted to identify the man. He might come after them again. She'd never forget those frightening eyes. But Cody was already mounting his buckskin. With a slight nod, he whirled the animal out into the thoroughfare.

She stared at his powerful, broad shoulders and struggled against a wave of wanting.

Shivering in a sudden gust, Sky hurried into the store. Maybe Cody did care about her. Or maybe he simply wanted to reprimand the driver before he ran down some other unsuspecting traveler.

With renewed anticipation and anxiety, she approached the

mail clerk at the rear of the store. *Please let the divorce papers be there, so I can put this all behind me.*

Yet, once again, he shook his head. No mail for her. No divorce papers.

Her heart torn, she thanked him and turned away.

Cody rode over to the County Clerk's office, his temper rising. Wickham.

It had to be him.

Wickham must have heard that his sidekick Ratcliff squealed about Abe Fitch's murder to Cody before he got cold feet and disappeared. So, the devil had tried to run Sky off the road as a warning to Cody. Intimidate him.

Cody's gut twisted with rage. He'd get the vermin, arrest him for suspicion of attempted murder. After that, he'd give him a real incentive to confess—he'd squeeze his scrawny neck till his frog eyes popped out of his worthless head!

His hand curling around his gun, he checked the side office but found it empty. He strode through the open doorway to Samuel Keefer's office.

"Where's Wickham, Sam?"

The portly county clerk glanced up from behind his desk and focused through thick spectacles. "Where's the fire, Marshal?"

Cody knew his demeanor was abrupt, but he couldn't help it. His jaw tightened and he spoke through clenched teeth. "I need to find Wickham. I want him."

Keefer shook his head. "Don't know where he is. He hasn't shown up for work in a couple days. Far as I'm concerned, he's fired."

"Great." Cody snorted. "He's dangerous, Sam. I gotta get him before he does any more dirty business."

He turned on his heel and headed across the rough plank floor.

"I'll get word to you if I hear anything."

Cody gave a quick nod then charged through the outer door to the street. Of all the stinking luck. The bastard kept evading him!

He was so damned mad, he kicked at the hitching post before mounting Buck.

What rock are you hiding under, Frog Wickham? Better watch your worthless ass because I won't stop until I find you.

"Antonio, watch what you're doing!"

Peering through a mass of musty-smelling white feathers, Sky sent the boy a mock scowl. One errant cluster floated up her nose and she sneezed.

Next to her at the kitchen table, Antonio continued his frenzied plucking and grinned impishly. Chicken feathers continued to fly.

"*Caramba!* You said to get these chickens in the oven, so they be done for Thanksgiving dinner."

Sky blew a stray lock of hair out of her eyes. "And, didn't I also say a good cook doesn't make a mess of his kitchen?"

"I am a good cook," Antonio insisted. "I helped my ma stir the beans and fry the tortillas."

She ruffled his hair and smiled in spite of the sea of fluttering feathers taking residence in faraway corners. "I'm glad the pies are done," she said, tucking the last one into a cupboard, and smelling its aroma of cinnamon and tart-sweet apples.

As soon as the chickens were baked to a golden crispness, she and Antonio would load up Burtram's wagon and deliver the food baskets to the local Methodist Church. Ladies from the church would distribute them to several of Leadville's needy families.

She wished their Thanksgiving offering could have been more, but after purchasing the chickens from a neighbor and half a bushel of dried apples from the grocer, her earnings were stretched to their limit. It was the deed, after all, not so much the amount, Granny Saunders always said.

That afternoon, as they trundled through town, a light snow fell. Although Sky planned for the Methodists to be their main beneficiary, when they approached the Annunciation Catholic Church, she felt a sudden twinge and guided Miss Fanny over to the sidewalk.

"Wait here, Antonio." She hopped to the ground and fetched one of the baskets from the wagon.

"Where are you going, Miss Sky?" Antonio asked suspiciously.

"Wouldn't you like to share some of our Thanksgiving with the sisters?"

The boy's dark eyebrows shot up in surprise. "Not with Sister Prunella," he replied with the indignance of an eight-year-old who remembered scrubbing courtyard stones on his knees in the rain.

"Hush now. I won't be long."

"Caramba!" she heard him mutter under his breath.

Although Sky resolved to show some Christian charity, she hoped not to come face to face with the spinsterish sister again. When the smaller plump sister answered the rectory door, Sky was relieved to bestow her gift and make a quick departure.

The Methodist Church minister accepted the food baskets with delight and invited them to the kitchen for a cup of hot cider. Satisfied with their good deed, she and Antonio climbed aboard the wagon and made their way back through quieter-than-usual streets.

If the fire hadn't gone out, a warm dinner awaited them at the cabin. Sky's stomach rumbled in anticipation.

At the edge of town, two horsemen rode toward them through the light snow. Recalling the phantom driver's attack that recent dark night, her body tensed.

But as the horsemen came nearer, fear blended into a surprise of mixed emotions.

Cody tipped his hat. "What brings you to town on Thanksgiving Day, Mrs. Saunders?" he asked, his voice velvet-edged yet straightforward.

Deputy Jim Hacker rode beside him. With his drooping black mustache and chest-length beard flecked white, the huge man resembled a snow bear. He nodded. "Ma'am."

She pulled back on Miss Fanny's reins, slowing the animal's pace. "We've been delivering food baskets to the church, Marshal," she answered, her heartbeat rising slightly in her throat.

"I plucked the chicken feathers," Antonio boasted.

From the corner of her eye, she saw Cody's amused smile.

Sky felt tiny licks of heat in her chest beneath Cody's observant gaze. What was he thinking? Should she invite him to dinner? Remembering his hostility toward her, she instantly decided a dinner invitation was not a good idea.

Riding alongside the wagon, Cody interrupted her thoughts. "It'll be dark soon. Think Jim better escort you two home."

"Well, thank you, but I don't think it's—"

"Hope you enjoy your chicken dinner, Antonio. Good day." Cody gave a salute, his unreadable gaze resting on her for a brief moment. Then he turned his buckskin around and rode back toward town.

Her heart sank despite her vow to avoid emotion when around the marshal. Sky glanced over at burly Jim Hacker. "Guess we'd better get going if we want to reach home before dark."

She snapped the reins and the trio set out beneath spirals of swirling white.

Cody looked back through the light snow at the receding buckboard wagon and its occupants. At Sky's peacock-blue bonnet and the way she held herself so smartly, giving rein to that silly-looking mule. Beside Sky, Antonio leaned closer, almost touching her shoulder.

Jim Hacker on his big-rumped bay trotted alongside them.

Cody was glad he'd seen Sky and the boy before they'd started back to the cabin, and that Jim was with them. Not many a thug would dare come up against his deputy, a man built like a two-ton locomotive.

Watching the trio until they faded behind the snow curtain, he felt an ache of longing wind like a rope within his chest.

Ned's recent admonition filled his mind.

"Don't blame Sky for not telling you that she was still married when she first came to town. She'd run away from that pompous, no-good crook who abused her. She wanted to start a new life.

"Until her divorce is final, she decided to go by Miss instead of Missus. For her own protection."

Ned's comment gnawed at Cody's judgment of Sky, wearing thin his earlier reaction of mistrust. He understood her fears.

Now he could only wish he was the one escorting Sky home and maybe getting invited inside for Thanksgiving dinner.

A chill December gust accompanied Cody through the office door a fortnight later.

"Where is that damned Wickham?" he barked at Ned and slapped his hat on a wall peg behind his desk. "I've turned over every rock and dug out every coyote hole in the county—and the yellow coward's disappeared! Where is he hiding?"

Cody had tracked down many an outlaw in Leadville and other towns. Why couldn't he sniff out Wickham? What if the slimy Frog tried to hurt Sky again?

Ned shook his head slowly, a baffled expression on his face.

"Beats me. He could be in Texas by now."

Cody shoved his fingers through his hair. "Yeah, but he wouldn't leave all his stuff behind at the boarding house. I check with the manager every day, and he hasn't seen the skunk since he walked off his job."

Jim Hacker shrugged through the doorway from the back room. "Why don't you two quit bangin' your gums? Ol' Frog will show up sooner or later."

Cody scowled and stared out the clouded front window.

"Ya know, there's gonna be a bonfire and a street dance tonight. I seen folks decoratin' up for it. Ya oughtta go, Marshal. Get your mind off that scum Wickham."

Cody rubbed the back of his neck. "Maybe I'll do that, Jim. Sure would like to think about something else for a change."

Harrison Avenue glittered with gaiety, its inhabitants in a festive winter solstice mood. Bedecked with fir boughs and streaming red ribbons, street lamps glowed.

Cody sauntered past decorated storefronts, his heels tapping along the boardwalk as he headed for the center of town.

A lively tune tinged the crisp night air and stars flickered across the clear December sky. It was good to take a night off from the vigilance of previous weeks, set aside his hatred of Wickham and longing for Sky for an hour or two.

A block ahead, in front of the Briar Rose Hotel, a large cluster of townspeople gathered around a street band. Ben Drysdale, Leadville's mayor, beckoned to him. "Cody, you know this town will be needing a new mayor after I move down to Boulder. The town council is breathing down my back. Would you consider running for the job?"

Cody took a step backward, stunned. He knew a lot of the townspeople were upset with Drysdale for giving notice so soon after being voted into office. But Cody had his own responsibilities. "Thanks for asking, Ben. I've got all I can handle right now."

"Good evenin' to ye, Marshal," Peg O'Connor called out as Cody broke away from Drysdale. "Find yerself a lassie and go have a jig!"

Cody smiled and waved at the crimson-faced shop owner, already three sheets to the wind. He skirted a group of revelers, considering whether to stop in at a saloon and buy a drink before joining the merriment.

"Hello, Marshal." The familiar voice hit him like a lightning bolt. He halted not six inches from Sky. She looked radiant, her auburn hair cascading around her shoulders above a soft wool dress and matching short cape the color of evergreen.

"Good evening, Mrs. S—"

"Please don't call me that."

"You're right, Sky," he said. "I shouldn't call you Missus, even if you are still—"

She stood taller, lifting her chin a notch. Tempting as a summer strawberry, her lower lip curved upward. "I'm as good as divorced."

How he wanted to believe it. If she were a free woman, he'd move mountains to have her. Without speaking, he held her gaze for a long moment until she averted her veil of sweeping dark lashes.

"Enjoy yourself tonight, Cody," she said, her tone low and silky. "And I'll do the same." She glided away into the lively crowd.

He stood on the edge of the merrymakers feeling very much alone. But before he could dive into the nearest bar and have a drink to dull his frustration, he saw a tall, muscular fellow lead Sky into the circle of dancers and draw her close. The way her lips curved upward as they danced, he could swear the stranger's familiarity pleased her.

Despite his self-control, Cody's entire body burned with jealousy. He cursed it. Cursed his wanting. Whether she was married or not, he wanted Sky with a need bordering on obsession.

He forced himself to wait until the waltz had ended. Then, unable to hold his emotions in check one second longer, Cody pushed through the crowd, straight toward Sky and the man who held her in his arms.

CHAPTER TWENTY-THREE

"Pardon me, friend." Cody slipped Sky's fingers from her dance partner's shoulder and stepped between them. "The lady's promised the next dance to me."

The man's gray eyes narrowed resentfully until his gaze dropped to Cody's badge. "Sure, Marshal."

Before Sky could respond, Cody spun her around, guiding them into a quick-stepping polka. Reluctant at first, but having little choice, she followed his lead.

"I hadn't promised you this dance," she said, slightly out of breath.

"Nope." He winked. "But I didn't think you'd mind."

He was slick, Sky had to admit.

When a fiddler, with two missing front teeth, eased his bow into a melodic waltz, Cody drew her into his arms. Unbidden, a sweet ache thrummed along her veins.

"Why did you ask me to dance?" she asked, "I thought we were barely on speaking terms, since that night at my cabin."

His eyes softened in the glow of the street lamp. "What man here wouldn't want to dance with you, Sky? I owe you an apology for what I said, for my hasty judgment."

The sincerity of his words and the strength of his large hand holding hers radiated through her. His breath came warm on her cheek as he held her closer, his lips brushing her hair.

She sighed. "I should have explained my circumstances earlier, but there was never a right time." She thought of the long-awaited news she'd received today. News she was somehow not ready to reveal.

They danced to the edge of the crowd, and Cody led her to a place on the boardwalk where their conversation could be more private. Looking down at her intently, he said, "I'll admit I was more than disappointed to find out you were married. Then Ned told me about your tyrant husband. I admire you for having the courage to leave him."

Dazzling sparks burned within his gold-flecked gaze. He moved closer, lifted his hand to cradle her chin gently. "Even though at first I couldn't imagine you being here, Sky, I'm so glad you came to Leadville."

The tone of his voice, the virile emotion he projected, caused her knees to go weak. At the base of her throat, her heartbeat fluttered.

His warm fingertips released her chin, but his hazel eyes still held hers.

If she lifted herself on tiptoe, her face would be on the same level as his inviting lower lip. She recalled the tender flesh of his lip and the softness of his full tawny mustache. The memory and his nearness sent her senses spinning.

From the way Cody leaned toward her, his eyes caressing her face and mouth, she knew he must be feeling the same magnetic force. In a moment he might kiss her.

Her fingers touched the envelope tucked inside her pocket and a jolt of apprehension made her shiver. Should she tell him now? No. This wasn't the right time or place.

She cleared her throat abruptly. "Could we find something to drink?"

"I'll bet you'd like a hot rum. There's a vendor up the street." He gestured in that direction.

"A hot rum." She grasped at the offer, realizing a kiss in public would have embarrassed both of them and loosened her tongue. "I can't think of anything I'd like more right now."

He grinned and took her arm. They walked down Harrison, past the Clarendon Hotel and paused at the street vendor's wagon. In the center of the wide avenue, a crackling bonfire set to ward off the winter chill undulated beneath the stars. After Cody purchased two spiced rum drinks, they sipped and stared into the shimmering light.

"Antonio would have loved this. I had a hard time telling him it would be a grownup's party."

Cody frowned. "Where is Antonio now?"

"At the cabin, with Chico."

Cody's expression set off an instant alarm inside her head. "I think I'd better be getting back, before it gets late."

He gave their empty mugs back to the vendor. "I'll be glad to take you."

"Thank you, but I came with some neighbors."

Clasping Sky's elbow, he steered her down the boardwalk. "I insist." He smiled his assurance. "I haven't escorted a beautiful woman home in a long time."

She glanced up at him. "Certainly not a soon-to-be divorced woman."

"Only my deputies and I know that. Besides, I think I can trust you not to encourage me."

An imp gave a twist to her insides. She wondered if it was such a good idea. Could she trust herself, if he invited himself in?

He gave her a little nudge. "Go tell your neighbors, and I'll go get Buck."

Stars lit the road out of town. Seated in the saddle in front of Cody, Sky felt ill at ease. Misgivings flourished like fast-growing weeds, tangling her thoughts. "I should have left Antonio at the Hemmingses'. He's too young to stay alone at night," she brooded. "But he and one of their boys had a fight today, and I thought they should cool off."

"Don't worry. He's probably fast asleep and dreaming about what he wants for Christmas by now."

Even Cody's powerful frame surrounding her failed to provide reassurance. "Chico is a good guard dog," she emphasized, attempting to ease her guilt.

"I'll bet Antonio's own mother didn't worry about him any more than you do," Cody said. "He's a lucky kid."

The buckskin's hooves clopped along the hard-packed snow. A quarter-mile to Sky's cabin. Cody tamped down his own concern for Antonio's safety. With Frog Wickham on the loose, he should schedule one of the town's officers to check on Sky's cabin every night. Every day was not enough.

He inhaled the floral fragrance of Sky's hair, cascading abundantly so close to his nose, and wished she didn't smell so damned good.

When he saw her to her door, would she invite him in? How could he refuse even if she was still married? He'd be happy as a coon with a honey pot just to hold her in his arms like this all night long. If only she were free to make that invitation.

Cody let his eyes close as he breathed in Sky's sweet nearness and the crisp night air.

The barking jolted him from his reverie.

He peered ahead through a scattering of tall pine. Smoke billowed between the matchstick trunks.

Sky's fingers pricked the empty space in front of her. "There's a fire," she croaked. "It's my cabin!"

Cody's gut twisted. "Hang on. We'll get there." He dug his heels into the buckskin and they tore up the road.

As they approached the clearing, poker-red flames licked at the small cabin's walls. One look at the rising flames, and the chilling memory of Abe Fitch blazed before him.

Antonio. No! This time it would be different.

But, were they in time?

Chico bounded up to them, his bushy tail flickering with tiny fire sparks, his bark high-pitched and frantic.

Reining Buck to a halt, Cody slid to the ground and pulled Sky after him. "Antonio!" she called out in a strangled voice.

Cody yanked the bedroll from behind his saddle as Sky raced toward the door. Holding the bedroll under one arm, he tackled her around her waist. "You can't go in there. Wait here."

Stark fear glittered in her eyes. "Antonio's in there! I'm going in!"

He stood firm. "I said wait here."

She struggled fiercely, her nails clawing at him like a mother cougar. There was no time. With a sweep of his arm, he pushed her backward. She landed hard, her skirts bunched up around her, tears raging in her glazed stare.

Flinging the bedroll blanket over his hat and jacket, Cody lurched through the cabin door. The smoke was so thick, he choked, then hunkered down, half-crawling through the main room.

"Antonio!" he shouted, his nostrils burning.

Cinders snapped around him, lighting on the blanket like fireflies. A wall of fire surrounded him.

Antonio—Please be alive!

Through the haze, he saw the boy's small body sprawled outside the woodshed doorway. Trapped by a fallen beam.

In an instant, he reached Antonio and hurled the heavy beam from his leg. Molten heat seared his left palm. He swallowed a silent scream.

Ignoring the pain, he knelt by the boy. "Hang on, son. I've got you."

Cody lifted Antonio in his arms. A faint moan escaped the boy's lips. Dodging under falling roof chinks, Cody nearly stumbled over a chair. The blanket slipped from his shoulders as he zigzagged to the door.

Gasping for air, sparks sizzling around him, Cody carried Antonio's limp form into the side yard.

Her face terror-filled, Sky rushed to them. "Oh, God. Is he alive?"

"He's got a chance." Cody laid Antonio on the ground, then pulled off his jacket. Sky fell on her knees beside him. He handed her the rolled garment. "Put this under his head." Scooping up some crusted snow, he rubbed the boy's cheeks.

"Antonio!" Sky sobbed. Chico whimpered, hovering near.

Then a loud popping sound. A bullet whizzed past Cody's ear.

Sky shrieked and flung herself over Antonio.

Pivoting, Cody whipped his Colt from its holster and fired in the direction of the shot. Giddy laughter ricocheted into the night.

Another shot rang out. Cody ducked, quickly helping Sky to prop Antonio out of sight behind the well.

Squatting on his haunches, Cody fired back twice, splintering tree trunks ten yards away. He knew the devil hiding in the darkness was Frog Wickham, even before he spotted him silhouetted against the pale moonlight behind a scrub bush. Looked like he'd got himself another bowler hat.

Cody took careful aim. His next shot blew that disgusting bowler right off Wickham's head. Despite the blood boiling in his veins, he chortled. *My turn to laugh.*

Giving the scum no time to recover, Cody fired again. A howl and a thud set off a new barrage of barking from Chico.

"Get your worthless ass out here, Wickham!"

The outlaw gave no response. Only Sky's muffled sobs and Antonio's weak cough reached his ears.

Then, erupting like a geyser, Wickham leaped from behind the scrub. Clasping his right arm, he ran stoop-shouldered to his horse waiting in the shadows. Firelight emphasized his sloped forehead and long spindly legs.

"Stop, you bastard!"

Wickham mounted. Cody's last shot narrowly missed his horse's rear flank.

No time to reload. Cody slapped his gun into his holster and ran to mount. The carbine he carried on the buckskin was his best backup now.

"Be careful, Cody!" Sky warned.

"I'll be back," he called over his shoulder. A part of him longed to stay and help Sky and Antonio, but he couldn't let Frog Wickham escape.

Both riders galloped toward California Gulch. Frog had a slight lead, but Cody rapidly closed the gap.

Snow and ice covering the road made the chase treacherous. He dared not attempt shooting the carbine now. Closing in on Wickham was his focus. Sweat pooled under his arms and ran down his back, yet his mouth was dry as winter hay. He cursed the devil to hell.

I'll get you this time, Wickham!

They neared the gulch lying rocky and desolate in the moonlight. There was no way around it.

Ahead, Wickham's horse stumbled and fell to one knee. The outlaw propelled forward onto the road, scrambled to his feet and headed into the sparse trees. Cody rode up alongside him and jumped, landing hard on the ground. Pain streaked from his feet up his legs. But he swiftly tackled Wickham, sending both men crashing.

They rolled back and forth, each trying to gain an advantage. With a grunt, Wickham jerked his knee upward, grazing Cody's groin. Cody returned the favor with a fist to his jaw. Stunned for an instant, Frog wriggled out of Cody's reach and hopped to his feet. Holding his right arm to his side, he sprinted away with Cody on his heels.

They neared the rim of the gulch. Cody lunged forward, spinning Wickham around. His good fist swung out, knocking Cody's hat from his head. Cody swung back. Knuckles smashed flesh. Wickham yowled, his nose spurting blood across his face.

"Give up now, Frog, or you'll never live to tell about it."

"Kiss my ass—big shit Marshal!"

Seething, Cody lashed out, "You killed Abe Fitch in cold blood. You robbed and burned out others. Tonight you almost killed an innocent child." He glared at the greasy creature before him. "What do you think you deserve?"

A sneer split Wickham's face. "Here's what you're gonna get." He snatched a stiletto from inside his jacket. Its blade gleamed in the starlight.

Cody stared into the killer's defiant eyes. Taller than the man by several inches, he knew he was also stronger. But was he faster?

Guttural laughter bubbled up from Wickham's throat. He waved the knife, slicing the air. Then, with a bold swipe, he charged at Cody.

Kicking upward, Cody's boot slammed into Wickham's hand. The stiletto spun out of his grasp. Rage flaring in his eyes, Wickham leaped at Cody.

Repelled by his rancid breath, Cody peeled him off his chest and tossed him backward. Snarling, Wickham lunged forward again. Cody gave a mighty shove that sent him reeling. Over the rocky ledge of the gulch.

His keening wail pierced the night.

Heart thundering, Cody rushed to the edge and looked down. In the moonlight, Frog Wickham lay on a boulder thirty feet below, his head twisted at an odd angle. His bulging eyes stared grotesquely up at the starry sky.

Cody stepped away, fighting back nausea. He stood for a long moment, gulping in the cool night air. Tomorrow, he'd send his deputies, or whoever would volunteer, to scrape Frog's corpse off the boulder and bury him somewhere far away.

He looked forward to chasing down the rest of Wickham's cohorts. If he couldn't send the rats to jail, he'd like nothing more than to escort them out of town on a rail.

Cody whistled for Buck. He prayed that Antonio would survive—that he wouldn't be too late.

CHAPTER TWENTY-FOUR

With terror in her heart, Sky watched Cody chase after the madman who'd just torched her home to the ground and left the child she loved clinging to his life. Would Cody succeed and bring down the demon, or would the demon kill Cody? She shuddered in the cold. Her life was going up in smoke as well as the cabin.

Antonio gave a rasping cough and Sky cradled him to her. She breathed in his smoky hair and singed clothes, and fresh tears blurred her vision.

He must live. Dear God, he must live!

She'd lost the promise of one child. Might not be able to have another. She couldn't bear the pain of losing Antonio, too.

In the shadowy light, his eyelids flickered, then opened. "Señorita Sky . . . I tried to run . . ." Another spasm of coughing shook his small frame.

"I know, Antonio. You were so brave." She removed the cape from her shoulders and drew it around him.

"Chico," he called hoarsely. The dog padded up to him, his tail wagging furiously, and licked Antonio's smudged face. Antonio dragged his fingers through Chico's charred coat.

"We're all safe," she encouraged with an effort. Scanning the dark gulch road, Sky fought the fear gnawing her insides. Where was Cody? Would he ever come back?

She heard a rumbling and looked down the road in the opposite direction. A horse and buckboard trundled into the yard.

"Miss Saunders, is that you?" a male voice called.

Recognizing the Hemmingses, her neighbors half a mile to the east, she jumped to her feet. They sat on the wagon seat, their oldest boy, Jerry, in the back.

"Sky, are you hurt?" Beth Hemmings climbed down to the ground and rushed over to her. "We came as soon as we saw the fire."

"I'm fine," she answered, grateful to see Beth. "But Antonio was overcome with smoke and his leg was injured. Marshal Cassidy carried him out of the cabin."

Beth knelt by the boy, examining him. Antonio moaned an objection. "His leg doesn't seem to be broken," she said.

Lucas Hemmings grabbed a bucket of water from the well, raced toward the cabin and tossed it into the billowing flames. Sky could see the effort was futile.

Lucas returned to the women, shaking his head. "Afraid we can't save the place," he said with regret. "Did you say the marshal's here?"

Clinging to her fragile control, Sky blurted, "He was—but someone shot at us just after we got here—and Cody chased him toward the gulch."

She looked off toward the road and her body trembled. "I'm sure it was the man who started the fire."

Beth wrapped a sturdy arm around Sky. "You come home with us. We'll take care of Antonio."

Jerry brought a canteen from the wagon and helped Antonio drink from it.

"Don't worry, ma'am, the marshal can take care of himself," Lucas assured her. How desperately she wanted to believe him.

They heard a cracking sound, and the last of the cabin's roof beams sank into the middle of the smoldering foundation. Smoke and cinders from the burning wood permeated the air, pricking her nose and stinging her eyes.

Sky stared at the disintegrating structure, a suffocating cloak of loss smothering her. Every earthly possession she owned was gone now. All she had left was Antonio; God willing that he would recover from his injuries.

Cody? Was he still alive? Or shot and left for dead in some dark ravine?

Her throat constricted and she sagged against Beth. "I'm so afraid for the marshal," she cried, tears filling her eyes.

In the shadowy light, Beth's features reflected compassion and courage. "You love him," she said, knowing it without Sky having to tell her. She enfolded Sky's hand in her callused palm. "Be strong."

Lucas lifted Antonio carefully into his arms. "We need to get the boy over to our place, Miss Saunders. I'll put him in the back of the wagon and you can ride with him."

Anxiety coursed through her. As much as she wanted to help Antonio, she didn't want to leave. If . . . when Cody returned, he wouldn't know where she and Antonio had gone, and if they were safe.

But Lucas and his son were settling Antonio into the wagon bed. Beth took her arm. "Come, now."

The sound of hooves and a sharp whinny spun her around. Horse and rider flew into the side yard. Moonlight flickered off the buckskin's glistening chest; its nostrils flared.

Reining in the animal, the marshal stared at the small group gathered around the wagon. His overpowering gaze riveted Sky to the spot where she stood.

"Cody," she stammered, relief crashing through her.

His tall imposing frame slipped to the ground. "Sky . . ."

Impelled by longing, she rushed to him.

He embraced her, his heart thudding against her own, his breath hot against her cheek. She leaned into him, absorbing his powerful strength.

"Thank God, you're back. What happened?"

"I chased Wickham to the gulch," he rasped. "We fought. He fell backward—and broke his neck."

A sense of justice filled her. "He deserved to die. But why did he want to burn down my cabin?"

"I think, in his twisted mind, it was a way of taking revenge on me for tracking him and revealing his identity."

Cody glanced back to the wagon where the Hemmingses stood. "How is Antonio?"

Lucas Hemmings introduced himself. "Antonio's a strong kid. I think he'll be all right. We want to take care of him back at our place."

Cody nodded. "Sure. I'll ride over there with you."

Sky climbed up beside Antonio, whose breathing was still labored. Her own pulse fluttered in her breast. But for the grace of heaven, Cody could be lying at the bottom of California Gulch instead of that monster, Wickham.

At the Hemmingses's place, she nursed Antonio, watching Cody from the corner of her eye. His dirtied and bruised face. The bloodied knuckles.

He called no attention to his own wounds, showing only concern for the boy and his injured leg. When she saw Cody's burned palm, she insisted on cleaning and tending it with a salve Beth produced. He objected but finally let her bandage his hand.

The touch of his warm flesh brushing hers sent her heart swaying. She, who was now a free spirit. An independent woman. Yet when he went to leave, she could not stop a hot ache from growing in her throat.

"Take care of yourself, Cody," she said at the front door, an undeniable need for him tearing at her. "And thank you for rescuing Antonio."

He gazed down into her eyes. "I wish I could do more." The

double meaning of his words was obvious.

She watched him turn toward the dark. A stabbing pain of regret twisted inside her. "Cody—"

He whirled and caught her by her arms, pulling her into the yard, taking her breath away. "This is crazy. I won't walk away from you this time. I don't care if you're still married, Sky. I'll wait until you're free. Will you marry me, then?"

His words rocketed through her. For months, she'd denied her attraction to Cody. The last thing she'd wanted was to marry again. Until he'd shown her his goodness, his commitment to others. Nor could she deny the intense sensual attraction between them.

She wavered. "You'd feel no regret marrying a divorced woman?"

"It doesn't matter." He shrugged. "Folks will understand. They left their pasts behind when they came to Leadville. Like you, they came to make a new start." He gently stroked her arms. "I admire so much what you've done. Getting a respectable job, even if it is working for that dratted Burtram, and making a home for Antonio."

She smiled to herself. At least he admired her for her courage and hard work.

Inside her pocket, Sky touched the edge of the envelope and her nerve endings began to tingle. "Could you trust me to be faithful and never leave you?"

Light from the cabin window reflected the burning light in his gaze. "I haven't trusted women for most of my life, but I trust you, Sky." He lifted his large hand and caressed her cheek. "The same as you could trust me."

Her heart took a perilous leap. "I have something you should see." Plucking the envelope from the depths of her pocket, she held it out to him. "My divorce papers. They arrived today."

He stared at the envelope, complete surprise on his face.

"You've been carrying this around all night and didn't tell me?"

She slipped the papers back in her pocket. "Well, I could hardly announce my divorce to everyone at the town dance."

A grin started at the corners of his mouth and spread outward. "Maybe not, but I'd sure like to announce something else to them." Gathering her into his arms, he held her snugly.

Anxiety tinged her rising joy. She drew back a few inches. "There's something I need to tell you, Cody. I had a miscarriage a little over a year ago. I might not be able to have more children."

A tear slipped down her cheek. But she bolstered herself. If he really wanted her, he would have to take her as she was.

To her surprise, Cody held her tighter, her breasts flush against his broad chest. "Did you think that would make any difference to me? I'm so crazy in love with you, Sky."

Every nerve hummed with the delicious sensation of his body heat.

She looked up into the heart-stopping desire of his gaze. "I love you, too. And so does Antonio."

He pressed his lips to hers, caressing her mouth, then taking it hungrily. The tip of his tongue, hot and moist, coaxed her lips to part.

Her pulse pounding, Sky opened to his entry, mating her tongue with his.

Dizzying moments later, his husky voice whispered into her ear, "All I want is to take care of you and Antonio. Marry me."

Breathless, she said, "I'd be proud to be your wife."

Cody's lips captured hers in another velvet-warm kiss. Shadows from her past melted away. Welcoming the sanctuary of his strong embrace, Sky returned his kiss with all the love in her heart.

Christmas—one year later

The enticing aroma of Granny Saunders's apple spice cake filled the kitchen as Sky slid the metal pan from the cook stove and set the cake on the sideboard to cool. Cody's father and Ned and Cindy were coming for dinner. It would be their first Christmas together as a family.

"Are you gonna drizzle some cinnamon and sugar over that cake?" Cody asked, trailing kisses across the back of her neck.

"If it would please you."

He turned her around and kissed the tip of her nose. "Everything you do pleases me, Mrs. Cassidy."

She responded with a light peck on his mouth, then pushed him away, knowing where those kisses would lead if she didn't. "Have you set up the Christmas tree?"

"It's done." He moved toward the parlor. "Come see."

She hung her apron on a wall peg and tagged after him.

In the parlor, a magnificent ten-foot fir stood before the front window. "We'll decorate it tonight," she said, smiling at Cody with eager anticipation.

Her gaze fell to the stone hearth before the fireplace where Antonio had arranged a Nativity scene of woodcarvings he'd whittled from scraps of kindling. Mary and Joseph, a shepherd, an angel, the Christ babe in a manger, and a scruffy dog that somehow resembled Chico.

She smiled. Life was so good in this house at the top of the hill. Now that she no longer worked for Burtram, she had more time to entertain their friends, and take an active part in Leadville's promising future.

Now that she was the mayor's wife.

Much had happened in the past year. Members of the town council had asked Cody to run for mayor after Ben Drysdale vacated the office. He had easily beat out his opponent. Of course, Sky knew Cody had the best credentials for the job. Honesty, integrity, and courage. She was thrilled when he'd won. Being mayor of Leadville would be much safer for Cody than continuing as town marshal.

Antonio's beaming face appeared at the parlor threshold. "Mom. Dad. Come out to the stable. I want to show you something."

She draped a woolen shawl over her shoulders. "All right, but only for a minute. I have to start dinner." As they followed Antonio outside, she noticed that he'd shot up nearly two inches in the last year.

Inside the stable, Miss Fanny waited, decorated like a Christmas package. Evergreen boughs wound around her harness, crimson and green ribbons adorned her bridle and were braided through her tail.

"See," Antonio giggled. "I make a present for you."

She laughed. "You mean for Miss Fanny. How dear you are, *mi hijo*, my son, always full of surprises." She hugged him to her.

Cody stroked the mule's neck. "You can ride her when we go to the church service tonight."

Miss Fanny gave a short bray as if in agreement.

Antonio's eyes shone with delight. "She'd like it."

On their way back to the house, Sky glanced across the valley. Glorious colors of a Colorado sunset painted the snow-draped Mount Massive. She thought of the Lady Luck Mine, which had truly brought her good fortune. Not from a great silver strike, as yet, but mainly having given her the opportunity to reach beyond limiting self-doubt to an inner freedom. Finally, to the realization of her own self-worth.

A tiny sensation in her womb brought a rush of excitement. New life growing within her.

She stopped. "Cody, feel this." She guided his large hand to her belly.

His eyes widened. "A baby! You didn't tell me."

"I wanted to be sure."

His grin was broad and full of love and pride. His hug nearly smothered her. Joy, like a fountain, rose in her breast.

"Antonio!" she called. "We want to tell you something."

He emerged from the stable, curiosity flickering in his dark brown eyes. Then his mouth curved up at the corners. "Is it about my Christmas present?"

Sky glanced up at Cody. His conspiratorial wink set her spirit aglow.

Antonio approached them and she took his small, sturdy hand in hers. "Yes. A very special present."

ABOUT THE AUTHOR

Leslee Breene creates stories from the heart, depicting heroes and heroines of western romance. *Foxfire* was her debut novel and a second place winner of the RWA Valley Forge "Winning Beginnings" contest. *Foxfire* is available as a print-on-demand at www.lesleebreene.com.

Her short fiction has won or placed in the Moonlight & Magnolia national short fiction awards, *Byline* magazine, and *Writer's Digest* annual competition.

Ms. Breene attended the University of Denver, was awarded a Denver Fashion Group Scholarship, and graduated from the Fashion Institute of Technology, New York City.

During leisure time away from her computer, she enjoys scouting for book settings with her husband in the Colorado Rockies and Jackson Hole, Wyoming.

A believer in supporting fellow writers, Ms. Breene is an active member of Colorado Romance Writers, Rocky Mountain Fiction Writers, and Romance Writers of America.